Closer to God

Closer to God

JOHN MOEHL

RESOURCE *Publications* · Eugene, Oregon

CLOSER TO GOD

Resource Publications
An Imprint of Wipf and Stock Publishers
199 W. 8th Ave., Suite 3
Eugene, OR 97401

www.wipfandstock.com

PAPERBACK ISBN: 978-1-5326-1987-8
HARDCOVER ISBN: 978-1-5326-1989-2
EBOOK ISBN: 978-1-5326-1988-5

Manufactured in the U.S.A.

Contents

Foreword

IN MY FIRST EFFORT to confront my binary life (*Phobos & Deimos: Two Moons, Two Worlds*, 2016), I was blazing my trail—clearing the brush, trying to find the way to describe a lifetime divided between two continents. Through this inaugural book, my first endeavor to compose fiction for wider public consumption, I attempted, as an outsider, to look through the eyes of a variety of insiders—people into whose lives I had plummeted, people with different cultures and norms, but a common humanity. I was trying to look closely at the day-to-day activities of others to try and understand better how they themselves adjusted to the unknowns we all find in our paths.

The present text is still very much a part of my double life; this time, attempting to look through the eyes of another foreigner who, like myself, is an incomer, but whose mission and expectations are very different from mine. This work is fictitious, albeit some of the geographic features are those of Central Africa. The individuals, institutions, and settings of the characters, as well as their actions, are all fictitious—an amalgam of my time working in this region in the 1980s—and any seeming relationships with or references to persons living or dead, or institutions, past or present, is purely coincidental.

For both of these writings, and for all aspects of my life, I have relied heavily on the guidance and insight of my wife of four-plus decades. She has helped me see life through a unique and highly sensitive lens, understanding others' joys and sorrows, and respecting others' individuality. She has cautioned me to watch where I stepped, as I have sometimes catapulted along life's path, having far too often dragged her through the brambles. In the face of many sacrifices, she has always been my touchstone and it is with love and profound gratitude that I dedicate this, and all that I do, to Elisabeth.

Acknowledgments

With Elisabeth at the heart of my efforts, there are many who should be acknowledged for their contribution to this work. The people of Central Africa, the Land of Eternal Spring, have left an indelible imprint on my life—a mosaic built layer by layer during the five years we lived and worked in this beautiful and troubled piece of a beautiful and troubled world. The farmer, the fisher, the shopkeeper, the barman, the taxi driver, the student, the teacher, the priest, and so many others lived, and often shared their lives with me in ways that were at once unique to the Afromontane Region and common to global civilization. Through them and their generosity, I have learned so much and can only hope that my presence may have, in some small way, made a tiny down payment on all the knowledge and hoped-for wisdom I have gained. I would also like to offer special thanks to Marie for her help with this text—she so unselfishly offered assistance and ended up providing much more in terms of guidance and a common sense approach to the challenges of getting words down on paper. My thanks are also extended to Nancy who worked hard to polish an imperfect product.

From the hilltop

The scent of eucalyptus and cypress mix with wood smoke to perfume the morning air.

Long-handled hoes slung lightly over sinewy shoulders, men and women deftly head for steep, rocky fields.

The lilting song of school children echoes off the hills—carried on the breeze with the harsh caw of a peevish pied crow.

Down the palisade's path, four stout youth, carrying an ailing veteran on a papyrus stretcher, add their chants to the morning melody to lighten their load.

The fertile valleys, crops of cabbage and beans peering from the rich soil, are still cloaked in the mist, seemingly rising from the morning dew.

Long-horned cattle, with their sheep stewards, head down pitched trails, leaving their corrals for morning pasture under the watchful eye of a family son.

The fresh air seems to vibrate, as if in anticipation of a momentous event— in the mountains, valleys, and perpetual spring, the day begins.

Author's Note

CENTRAL AFRICA IS THE setting for this tale. This should not be confused with the Central African Republic—at one time, the Central African Empire. The Central African area described in the following writings is a high-elevation undulating terrain, alternating between populated hills (*collines*) and cultivated marshy valleys (*marais*). This terrain, just south of the equator (1° to 5° south latitude), some of the most heavily populated in Africa, is the source for the great Congo and Nile Rivers. This land is also the home of Lakes Kivu and Tanganyika; hence, at times referred to as the Great Lakes Region. Casting a wide net, this area encompasses present-day Congo (Zaïre), Burundi, Rwanda, Tanzania, and Zambia; historically, these countries have had Belgian, English, and/or German colonial rule. The epicenter, the focus of this text, is the former German Colony of Ruanda-Rundi; foreign control of these lands was assumed by Belgium in 1916, and lasted until 1962 when the independent countries of Burundi and Rwanda were established—each circumscribing kingdoms dating back to at least the 15th century.

Our protagonist, Michel van Leuven, a son of Flanders, Belgium, came to this region as a young man after Independence. At the time, 250 km to the east, Bob Denard and Jean Schramme, accompanied by other mercenaries and Katanga separatists, were engulfed in a bloody battle in Bukavu (Democratic Republic of Congo) with Mobutu Sese Seko Kuku Ngbendu (born Joseph-Désiré Mobutu). Mobutu had taken power two years earlier and would remain as head of state for another three decades of what had been the Belgian Congo. However, the affairs of what was once King Leopold's private domain are another story. At this juncture, our target is a now more mature and worldly Michel van Leuven who has traded the industries along with the barley and beet fields of Belgium for the hills and valleys of Central Africa.

Prologue

Rift Valley Gazette, Nairobi, 9 November 1994

GREAT LAKES REGION. *A Belgian monk, transporting potatoes for his religious community in the south of the country, is reported to have saved the lives of eleven women and children. First-hand accounts indicate the monk, when stopped at a militia checkpoint 26 km from the Nyabugogo River, saw a mob violently attack the villagers, assailing them with ethnic slurs. He drove his pickup into the midst of the aggressors, offering them the load of potatoes in exchange for the safe passage of the women and children. The hungry throng agreed, and the Brother pushed bags of potatoes to the ground, shepherding his charges into the now empty truck bed, and drove them to the shelter of St. Michael's Cathedral in the capital city, only an hour away.*

1

BROTHER MIKE LIKED TO fish. In his youth, the Leie River near his home in Ghent, before it became polluted beyond recognition, had provided good fishing—even offering up the occasional prize pike. But today, as for every outing over past decades, Brother Mike was far from the river of his childhood. He now baited his hook for bream in the large pond below the monastery in Central Africa.

Here, the bream were no pike. There was no thrashing, no violent fight of life and death, good and evil. But there was a good battle, nonetheless. There was the battle of being pulled in this direction and that—being dragged against one's will. The bream would indeed fight nobly, splaying his fins against the unwanted, the feared pull of the line. The bream would not give up easily. Many had flopped off the hook right at the water's edge.

Brother Mike frequently wondered if the Church brought its flock together as though they were caught on a line. Were they pulled against their will? Was he? The world was changing. Perhaps faith was not enough. In the olden days, even in the days of his youth, you did what was right—you did what you were told. Today, it seemed not only countries were freed—so were souls.

Brother Mike also often thought of those early White Fathers, the first venturing forth nearly a century ago in North Africa. They were pioneers who brought God's Word to these hidden regions, many a time at such a high price to themselves, their sponsors, and even their hoped-to-be beneficiaries. They must have felt closer to God when they built churches on the hilltops around these verdant valleys of Central Africa, with their spires pointing to the stars, oftentimes silhouetted by angry tropical storms.

His own hilltop, the well-kept crest guarded by his community, was crowned by a small but elegant chapel, built nearly a hundred years ago. This sanctuary and launching pad for God's Ways had, over the ensuing years, metamorphosed into a vibrant and diversified religious community now overseen by the Brothers of Piety, a community that included a health center, primary and secondary schools, an orphanage, a butcher shop, greengrocer, and bakery, mechanic and carpentry workshops, as well as an impressive library.

Far from the hubbub of the nearly constant goings-on of the monastery, the fishpond offered a refuge, a calm that slowly intensified like the afternoon breeze blowing across the water's surface. Generally, Brother Mike returned to his apartment with no fish, but a serene soul. And, for Brother Mike, finding serenity was no small matter.

Brother Mike, or Michel van Leuven as he had been baptized a half a century before, had been raised by strict Flemish parents, attended strict Flemish schools, lived in a strict Flemish neighborhood, and was oh so happy to now be living in the not-so-strict heart of Africa. In spite of his solemn monastic vows of obedience and conversion to the monastic way of life, including chastity, Brother Mike felt liberated.

Brother Mike was a religious person. He was a true believer. He had studied his Catechism. He understood the aim of chastity was to integrate the powers of life and love. He understood chastity as an act linked to the virtue of temperance. He also understood chastity to be expressed in friendship and, while he was opposed to the fornication of the unmarried, he saw the expression of his friendship through love making as a very acceptable, almost sacred, deed. It was so that Brother Mike had many female friends; ladies married to their husbands or married to the Holy Spirit.

Brother Mike had come to his monastic life as a young man, barely out of his teens. He had started working for the betterment of all at the lowest rungs of the ladder. First as a kitchen helper, he had shown an aptitude for being a good organizer. Thus, he was put in charge of the pantry; maintaining the food stores to feed the not inconsequential number of mouths that accounted for the monastery's population of brothers, students, workers, the ill, and hangers-on. He was superb. He had an analytical mind that quickly ended the haphazard way in which stocks had been kept, and put in place an efficient and easily monitored system that shed light on any pilfering that was an unavoidable byproduct of such a varied population.

Brother Mike was so successful at supervising the pantries that he was soon promoted to a position where he oversaw the movement of all the goods with which the community dealt. As a philanthropic society, the Brothers of Piety imported a large quantity of material, including medications and medical supplies, books for school, parts for the mechanic's shop, appliances for the butcher shop and bakery, clothing for the orphans, and foodstuffs for the community itself—all duty free. On average, the monastery received a container a month. However, these containers were often not full, providing Brother Mike an opportunity to offer friendship to local businessmen who sought imported products but disliked paying the high import duties. This kindness was repaid in many forms, both in cash and in kind.

Brother Mike believed he practiced what he preached, including temperance. Thus it was that he shared his friendship with but one lady at a time. It was, moreover, divine providence that determined the depth of this friendship. At times it was purely a blessed chance encounter that flowered into something more profound, but as fleeting as the coffee blossoms on the hill. On other occasions, it was a more consummate friendship that could carry on for weeks or even months. Nevertheless, there was always an amicable ending as friendship was a blessing to be shared and not monopolized by one individual.

Brother Mike had few rules, thinking his vows were adequate to steer his life. However, whether as a survival instinct or a paternalistic sentiment, he strove not to have friendships with anyone at the monastery—no students, recovering patients, patrons, or workers. He fervently believed in separating work and socializing and his friendships were generally forged with sisters from the neighboring convent or the citizenry of the nearby provincial capital, the fortuitous congress notwithstanding.

Brother Mike could always be seen with his tattered canvas holdall slung over his shoulder. When he encountered a new friend, with an affable smile and an open demeanor, he would ask his new acquaintance to find a comfortable seat, be it in a public space, a restaurant, a grassy knoll, or an open market. He would remove from his bag a bottle of Courvoisier and two small glasses. In the blink of an eye, thanks to his clandestine import arrangements, he would be sipping fine cognac with his newly found friend.

Brother Mike was the kind of man who could easily have been elected burgomaster. But Brother Mike was someone who knew his place. He enjoyed immensely the pleasures of his position and in no way wanted to jeopardize these by being a threat, either real or perceived, to the power structure of the monastic community. He was very careful to follow the rules, at least most of them, to adhere to the prayer schedule, and to show due respect to his superiors. He was polite, respectful, disciplined, and well-kept. He was, in fact, often spoken of by the Abbot as the exemplary monk of the order.

This all meant that Brother Mike was very busy and very discreet. With his friendships and inventories to manage, he was always engrossed in one thing or another. It was often hard to find the ways to fit his formal and informal lives together, so his respites on the pond bank were frequently one of the few occasions to take stock and assess options.

Brother Mike's current friendship with Sister Alice was coming to an expected and logical end. They had been able to carry on their liaison for several months, exceptionally long from Brother Mike's point of view, as they were both involved in assisting some of the village clinics in the surrounding area—an accommodating spot always available when away from the curious eyes of the religious or civil society.

Sister Alice was a big-boned Walloon with equally big appetites. If the truth were known, she was more than Brother Mike would normally have chosen to take on as a partner in friendship. But she had a robust sense of humor and an appetite for cognac or any of its relatives. All in all, there was a mesh of similar life forces, but the friendship had run its course. The village public health program was ending and it was a good time to end the friendship before it got out of hand.

2

THE MONASTERY HAD A wide variety of quarters. In addition to the monks' cells in the Abbey, there were dormitories for the orphans and live-in students, wards for the health center, and nearly an entire village for those helpers who worked in the various branches of the monastery. All of these structures required general maintenance and repairs, and the purchase (or import) and stocking of these materials was among the slew of responsibilities assumed by Brother Mike. Accordingly, he would often go to the big market in the provincial capital in search of hardware and building supplies.

The core of the market was the food section. Fresh fruits and vegetables were sold in almost a piazza arrangement at the center, which was surrounded by a neat, shoulder-high brick wall and shaded by translucent fiberglass roofing sheets. Other items were arranged in concentric circles around this hub. Butchered meat and fish were on one side, with live animals further out on the periphery. Clothing, new and used, was on another side while miscellaneous household necessities such as soap, toothpaste, and pots and pans formed the first echelon as one entered. Slightly separated from this spiral of open-air merchandise were several parallel rows of small, enclosed shops, generally made of an *ad hoc* mixture of wood and galvanized roofing sheets. These shops sold fine fabrics, tableware, pharmaceuticals, and hardware along with building supplies, with the latter vendors often recognized by the stacks of sacks of cement adorning their entrance as though they were military bunkers.

Brother Mike was perusing one such cluttered shop when he found his aisle blocked by someone scooping nails out of a metal bin on the floor; only the person's derriere was visible in the filtered lighting of the emporium. He was taken as much by the shapeliness of the form as its evident musculature under the loose khaki trousers. This was obviously part of a hard-working person. A person who, when he turned, was not a he but a she.

She was short, coming to Brother Mike's chin and Brother Mike was not a giant among men, at least in terms of physical stature. She had a round, happy face with braided hair falling about both sides, adorning a crooked, mischievous smile, and a glowing mahogany complexion.

It would be an exaggeration to say Brother Mike was smitten. Brother Mike did not get smitten. But he did have his curiosity aroused. While he wore no collar or other sign of his religious affiliation, most recognized the monks when they were out and about. With this recognition came a degree of deference, especially among women who often bowed slightly and seemed to evaporate into the shadows. This woman, very much to the contrary, was right in his face in the confined space, and apparently very content to be so poised.

Brother Mike was taken a bit aback, and mumbled something about it being unusual to find a woman buying nails in a hardware shop.

Rather than accepting the brief pleasantry as simply the offhanded salutation it was intended to be, the woman replied, "And I suppose you feel a woman's place is in the home?"

Somewhat astounded by such a reaction, and even provocation from a woman in public, Brother Mike mustered his most expansive communication skills, replying, "Oh no Madame, I would never dare relegate you to the foyer whose dimness would hide your radiance."

He had imagined his effusiveness would have engendered a modest grin that would announce the end of the encounter. However, to his even greater surprise, she intoned, "Now, who would you be to relegate me anywhere?"

He was looking for brass hinges and not heated debate. He thought peaceful thoughts, then, in an effort to disengage, he replied, "Indeed Madame, my humble apologies. We are in a brave new world without borders, and I hope you secure the necessary supplies for your project—wishing you the greatest success with its prompt completion."

Surely that was adequate to stifle any further exchanges and allow Brother Mike to continue his search for the obviously elusive brass hinges. Alas, the lady rose as if on her tippy toes, locked eyes with him and expounded, "Maybe your world is limitless, but mine is very real and very cramped; especially right now. Good day to you sir."

Well, at least an ending was accomplished and Brother Mike moved down the aisle where he found his hinges on a dust-covered bottom shelf.

ỡ ỡ ỡ

The monastery had a rather typical, for a monastery, schedule. The first prayers of the day, Vigils, were held at 6:00 a.m. These were followed by Lauds Prayers at 7:15 a.m. There was midday prayer at 12:30 p.m., followed by a large midday meal and gathering at 1:00 p.m. In the evening, Vespers were held at 6:00 p.m. and Compline at 8:00 p.m. For some, the day was totally absorbed in prayer, adding a mass at mid-morning and afternoon prayer at teatime. But for many, given the multitude of activities at the monastery, the daylight hours were a time of working in God's name. Thus, the entire community was required to attend Vigils, Lauds, Vespers, and Compline; other services attended as time and responsibilities permitted.

Brother Mike followed the schedule, using all his self-discipline. While this imposed restrictions on budgeting his own time, he was only glad that, unlike at some monasteries, Vigils did not take place at 4:00 a.m. He made all efforts to organize his activities so as to be present for the morning and evening prayers, while also trying to be a regular at the midday gathering where internal politics were discussed and decided.

However, on Saturday he was consistently absent from the Abbey at midday. He had developed the habit of passing by the Crane Hotel in the early afternoon after doing his regular shopping. This hotel, dating back to before World War II, had been operated by the same Belgian family for decades. The current owner-operator and his son had a large table permanently reserved for them in one secluded corner of the veranda. This was called *Petit Bruxelles*. Members of the local Belgian community would congregate here to play cards, drink Stella beer, and on special occasions, eat imported European mussels. Older members of the group had been around since before Independence, while younger newcomers generally worked for bilateral or multinational development agencies, although some were local Belgian businessmen or farmers. On nearly any night there was a full table of Europeans adorned by empty beer bottles and coagulating mayonnaise near mostly eaten *frites*.

However, whatever happened the night before, Saturday morning was the time for all hands on deck. This was the period for national community labor. Everyone in fit condition was expected to undertake some activity for the benefit of the state: sweeping a street, cleaning a gutter, planting a tree, or clearing a field of weeds. Although, to Brother Mike's great satisfaction, religious communities were exempt from these wearisome duties—the principle being they were thus engaged full-time—nearly all who could stand did turn out, expat and local resident alike. After these purported arduous Saturday morning humanitarian duties, the duty after the duty was to fall upon the city's drinkeries and replace lost bodily fluids. To this end, the veranda of the Crane was a wild and wooly place on Saturday afternoons and Brother Mike liked nothing more than observing the spectacles clandestinely from *Petit Bruxelles*.

Brother Mike was not a typical denizen of *Petit Bruxelles*. Unlike many of his countrymen, his tastes ran more to local than imported brews, when he was forced to forego his much-loved Courvoisier. Moreover, he put little value in reminiscing about a homeland of which he was so happy to be rid. In a sort of abstract way, he was, however, fascinated by the nostalgia-laced discussions of those seated around the table and equally enthralled by the drunken outspokenness, even lewdness, that could emerge from any point on the veranda as the levels of inebriation and free-spiritedness mounted.

These public displays of depraved lack of self-control were usually even more riveting than the continuous lamenting by old Europeans of times of yore—bemoaning that, in their view, today all was headed to rack and ruin due to the new order of things—in short, due to decolonization. These open theatrics, at times melding into pointed accusations by outsiders, were the very opposite of (indeed, perhaps the motive for) the government's manifesto that the country's neotraditional society should be stoic and detached from corrupting foreign ways—an isolationist message delivered at regular intervals over the airwaves.

To most, however, the political rhetoric was far removed from the daily challenges confronting many foreigners and native-born citizens alike. Life could be tough, and the exhaust valve of the Crane's terrace on a Saturday afternoon was a welcome relief to plenty of those feeling weighed upon by the rigors of the previous week.

During his stopover at the Crane early one such Saturday afternoon, the table of *Petit Bruxelles* was joined by a young man introduced to Brother Mike as Philip. Through the course of the exchanges, it became clear that Philip, although previously unknown to Brother Mike, was no newcomer. He worked at the provincial hospital as an eye specialist. Since the monastery's clinic was not a part of the core public health system, but an adjunct institution, the staff of the larger public program was often unaware of the sectarian facilities, and vice versa.

Brother Mike and Philip seemed to have been born under the same star. They both disclosed they could only take *Petit Bruxelles* in small doses, that they felt exceptionally blessed to be where they were, doing what they were doing, and that they really didn't give a damn about the rest of the world. They were truly kindred spirits.

Brother Mike and Philip continued to meet on the veranda of the Crane most Saturday afternoons, ultimately choosing their own table a safe distance from *Petit Bruxelles*. Well-chilled beer and heated discussions further cemented their relationship and one day Philip asked Brother Mike if he played poker. Brother Mike loved poker. He loved taking the risks and loved even more winning, which he did frequently. Here was another nail reinforcing their bond.

Philip explained he had hosted a group of four to play poker at least one evening a week. One of the group, a professor of geography at the local university, was retiring and moving back to Belgium. Philip wondered if Brother Mike would like to take his place?

Brother Mike did very much want to join the group. Alas, he immediately foresaw a conflict with his ordinary routine: he had evening prayers every day. He clarified his conundrum to Philip. He would very much like to enter the group, but he had Vespers every evening, a convention he could not break without incurring the wrath of the Abbot.

Philip very much liked Brother Mike and even more, he was curious how he would be as a card player. In their weekly reunions on the veranda, Brother Mike demonstrated an affable camaraderie and open mind. But when they entered into frank and often serious discussions as the beer loosened the spirit, Brother Mike ever so slightly lifted the cover on a much more deliberate and calculating core that seemed to reflect a very strong dose of *sangfroid*. How would this circumspect personality fair on the combative and, at times, insidious terrain of poker?

Philip thought for a while and came up with a proposal for Brother Mike, "Wednesday afternoon my eye clinic is closed as the space is needed for a program focusing on pregnant and soon-to-deliver mothers. Another member of our group, Karl, is also a professor at the university, an international law specialist. I happen to know he has no academic responsibilities on Wednesday afternoons. Finally, the third member of our group is Antonio. You may know him? He has the small grocery store before you get to the main market. His time is his own and his sons generally take care of the store, so I am sure he too could be free on Wednesdays. So how about it? We could arrange our game for 3:00 p.m. which would give us a good run at the cards and still allow you to get back for prayers."

Brother Mike was most appreciative. It seemed where there's a will there really is a way and he really wanted a way to play poker with this man whom he saw as an able adversary as well as potentially a genuine friend. If Philip was as good at cards as he was at organizing a card game, the planned contests could be most interesting.

Brother Mike thanked Philip for his ingenuity and efforts to arrange things such that he could partake of this worthy pastime. They agreed to meet at Philip's house, not far from the Crane, the next Wednesday.

Brother Mike then took his leave as, exceptionally this Saturday afternoon, he had to attend to some monastic business. A young novitiate, Jean-Baptiste, was being proposed to be assigned to him as a sort of assistant. Given the delicacy of his affairs, he was not sure he could accommodate an assistant without jeopardizing all he had put together over the years. Accordingly, he had agreed with Jean-Baptiste to meet for a drink at a well-known outdoor cabaret on the road to the southern border.

With his religious life of piety and penury, Brother Mike did not own a vehicle himself. However, this curtailment was no obstacle. As the responsible person for the community's logistics, he had access to the monastery's motor pool which, to support their assorted tasks, was large if not exhaustive. Consequently, he was assigned a rather aged Toyota pickup that now, with a score of bunches of bananas in the back that he had picked up earlier in the day for the orphanage kitchens, he drove south to his rendezvous with Jean-Baptiste.

He found Jean-Baptiste sitting at a shaded table, enjoying the cooling gusts that began to whirl around the hills in the afternoon, while consuming an equally cool brew. Jean-Baptiste was in his late twenties. Brother Mike knew that he was the son of a major entrepreneur, one of the chief petrol importers into the country. Given the weaknesses in the public school system, Jean-Baptiste's father saw a life in a religious community as the best means for a good education—something he valued greatly as not having benefited from the same himself. From his early teens, Jean-Baptiste had attended Catholic schools and then migrated into more specialized studies and training with several religious communities, ending up with the Brothers of Piety. There was always a worrisome parallel agenda that, should he lose his enthusiasm, Jean-Baptiste could opt to leave the religious world and return to the world of money, politics, and power that flowed around his father. The various religious community members who were engaged with Jean-Baptiste were always praying that he stays the course and remain a strong proponent of monastic life because, through this moral support, the various communities received considerable financial support from the father, support they feared they would lose if the son left.

To the surprise of many, in spite of his good looks and joie de vivre, from all appearances Jean-Baptiste was leading a devout life, still passionate about his calling and serious about his studies. One unexpected detour had been the revelation that Jean-Baptiste had a talent for sculpture, an art form for which he also seemingly had the necessary fervor to be able to transform thoughts into tangible objects. It was perhaps a bit unfortunate that his father still wanted to micromanage Jean-Baptiste's ecclesiastic life. Apparently trying to cover all his bases, his father promoted a business orientation to his son's intellectual growth such that, when the day came, the son would be able to leave his theological pursuits and assume control of the father's empire. It was in this vein that he had been pushing the Brothers of Piety to get his son more involved in the business side of things and in this way that the son had landed on Brother Mike's doorstep, unexpected and unwanted.

Brother Mike put on his most congenial smile and sat across from his would-be protégé after giving him a strong embrace and heartfelt wishes for a good Saturday afternoon. He had been planning, as he was wont to do, for some time how he would handle this dilemma. He could not alienate Jean-Baptiste as this might raise some eyebrows at the Abbey and cause far more in-depth looks into his various practices. Yet, he could not afford to have an attendant of any sort—his affairs were his alone and must be overseen by but one person: Brother Mike himself. He had a plan. He had to test the ground to see if it could stand up to the rather complex requirements of the situation. But, as everyone knew, Brother Mike was good at organizing things.

He had considered starting with a "How are you my son?" type of father-son approach, but he quickly sensed this would be to no avail. Strategically, he needed to start on the upper hand. With complete openness, he asked, "Tell me about your sculptures."

With no hesitation, Jean-Baptiste flowered and expansively described the various statues he had created and how thrilling it felt to be able to see these objects materialize from amorphous stones. He went into great detail as to how the process was one with his religion and how it was through his faith that he saw the stones transform into divine works.

Brother Mike ordered more beer and enquired as to how much time Jean-Baptiste was able to devote to his sculptures given all the rigors of the Abbey. A frown entered the corners of Jean-Baptiste's eyes as he conceded he was frustrated because his sculpting time was minimal with all the obligations he must fulfill to take his final vows and enter the order.

It would work.

Brother Mike smiled to himself, maintaining a solemn air as he offered, "If you were to be assigned to me, I have a vacant room near the panel beating shop where you could set up a studio and spend all your time, at least in that part assigned to me, developing your wondrous works of art."

Yes, this would be fantastic, an excellent solution. So let it be written, so let it be done.

Brother Mike shared a few more beers with Jean-Baptiste, steering the conversation to an analysis of the late rains and the impact these might have on the harvest. As the sun moved further west, Brother Mike reminded Jean-Baptiste of Vespers and offered him a ride back to the Abbey.

3

WEDNESDAY ARRIVED AT ITS own speed and Brother Mike prepared for poker. He left early to get a few sacks of cement at the market, thereby justifying his taking the Toyota. He then found Philip's house with little difficulty. Typical of this expat neighborhood, his bungalow was set back in a small but well-kept garden, set off by a small garage and a large apron with parking for several vehicles including Brother Mike's pickup. The entryway was through sliding glass doors, directly into a modest living room with an adjacent dining area. The living area was appointed with locally made armchairs with foam rubber cushions covered in bright African prints surrounding a large glass-topped coffee table.

Philip met him as he approached the sliding door, guiding him to one of the chairs; the others were occupied by two gentlemen he assumed to be Karl and Antonio. His suspicions proved correct as Philip made the introductions, thereafter offering beer and cigarettes all around. Brother Mike did not smoke, but he was a minority of one and the room was soon redolent with tobacco smoke.

They chatted while Philip's houseboy adjusted the dining area to make room for a folding card table under the central hanging light, placing a similar folding chair on each side. As Brother Mike was not only new to the game, but also to the group, the preliminary conversation was more biographic. Brother Mike by now knew Philip well, knowing he was starting his second decade in Central Africa after lengthy schooling in ophthalmology, specializing in tropical eye diseases.

Brother Mike now learned by current standards Philip was still wet behind the ears in terms of experience living abroad. In fact, for the others, living abroad was really the wrong term, applied only because both Karl and Antonio were from European stock, but neither had ever really lived in Europe. Karl had been born in Central Africa where his father had been a doctor in the colonial service. Antonio's equatorial roots were even deeper.

His family had migrated to German East Africa in 1888, and started a bodega in Bagamoyo in what is now Tanzania. His family had considerably expanded their business interests from those early days, but in 1962, when Nyerere was elected president, it became hard for the family to hold onto its investments in an environment of African Socialism. They had moved further into the hinterland, into the Great Lakes Region. Today, after two decades of rebuilding, Antonio and his family had a thriving supermarket as well as commercial and residential property and a profitable poultry farm.

Brother Mike wondered how it was that he had never met these gentlemen before. After all, the provincial capital had a population of less than 70,000 inhabitants; it was not a big city—the expats of all varieties, including the religious orders, accounted for less than three percent of the census. It would seem logical that everyone knew everyone else, but this was obviously not the case. Everyone may well know the rumors and tall tales of everyone else, but they certainly did not know everyone else in the flesh and blood. Karl and Antonio definitely had stories to tell. They were people from whom lessons could be learned.

But this was not the time for introspection. The card table was set with a fresh deck of cards impatiently waiting to be shuffled, not to mention Vespers getting all the closer with each passing minute. Everyone picked up their sweating amber beer bottles and moved to the square field of battle.

The cards were shuffled and dealt and then reshuffled. The conversation was mainly monosyllabic. At one critical point when Brother Mike was considering his wager, there was a loud call of "Bullshit!" When Brother Mike looked up from his hand, he could not tell which of his adversaries had made such a pronouncement. As he stared at his opponents, a resounding "Bullshit!" was again uttered, but by none of the players. His consternation was clear on his face.

Philip saw Brother Mike's predicament and laughingly pointed to the corner of the room. There, for the first time, Brother Mike noticed a tall cylindrical cage with a domed top. He placed his cards face down on the table and got up to see, more closely, the creature that had so rudely interrupted his concentration.

As he approached the cage, he saw it was occupied by a most impressive African grey parrot. As he got nearer, the parrot scooted across his perch and bowed his head, almost as if to seek Brother Mike's blessing. Brother Mike extended a finger to try and scratch the proffered head.

"Don't do that," said Philip in a stern voice. "You get your finger in there and he'll flay it. He doesn't like men.

"That's Kasuku, Angela's naughty bird. They say the female parrots bond with men and the males with women. We don't know which sort this one is, but by its behavior we assume it's a male and it sure is tight with Angela and enjoys inflicting great pain on us boys."

Brother Mike withdrew his finger and was turning to regain his chair when, as if understanding the full conversation, Kasuku bid him goodbye with a loud "Asshole!"

Time passed quickly with no big winner nor loser. Soon the shadows lengthened and Brother Mike knew he would have to race the sun to its setting, the hour of Vespers corresponding to sundown at these latitudes.

The next Saturday, as the veranda at the Crane began to simmer with weekend energy, Philip confirmed to Brother Mike that their Wednesday game would be on and would be on for the foreseeable future, as all the players were now committed to the new schedule, which they found to be the most agreeable way to pass a midweek afternoon.

With due precision, the group assembled at Philip's on the next appointed date. As the introductions and biographies had been taken care of, they were able to plunge directly into their cards. Each was engrossed in evaluating what the Fates had given them when they heard the door slide open. With a quick glance, Philip said, "Do you all know my wife, Angela?"

Karl and Antonio looked up from their cards and offered a familiar greeting to Philip's spouse who they obviously knew well. When Brother Mike looked up, she had her back turned, as she was removing her scarf. He mumbled a brief salutation and was just about to look back to his cards when she did an about-face and, to his shock, he realized that Mrs. Philip was the lady with whom he had exchanged words at the hardware shop all those weeks ago.

There was a twinkle in her eyes as she came over to the card table and offered her hand to Brother Mike. He politely stood and took her hand, noticing the firm return pressure and the dry palm. She then softly intoned, "My pleasure Brother Mike, Philip has told me so much about you. And, as I see you now before me, I wonder, have we met before?"

"Indeed," replied Brother Mike. "You may have long forgotten a modest monk who exchanged a few words with you in a hardware store some time back."

"Hmmm," she followed through. "I have no idea of the modesty, but I do recall the conversation. I also recall our discourse being a bit one-sided. I hope your cards treat you better than did my dialogue."

With this she excused herself and went into the interior of the house.

Brother Mike felt obliged to add some background to their somewhat cryptic exchange, explaining to his fellow players that he had met a charming lady at a hardware store when seeking supplies for the Abbey, having no idea this lady was Mrs. Philip.

Philip seemed to want to fill in the blanks and added, "I tell Angela she's the slum lord of the town. She has lots of small rentals scattered hither and yon. Although these don't seem to put much meat on the table, or money in the pot, the oversight and upkeep do seem to fully occupy her time. Therefore, if you ever have to move out of the Abbey, she has a place for you. You would probably not find her accommodation that different from the monastery's cells."

At this, all had a good laugh followed by a good swallow of beer before they got back to the serious business of poker. Again, time dictated their play and soon Brother Mike was bumping along the road to the Abbey, unsure if it was the stiff springs of the pickup or the potholes of the laterite road that were most answerable for the jostling he was receiving as he headed toward Vespers with his pockets full of considerably more francs than he had had when he had departed early in the morning in search of a valve for one of the clinic's toilets.

The next day after Lauds, Brother Mike snuck away to his refuge on the pond bank. After he had impaled a worm on the hook of the cane pole he secreted in a nearby banana grove, he leaned back against the acacia tree that had pierced the dike and took score, not of his poker hands, but of his life.

Things seemed to be as well as they could, with the knowledge that the unknown always offered both greater riches and a shortcut to Purgatory. His management of the Abbey's affairs continued to be impeccable, if slightly embellished for the benefit of his good self and a few other selected entrepreneurs in the nearly area. He had managed to get Jean-Baptiste set up in a secluded room where few would know he was there and even fewer would care. He had successfully ended the friendship with Sister Alice and, for the moment, was relishing his monastic solitude. He felt comfortable he was living up to his vows and his expectations, with only two sorties a week: Saturday and Wednesday afternoons.

Brother Mike pulled in his line, reached into his ever-present holdall, extracted his bottle of Courvoisier and a small glass; things were good. The breeze picked up, rustling the fronds on the nearby banana trees. The gust startled a hamerkop that scolded all as it flew from its hiding place along the shore where it had been hunting small fishes. Children laughed and played at the school on the hill on the far side of the swale, their melody vibrating off the rich lowlands where cabbage, carrots, and tomatoes sprouted like buds on a rose. Life was good.

Brother Mike's routine now seemed fixed and his situation stable. He approached new friendships with caution after a lengthy break following Sister Alice. He managed short, almost ephemeral, friendships with a sister visiting from a northern order and a public health specialist from the Ministry who was touring centers in the area.

He enjoyed the challenges of keeping things moving—the logistics of intertwining the Abbey's supply chain and his own substantive network. But his real pleasures were still to be found crowd watching from the Crane's veranda and placing his bets at Philip's.

The seasonal changes were very nuanced in these hills, and Brother Mike was scarcely aware of the passing of time. The arrival of a new container was the main milestone, and this, too, was routine enough as to not create any feeling of exceptionalism. The Christmas season was always a joy, but the abstemious spirit of the Abbey made this a modest festivity, with the exception of a splendid and ornate Christmas Eve Mass.

The ascetic lifestyle notwithstanding, the monastery was not to forego opportunities. The Christmas season was a time when the bakery and butcher shop produced baskets of seasonal favorites to entice their customers: special breads, exotic sausages, and heavily scented cakes and cookies. There was a cornucopia of holiday gastronomy that required a whole new stock of supplies. It was, thus, that at this time there were no less than two containers a month to ensure the brothers had all the fixings to satisfactorily serve their clientele, some coming from as far away as the national capital.

After the holidays, there was a respite—a deep communal sigh of relief that yet another season had successfully passed. This lull was generally filled with a quite good cheer such as one has after consuming a well-prepared feast. In fact, the comparison was very apt as the brothers themselves also tended to up consumption of all sorts during the festive season.

Brother Mike was enjoying the seasonal afterglow during his first go at the cards for the New Year. They had just dealt the first hand when there was a raucous pounding on the sliding glass door. All looked up, but only Karl recognizing Etienne frantically knocking on the door.

As Karl escorted Etienne into the room, he announced to all that Etienne was the houseboy of Mr. Goldfarb, the math teacher at the Catholic High School. While none of the other players knew Mr. Goldfarb, they had heard of him, as he had been here for ages. Now in his advanced years, he still walked to school every day, wearing the same old charcoal gray three-piece tweed suit with a red fraternity tie. No one knew if he had but one set of clothes, but he was only seen wearing the same somber attire when he marched to and from school, through the years with the same strong gate.

Like Karl, Mr. Goldfarb had sent his wife to back Europe, or she had opted to return. In any event, as with many expats in town, they lived separate lives. Since *La Coopération*—the international assistance agency that employed most of the expatriates ostensibly assisting the country in various capacities—paid travel for the whole family, a spouse living in Europe could come to Africa on holiday while one working here could return at regular intervals to reacquaint him- or herself with the homeland.

These somewhat fluid spousal arrangements led to a variety of accords. While Karl found in this detached connection a new freedom to sow the wild oats he had forgone as a youth, when he was consumed by his academics, Mr. Goldfarb had preferred a more staid arrangement—setting up house with a young girl for whom he could more likely have been a grandfather than a lover.

This relationship, so scorching at the onset, had cooled and assumed another form of detachment as Mr. Goldfarb's years continued to climb. While the flame may not have been fully extinguished, the young and striking (and for all intents and purposes, the second Mrs. Goldfarb) frequently sought the attention of younger men—often on the veranda of the Crane. Many an evening, the still comely but aging second Mrs. Goldfarb could be seen on the portico encircled by a gaggle of would-be suitors. After leaving the Crane Hotel, whatever, however, and wherever things happened was only the object of the community's active rumor mill, as the second Mrs. Goldfarb, to her credit, masked her extracurricular flings in nearly complete secrecy. The onlookers could only, as they did so well, wonder with whom and how.

While his spouse was assessing the evening's crop of young admirers strutting their virility at the Crane, Mr. Goldfarb could be seen in his study through the rarely drawn drapes, pacing back and forth in his shirt sleeves, a whisky glass in his hand, a well-used bottle on the coffee table, listening to cassettes of François-Joseph Gossec and seemingly talking to himself between sips.

But now the delicate spousal equilibrium had shifted, as a frantic Etienne was anxiously trying to explain to any who would listen. The second Mrs. Goldfarb had locked Mr. Goldfarb out of the house. When he had returned from his day at school, perspiration drenching his face as it was now the hot season, he found no way to enter his home. Madame had barricaded the doors and was deaf to his calls. Etienne had been returning from the market when he saw the sight. He was now concerned his patron could succumb to heat exhaustion, as he was hammering and hammering on each and every door and window, all to no avail, but with the sweat now soaking his three-piece suit.

The players decided they had to intervene. If they could not penetrate the ramparts on Mr. Goldfarb's behalf, they could at least bring him back here where he could have a cold beer and a sympathetic ear.

Antonio had driven the minivan from the store, so there was room for everyone as they drove the few blocks to the colonial style house that had been occupied by Goldfarb for years and years and years. Pulling into the drive, they spied their prey sitting in a heap on the stoop; his coat still on but his tie loosened around a sweat-soaked collar. He was so still they were worried he may have expired, but when they shook his shoulder, he revived and meekly accepted a ride to Philip's, apparently having lost all will to access the habitation now apparently overseen by the second Mrs. Goldfarb.

When finally seated in one of Philip's armchairs, Mr. Goldfarb resembled a blow-up Saint Nicholas that had suddenly lost all its air. In fact, like air hissing from a leak, his lungs seemed to be voiding their very essence. Nonetheless, when a frothy pint of beer was passed before him, he eagerly took it, instantaneously consuming the entire contents. After a third pint, Mr. Goldfarb's hooded eyes fluttered and he looked as though he could speak. With the four men perched over him like a kingfisher at the fishpond, and Etienne shadowing them in the corner, unwilling to leave his long-time patron, Mr. Goldfarb uttered but a word, "Damn!"

It took yet a fourth pint before the tale could be spun.

Goldfarb knew it was in the offing. She was still a prime specimen and he offered little to keep her close to home and hearth. Heretofore, the long parade of young men had been able to assuage the urges, while she still found safety and security in remaining the second Mrs. Goldfarb. However, as was bound to happen, she finally met a man who was not just there to satiate her but who said he really loved her; he wanted to marry her and build a house for her. This seemed so little to ask. A normal life was now so attainable—no more galavanting, no more evenings on the terrace. The opportunity for a real home with someone to whom she could relate and with whom she could communicate. Was it too much to ask? She certainly did not think so and had said as much to Goldfarb that morning. She only wanted her freedom and a stipend that could help with building the new house. She was not greedy and she bore Goldfarb no ill feeling. But it was time for change.

Yet, upon hearing the early morning news, Goldfarb, as usual a bit hung over from his nightly concert with his whiskey, had reacted violently and negatively. No! Never! Never, never, never! She was his. She had come to him as almost a child. All she had, all she knew, all she had learned was thanks to him. She was not only his wife, she was his product. She owed him. She could not abandon him—absolutely not.

However, now among his own, he saw the futility of his actions. He could not control her. He could not refuse her. He had no choice, he had to acquiesce. Maybe his first wife would come back. Then another "Damn!" He remembered his first wife was now living with a young tennis pro. What would he do? He was too old to think of a third Mrs. Goldfarb.

Even though Goldfarb was not close to the group, he was a member of their wider expat community. They wanted to help him as they wanted to believe he would help them if the tables were turned.

They called Etienne to a group huddle and then approached Goldfarb before he could down his sixth pint. Etienne, who has been living at his farm outside town and coming to work every day by bicycle, offered to move into the boy's quarters at the Goldfarb house if *le patron* agreed. Etienne's oldest son wanted to marry but could not as he had no house of his own. This son already did most of the farming, so Etienne could give his country house to the boy, who could then marry while Etienne and his wife moved into town, albeit into accommodations that were not their own. His other children were nearly grown and could live on the farm as they had been doing, their older sibling now the head of the household.

They had to repeat this proposal three times before Goldfarb grasped what was being suggested. Yet, once he did seize the idea, he accepted immediately, offering to spruce up the quarters before Etienne moved in.

In this way, another in the continuing dramas had been contained, but at the cost of a game of poker.

࿔ ࿔ ࿔

Brother Mike had little contact with Goldfarb and could only assume the arrangements with Etienne had taken place as planned: the second Mrs. Goldfarb was now missus somebody else and Goldfarb's suit had finally dried after the ordeal of restructuring his household.

Brother Mike understood, moreover, that situations like Goldfarb's arose more often than most knew. Men often entered the Foreign Service fresh out of their tertiary studies. Many—married and even fathers at this time—had had little opportunity to, as they liked to say in this part of the world, "play life." While they may have been long on education, they were very short on life experiences. When they came here, they found a lot of their traditional social barriers absent or replaced by new and often more liberal codes of conduct, certainly a concept well appreciated by Brother Mike.

Here there were frequently totally different value systems and protocols. Marriage, age, sex, friendship, respect—all were subject to new interpretations. Brother Mike had seen his European brothers completely burn out on the excesses of a less encumbering and more open life, even though the social liberties here in the central part of the continent were said to be stringent by comparison to those further to the west.

Brother Mike often wondered about these social norms, thinking frequently of the time he was driving to the country's capital and was overtaken by the shiny black Mercedes of the Archbishop, with his Holiness seated regally in the back, his wife next to him, her headscarf piled high in the rear window.

4

SLOWLY BROTHER MIKE BECAME more acquainted with Philip and his family. With only two windows a week, the process was at times almost imperceptible, but somehow enjoyable, like peeping through a keyhole at the lives of others. He wondered if Father Alphonse from his church back home had felt this way when he had heard his confessional?

Philip had come "out" to the real world, as he liked to say, as soon as he finished his internship in a prestigious hospital in Bruges. His story was very similar to Brother Mike's own. Philip's father had been a common laborer, working for the city, basically filling potholes and cleaning ditches. To make ends meet, his mother worked part-time as a cleaning lady, leaving their small, nearly bare home for the extravagant and rambling estates of the rich. He had one older sister who worked in a yardage shop after finishing secondary school. He was the star of the family. They had all pooled their resources for him to be able to attend the best schools and achieve the finest education. They were, thus, shocked and even wounded when, upon receiving his medical degree, he announced he wanted to go to work and live in Africa. He left with his family ties frayed, some to the breaking point.

But Belgium and his Belgian life faded as he immersed himself in his new career and his new environment. He found he had a great, nearly unquenchable appetite for two things: his work and beer; a close third was the ladies. As the first ophthalmologist in the country, Philip, or Doctor Bwana Phil as many of his patients called him, had many waiting at his doorstep. With great pride, he treated each equally and was as thrilled today to help someone see better as he had been when he helped his first patient (an 80-year-old man from a far-off village in the mountains of the North) all those years ago. He could and did spend countless hours in his clinic.

Early on, as a bachelor, he would stay in the clinic at night until the last patient was seen and then head to his favorite bar, a small off-license called Chez Martin, situated in a working-class neighborhood with few expatriates. This reminded him of the bars his father used to frequent in Belgium. He relished the frosty beer and took pleasure in trying to pick up the local dialect as he chatted with fellow customers who, once they grew used to a white man in their midst, treated him just like any other drinking buddy.

Philip avoided the expat watering holes and the expat social events. He had not come all this way to live as a Belgian in Belgium. That was the life he had forsaken to the great chagrin of his family, a family that had indeed sacrificed greatly to get him to where he was.

As he began sinking African roots, Philip moved into the small bungalow he occupied to today. He hired Joseph as his cook, launderer, cleaner, and live-in caretaker. The same Joseph who still cooked his *frites* just so, and kept the fridge stocked with ice cold beer.

For several years his life seemed like a record on a Victrola—when the needle got to the last groove, the arm lifted up automatically and gently placed the needle on the first groove and it all started over again. Up—coffee, cigarette, and baguette for a starter—to the clinic, closing when the last person had been seen—to Chez Martin (he used to keep the bottle caps in his pocket to know how many beers he had drunk, but this disgusted him so he abandoned the practice)—home at some point finding dinner prepared by Joseph and warming in the oven, to bed—either alone or accompanied. The next day it all started over again.

Then one day his routine changed forever. As usual, he went into his exam room to see a patient the nurses had prepped. As he glanced into the chair, he felt a lump in his throat—a sensation with which he was completely unfamiliar. Here in his chair was a rather diminutive youngish lady but who had the most mischievous eyes and enigmatic smile. He was truly taken aback. Aware of his reaction, he felt compelled to at least try and find out more about his patient than her vision problems. In fact, it turned out her eyesight was 20/20. She had been working in a garden, pruning a large Euphorbia plant, when her machete splashed the milky sap into her eyes and she felt she was blinded. Once Philip washed the eyes thoroughly and let them rest with some comforting ointment, her sight returned—uninjured and perfect. He sensed that her relief at his findings made her let her guard down and she did at least impart enough of her story for him to ascertain that she was single, the daughter of a rather prosperous businessman who had three sons and was disappointed that his last born was not also a male.

She seemed disinclined to give much more information. However, what she had provided—or more correctly, the cheeky fashion with which she had provided it—was enough to tweak Philip's soul and he knew he would go to the records to get her address so that he could call upon her later.

This was Angela. Philip had courted her with ardor and all the energy his compact but muscular body could muster. He had abandoned all the casual girlfriends he had lined up, focusing totally on this one indecipherable female who so intrigued him. As he had later recounted to Brother Mike, Philip had heard that in dental school, students had to learn to tie complex knots inside a matchbox with their eyes closed to practice the dexterity needed to perform all variety of maneuvers in the space of a mouth. In trying to court Angela, Philip felt like he was trying to untie a complicated knot in a matchbox. While Angela did not shun him completely, she certainly did not encourage him. She was often aloof, keeping him, and seemingly everyone else, at arms length. While her enticing smile that went all the way to the corners of her piercing eyes was at times tender, her mannerisms tended to be impassive, and at times glacial.

But if Philip was nothing else, he was determined. Slowly he thawed Angela's spirit, slowly they moved through friendship to something deeper and richer. Slowly she opened and told her story.

Philip had known that she had come from a well-to-do family that had a preference for male children. But what he now learned was that, when she had just entered university, she had met a young Congolese, a sharp and savvy entrepreneur who saw great opportunities in real estate. They became engaged. She was planning on leaving her studies to work with him. Her father was choleric. He had but one daughter and she would complete university—something he had always regretted he himself, like Philip's father, had been unable to accomplish. But she was equally resolute, she would marry the man of her dreams and they would create new, grander dreams together.

Angela had forged ahead regardless of the consequences and found herself banished from her family. They treated her as if she did not exist.

But she did exist and her love existed. Through this love she and her husband had formed a beautiful girl child. They watched their real estate holdings grow as the girl grew and life seemed to be on track. Then it had happened. In going to arrange for title documents at the national capital, her husband had been in a terrible accident; he was dead on the spot. Angela was now a widow with no close family ties, a young daughter, and an expanding business to manage. It took all her considerable will to stand up under these pressures, but stand up she did, and she transformed the real estate business into a portfolio of rental properties that, even if they did not bring wealth, would keep her daughter and herself in good shape, food on the table, bills paid, and enough for her daughter's education.

Then Angela met Philip.

They had now been married for nearly ten years. Angela's daughter, Lucie, was away at boarding school. Angela and Philip had had one son, Germain, who was now six. As Joseph continued to oversee the household, including Germain's daily upkeep, Angela and Philip were free to spend the necessary hours and days taking care of their respective jobs, being a landlord and an eye doctor.

Brother Mike had no idea how the marriage now faired with two workaholic spouses. But he had heard from Philip, reading a bit between the lines, that as in Angela's case, Philip's family had been apoplectic when they had heard their son was to be married to an African. It was already more than they could bear that their boy had gone to some hellish place where he hid his light under a basket and where the family would never receive any acclaim for his healing skills and their grand sacrifice that had led to these skills. But now this ungracious offspring had gone native and was going to take a heathen wife. They could not support the shame. His father had not toiled in the mud and muck to put his only son through school for this. His mother had not tolerated the abuse of the rich and rude to put food in his stomach for this. His sister had not struggled for long hours to help pay his tuition for this. No, the family was beyond the breaking point. Philip was no more. Their son was dead.

Two souls, having been cast off by disapproving families; Brother Mike wondered if it was a match made in Heaven. He had no idea, but it certainly was a pairing of two very strong forces. And, like strong magnets, these forces could attract or repel. Brother Mike was uncertain how they were joined. But he found himself nearly magnetically attracted to each, seeing each as so different yet somehow part of a whole.

Some afternoons when things seemed to be going as they should, Brother Mike would slip off to the pond, grab his pole, and let his mind fly as he hoped his worm would entice a nice sized bream. When the sky was that pale blue you-can-see-forever clear, the siesta hour gusts like gentle puffs from a snoozing calf, and the eucalyptus leaves rustling like shifting sands, Brother Mike's mind would soar like a falcon, riding the zephyr, looking down at mankind as though spying on termites in a massive transparent mound—each going his own way, order out of disorder, production out of decay.

Brother Mike could be a deep thinker. He could wonder about man's inhumanity to man. He could ponder a world overtaken by a tumescent population. He could even probe the furthest reaches of his intellect, asking himself, "Is God with us?" Brother Mike could do all these things or Brother Mike could drink a cold beer and play a hand of cards. While the former might lead to wisdom and divine understanding, it would also underscore the feeble human state. Brother Mike preferred the latter, which numbed the mind and allowed one to be indifferent as to humankind's almost certain degeneracy.

This particular afternoon on the pond back, Brother Mike wondered about his own direction, sensing he might be getting too mixed up with Philip and Angela. How had he spent all these years without even knowing them and now they seemed to preoccupy his thoughts? If there was a reason for everything, what was the reason for this? Two nearly antisocial souls who had been excommunicated by their families. A household that had nothing to do with the Abbey, a household that did not even attend church. What was the attraction? What was the magnetism?

Brother Mike tried, and usually succeeded to keep below the radar. He was thus a bit concerned when he was summoned urgently to the Abbot's office. He entered the sparse headquarters of the Abbey with some trepidation, knocking softly on the Abbot's stout door before entering, hat in hand.

The rotund and aging Abbot was silhouetted against the big windows that looked out over the courtyard that was the epicenter of the monastery as well as the concourse for the mission's impressive chapel. He turned as he heard Brother Mike entering, extending his right hand, a golden ecclesiastical ring clearly visible. Brother Mike genuflected on his left knee saying, "Father Abbot, may I ask your blessing?"

As the blessing was given, Brother Mike brushed his lips along the icy surface of the ring, stood and took the chair offered by the Abbot. Seating himself behind a rough-hewn desk, the Abbot entertained a few pleasantries before going after the meat, "Michael, my son, I believe you know Doctor van Hoot who comes regularly to our health center from the provincial hospital?"

Brother Mike indicated he did know the doctor, although in his mind he was wondering about the question as he and the doctor were certainly not close in any way; in truth, they rarely saw each other.

"Well, Doctor van Hoot has a bit of a problem and I would like you to look in on him as you are frequently in town and you seem to have good contacts across the board, including at the hospital."

"Thank you Father," Brother Mike interjected, "for thinking of me, but I scarcely know the good doctor."

The Abbot frowned a bit and replied in a neutral tone, "That is of no matter. I've just told our good friend the Doctor that we will extend a hand of help should he choose to accept it. Your connections and talents in dealing with the outside world make you perfectly suited for this assignment. Simply see our good friend and offer any assistance the Abbey may provide. If he chooses to decline, we have stood by him as we promised. If he asks for your intervention, do try and see how this can be done with as little disruption as possible. Come back to me if you feel this is an area where there are matters that could impact on the Abbey or the Abbey's population."

With that, Brother Mike was dismissed with the understanding that sooner rather than later he would seek out Doctor van Hoot.

As he walked along the corridor that took him out to the courtyard, Brother Mike wondered if there was deeper meaning in the Abbot's comments about his "talent in dealing with the outside." Were his machinations known to the Abbot? To others? Was he in jeopardy?

Ahhhh, he decided, this is much ado about nothing. If anyone knew they would quickly try and bring all to a halt. Having too avid an imagination was often not a blessing and he should not be looking for scorpions under every stone. This was about some sort of promise the Abbot had made to van Hoot and nothing else. The sooner he followed up on the Abbot's behalf, the sooner this would be a closed case and he could go back to his normal routine.

ề ề ề

Brother Mike found Doctor van Hoot in his office at the hospital. He was an internist and one of the senior doctors, the team leader for a project of the Belgian Government aimed at building local public health capacity while at the same time treating the needy.

Doctor van Hoot looked like anyone you might see on the streets of Brussels—a little overweight, a little balding, medium height—completely ordinary. Brother Mike knew that, not too different from Goldfarb, van Hoot had married a young local girl. However, he had never been married before and the word was that their marriage was sound. Van Hoot did not frequent the Crane or other sites of laxness or lasciviousness, and it was assumed he was a "good man."

Brother Mike explained he had come at the request of the Abbot as his Father had understood Doctor van Hoot might need some help from the Abbey?

"Help from God?" he quipped with a smirk. "Now that would be a solution to my problem that I had not considered. I need forgiveness, but I am not sure God is ready to intervene into the mess I've created."

"God is always ready to help those who ask for His assistance," replied Brother Mike.

"Thank you for the kind offer. Kindly tell my good friend the Abbot I am most appreciative, but must deal with this on my own."

"I will gladly inform my Father the Abbot, but I am sure he would appreciate a bit more detail as to the nature of the problem at hand to ensure the Abbey cannot offer assistance in one way or another, even if it is not Divine Intervention."

"This is truly not an issue that concerns the Abbey, the church, or any religious order or person. This is my problem and mine alone."

"Surely my Father would want me to offer to help you with your burden. God does not give us more than we can carry, but sometimes we need to hold hands to be able to carry the heaviest of loads."

"I can see your Father has given you strict orders and that you are unlikely to leave me in peace until you have more tidbits to carry to the Abbot." And so it was, without a blush and without missing a beat, Doctor van Hoot told Brother Mike his problem was that he had slept with his mother-in-law. He seemed to think a further explanation was really unnecessary, but did add, as almost an afterthought, that his wife had been away at the time of his mother-in-law's visit. They had both partaken of too much wine and found themselves in a compromising position. A position, he could not help from adding, that was most probably unknown to members of the religious community such as Brother Mike, who had taken a vow of chastity.

The once-off indiscretion had taken on new importance when his wicked mother-in-law threatened to tell her daughter of the union, not portraying it as an alcohol-induced mistake, but the sign of a maturing relationship where the Doctor had finally realized that he was more akin to an older, more experienced woman than a young child. This was nonsense and the Doctor had no intention of leaving his true wife. Nonetheless, he also wished to avoid as much drama and outrage as possible. He simply wanted to turn back the clock and find again the life that he had known and enjoyed.

Brother Mike's brain was ticking off the options, starting to idle like a well-tuned engine. His survival skills had often shown him that the best tactic was the lowest common denominator. This was a prurient subject that would benefit neither the good Doctor nor the Abbey. While it could certainly set tongues a wagging, it was destined only for ruin for the family and, by inference, friends. His task was to find a means of avoiding this nearly certain outcome, while restoring honor and peace to the Doctor.

There was no advantage to even fill the Abbot in on all the salacious details. It would suffice to say Doctor van Hoot had some delicate family issues which Brother Mike, on behalf of his Father the Abbot, had been able to address to the mutual satisfaction of all. The Doctor would then be in the Abbey's debt, the Abbot would, in turn, be in Brother Mike's debt, or at the very least see Brother Mike as an ally with sensitive secrets that were best kept suppressed. As the Abbot's emissary, moreover, Brother Mike might be able to call in a favor or two from Doctor van Hoot, and maybe even a few from his close associates.

The sordid affair of two old drunks doing things they wished they had not was as old as the hills. Stifling any negative repercussions in the name of the Abbey could bring benefits all around.

But, Brother Mike had no idea of how or where to start. Nevertheless, this was not a time for complete candor, so Brother Mike took his leave of the Doctor, thanking him for sharing his problem; hoping the intervention of the Church could bring some solace. He further assured the Doctor he would provide his Father with only the briefest summary while he himself would examine how it might be possible to mitigate any negatives from this unfortunate happenstance.

Brother Mike believed in taking prompt, but well thought out action. His first call was on Antonio. The shopkeeper knew all the businessmen and would-be businessmen in town. He knew not only their business, but their stories. He found such knowledge invaluable in optimizing the profits from his own investments.

When asked about Doctor van Hoot's mother-in-law, with no explanation offered as to why this person was of interest, Antonio's first reaction was, "Oh her!"

As Brother Mike dug deeper, Antonio unveiled a tale of many twists. The good lady's husband, now long departed, was seen by all, including the Doctor, as the father of the Doctor's wife. However, the madam had been more libertine than a Bangkok hooker. In her youth she had been known, in the Biblical sense, by many of the community, regardless of their age, ethnic origin, or social standing. Her daughter was a case in point. She was in truth not the child of the good lady's husband, but the child of an Arab trader who sold motorcycle parts, a Muslim merchant.

This presented a particular dilemma for the once so vampish lady. She was nonchalant about her many past imprudences, oblivious of her reputation, and unavoidably carried the baggage of her slattern past to the present. Nevertheless, at her husband's death she had inherited his considerable assets with the codicil that these riches be used for their daughter, both for her dowry and a stipend for her after her marriage. Any additional funds over and beyond the daughter's needs were to be available for his loving wife. And, the madam made sure her daughter's needs were modest at best, living a fine life on the residue. But these arrangements had been, and continued to be, much contested by the late husband's brother, with whom he had held many of the investments in partnership.

Brother Mike now saw light in the tunnel. If the wanton and now venerable madam went ahead with her scheme to try to turn her daughter against her doctor husband, then the daughter could seek retribution by informing her uncle of her mother's promiscuity, which would certainly make her father's will null and void as she was not in truth her father's daughter. Thus, the wealth of the dear man should pass to his brother, not to his wife and child. Ah yes, thought Brother Mike, circles within circles.

With the power of intrigue and innuendo now in his hands, Brother Mike could see about organizing things. He gave a scanty accounting to the Abbot with his affirmation that the Abbey would be seen as a unifier and peace-bringer to a common-day domestic problem, enhancing the monastery's standing and placing the good Doctor in the Abbey's debt. He then found the Doctor busy in his office, professing to him that he, Brother Mike, would be able to heal this unfortunate wound and that the Doctor and his wife would once again find joy and comfort in their home—the mother-in-law would be making no problems.

Finally, the most difficult of the trilogy of plans—convincing the most unpleasant madam to cease and desist. Almost as though bent on self-destruction, her notoriety indicated she would indeed be the toughest of the trio to get on board. But Brother Mike could be very convincing when he was committed.

Brother Mike found the lady in question at her home, a pre-Independence brick structure with what must have been at one time very nice ornamental gardens. Unfortunately, at least from Brother Mike's perspective, the home and garden were in need of a lot of loving care. The lady of the house herself was found in the parlor, sipping a glass of whisky, still in her bathrobe.

While she exuded an air of nonchalance, Brother Mike immediately sensed an aura of danger. Danger, yet in some way a sensual peril. This woman would be a testament to his skills.

She seemed to put out tentacles to test the waters, could she seduce or otherwise entice this religious man? Apparently her on-the-spot assessment was negative and, like an amoeba, she changed shape, assuming a less defiant and aggressive mien.

Politely declining her offer to imbibe with a charming smile and an imperceptible bow, Brother Mike sat upright in the rocker across from his subject. He realized diplomacy would be a wasted effort and cut immediately to the core of the matter: was she intent on making the otherwise honorable Doctor van Hoot pay for his recent and regrettable indiscretion?

She only smiled over the rim of her glass. Brother Mike, expecting as much, came forth with his carrot and stick: the stick first. In the most succinct of terms, he recalled how he had proof (perhaps a bit of a stretch on his part) that the father of her daughter was in fact a Muslim trafficker and not the upstanding businessman the community as a whole had taken to be the girl's sire. Were this irregularity to be made widely known, unquestionably the uncle would feel obliged to go to court to right this grievous wrong. However, to ensure that no such action was taken, and to allow all parties a respite, Doctor van Hoot was happy to provide the lady with a return ticket to Brussels where she could go to visit the family undoubtedly anxious to hear from her, passing a few leisurely months enjoying the climate and the food, free from the cabals spinning around her here.

Brother Mike had known instinctively when he entered the house that a threat would not be sufficient to achieve his aims—he needed a carrot. While he had not discussed the payment of airfare with the Doctor, he was sure he would feel this a small price to pay to get this lubricious event dismissed and have his family life return to normal.

Brother Mike took the lady's continued silence as acquiescence. He stood up, indicating that he felt the affair was closed and saw himself off. The lady took a gulp of whisky as he closed the door.

Bouncing back to the Abbey in the pickup, Brother Mike wished he were on the pond back where he could contemplate in a more suitable, calming setting. But here he was. This was not and had not been just business as usual. This was damage control for things that had run amok. The mess had not been a mess of the Abbey, and God knew there were many headaches there awaiting attention. The mess was not a mess of the Church, although God also knew His Church needed special attention in many areas. The mess was not even a mess of the town, province, or country. The mess was the mess of two inebriated foolish people, the same type of mess that foolish people everywhere get themselves into all the time. Why had this warranted his intervention? Not his intervention as Brother Mike, a relative nobody who was hopefully someone still relatively invisible to those surveying the landscape. This had indeed been an intervention by himself on behalf of the Farther Abbot and by inference, on behalf of the Abbey and even the Church. This role for him was either the pure and simple coincidence of the Abbot deciding he should provide a helping hand to someone, anyone, to demonstrate the Abbey's good faith. Or, this was a calculated intervention by the Abbot using Brother Mike as his agent. Flukes did happen. In fact, they happened with surprising regularity, but this did not feel like a fluke. This felt like the beginning of a movement or an offensive. The sands had begun to shift in some direction and Brother Mike needed to make sure he did not lose his balance.

Over the next poker game, Brother Mike fixed his sights on Antonio who had been so helpful in exposing the history of the van Hoot quandary. "Antonio," he asked, "who best knows the annals of the various religious groups hereabouts from before Independence to the present?"

After briefly pulling on his chin, Antonio recommended Brother Gustaf of the Jesuits, a member of the order that had a monastery in the north of the province where they raised a lot of bananas and made particularly potent varieties of banana beer and banana liqueur. Brother Gustaf, Antonio figured, must be in his eighties and, like so many of the community, he had come here as a young man during the colony and never left.

Brother Mike devised a plan. He went to his confrère who managed the kitchens, a sort of dietitian who decided what would be on the menu and when. He suggested the community would be most blessed to partake of a bit of the splendid local banana beverages so meticulously blended by their Jesuit brothers.

As was often the case with all things involving spirits, the debate was short lived as each saw things through the same lens: more drink made the Abbey joyous, and joy was good.

Accordingly, Brother Mike made arrangements for a day trip to the north of the province to procure banana spirits; and of course, to encounter Brother Gustaf. Most of the 80-km trip involved relatively well-maintained paved roads that wove between the hills, crossing several wide, papyrus-filled wetlands on stout concrete bridges built by the Chinese. However, the last 15 km was on a typical bush road—a washboard and rutted laterite passage that was rarely maintained. The Jesuits, as others before and after them, had chosen a beautiful hilltop for their Abbey. They had planted eucalyptus as a palisade, with coffee plantations, banana stands, and vegetable gardens spiraling down the hill in a most ornate fashion.

Brother Mike found Brother Gustaf waiting for him in a small gazebo sheltered away in the eucalyptus where the aroma of these fragrant trees filled the air, along with the whispering of their leaves. Brother Gustaf was a bit hunchbacked with slightly milky eyes, but seemed in generally good form for a man of his age who had spent a lifetime in the service of our Lord in Central Africa.

Without providing much in terms of background, Brother Mike posed his questions as he expansively anointed Brother Gustaf with the oils of ancestry—referring to him as the living legacy of their community, a treasure, and a font of knowledge.

Brother Mike only explained that his Father Abbot had asked him to be of assistance to Doctor van Hoot, who Brother Gustaf most certainly knew. To be able to fulfill the Abbot's wishes to the fullest, Brother Mike needed to know the history of the good Doctor and, if relevant, any relationship with the Abbot or the Abbey.

Brother Gustaf assumed a relaxed pose to where it seemed he was almost dozing, his eyes mostly closed, with his breathing deep and regular. Brother Mike could practically visualize Gustaf digging deep into his memories. After a brief interlude, he stiffened a bit and began, "You may recall that in 1940 there was a fascist party in Flanders, the *Vlaams Nationaal Verbond* (the Flemish National Union), that wanted an independent Flanders. With the German occupation of World War II, this party ultimately metamorphosed into the *Duits-Vlaamse Arbeidsgemeenschap* (the German Flemish Work Community) under the pennants of anti-communism and anti-clericalism, but also with the aim of integrating Flanders into Hitler's Reich. There were a number of young Flemish men who fought with Hitler in the Waffen-SS. Among these SS soldiers was a young schoolteacher from Gistel, outside Oostende. He was a mild-mannered man with two younger brothers, and although he was considered as compassionate by many, he was a fervent Flemish nationalist. His SS duties transformed this young man from the docile teacher into the efficient and ruthless killing machine and in due time, he was held responsible for the deaths of dozens of Belgians in the Resistance. Although he survived the war unscathed, he was brutally killed by vengeful Belgians after the Armistice. His disdain for the Church led to his burial in an unmarked grave somewhere west of Bruges. At the time of his death, his own parents had died but his two younger brothers and their young families had to go into hiding. Their older brother had been a truly diabolical person, scaring many families in both Flanders and Wallonia, and they feared retribution for his acts spilling over onto themselves and their families.

"The two brothers with their families ultimately changed their names and migrated to Congo. One family became the van Hoots and the other the de Graffs. The van Hoots stayed in what was Leopoldville at that time, becoming relatively well-to-do operators of a construction company. They were able to send their son to medical school in Belgium, from where he graduated and assumed the role of Team Leader here with us. The de Graffs moved to Costermansstad (later named Bukavu) on the shores of Lake Kivu, where they became successful coffee farmers. Their son went to seminary in Leopoldville (later Kinshasa) from where he became a member of the clergy across the border in Cyangugu. From there, he came here to join your order, ultimately becoming Abbot. Thus, the Abbot is the older cousin of the Doctor. Both are still hiding from the terrible souvenirs of their SS Uncle."

Brother Mike had learned what he had come to learn. He thanked Brother Gustaf, complementing him on his splendid memory. He then finished his assignment by purchasing two firkins of banana beer and one of the liqueur before regaining his pickup and heading south. The road was not heavily traveled, with more bicycles and cows than cars and trucks, so he had time to consider what he had learned. The facts would seem to speak for themselves. This was no indirect way to burrow into Brother Mike's affairs. Hopefully these were still buried under the layers of bureaucracy where he had safely interred them. This was the Abbot's way to try and really help a cousin in need, while maintaining the secrecy of their familial relationship, both for its past and present implications. The War had been a long time ago and it was uncertain if there were still wounds here so far from Europe that could be reopened. But, the good Doctor's role as Team Leader could be misconstrued if someone chose to document close ties to the Abbey. While there was officially the separation of Church and State in the government, the Church still had a powerful and often politicized voice. The President was a devout Catholic, his own sister a member of a convent not far from here. If international assistance programs were portrayed as being driven by religious priorities, this could have a negative impact on all fronts. Obviously, the Abbot felt it was in his interests and undoubtedly those of the Abbey, to not publicize the fact that one of the prominent physicians of the area was part of his family. Hence, Brother Mike's commission had been an act of caring and empathy, nothing more ominous.

Brother Mike was hoping there would be no more special commissions from the Abbot or from any other source and, thus far his wishes seemed to be coming true. He had entered into a period of calm routine where he was able to get to his spot on the pond bank at least twice a week. He took care of all his diverse responsibilities and still made it to the Crane on Saturday and to Philip's for cards on Wednesday.

The tranquility of this period included an extended stretch of complete celibacy, without any even fleeting friendships. This fact aside, Brother Mike continued to be preoccupied by his relationship with Philip and Angela. This seemed to be evolving into a special relationship by his standards and his general rule of thumb was to avoid sticky serious relationships with everyone. There were unavoidable, and often positive, relationships with members of his monastic community as well as relationships with those from the community at large, but experience had taught him to avoid serious personal relationships. He lived in a world of the transitory. People—expat experts, monks, sisters, all sorts—came and went. This was not the land of his birth, although he felt it to be his home. When he died, he would be buried in the Abbey's cemetery, but many of his confrères chose to be buried back in Europe. When people got sick, went on vacation, or had a family crisis, they left. Today's friend was gone tomorrow. This was just one of the transactional costs for the course of life he had chosen and it was, and had always been, his choice. But real friendships, true friendships, required one give a little bit of one's heart, and he did not have enough to give to all those to whom he could, or maybe should have over the years. It was, he knew, a coping mechanism, but perhaps—just perhaps—it kept him sane. Alas, these were thoughts best relegated to the pond bank, so he tended to lock them in a small room in his brain and only bring them out after he had baited his hook and could let his mind fly. Still, there was an uneasiness when he thought of Philip and Angela.

5

THIS RELATIVELY SEDATE AND pensive stretch proved to be short-lived as Brother Mike found he needed to go south to Lake Tanganyika to get regular supplies of fish for the monastery's kitchens. The Abbey purchased a pickup load of fish every three or four months—a mixture of various fishes caught by the commercial Greek fishery and sold at very good prices, all tax-free to the religious community.

He decided to go with Jean-Baptiste to help with the loading and un-loading of the cartons of fish. They left early one morning, hoping to be back in two days. The undulating hills and valleys dropped away after 120 km of the 160-km trip and they found themselves looking down almost 1,000 m to the long finger of the lake pointing south, all the way to Zambia, some 670 km away. Brother Mike was reminded of what a breathtaking view this must have been for the early traders coming from Zanzibar, looking for ivory and slaves.

The road wound down, slowly reaching the narrow plain that circum-scribed the lake. As the old Toyota sluggishly descended, it was overtaken by bicycles piled high with bunches of bananas, bicycles that could only be stopped by the laws of physics, the brakes useless with so much momentum.

Gaining lake level, they first sought the Cathedral, which would have some sort of guest accommodation within its complex. Once they had satis-fied themselves they would have a bed in which to sleep, they went to The Circle, a well-known watering hole on the lakefront where they could get delicious fresh fish and wonderful cold beer.

This open-air café was in no way special in terms of its decor. Like scores of other lakeside establishments, it boasted a dozen wobbly tables accompanied by numerous chairs, many equally unstable and most needing paint. Furthermore, its menu was certainly not the best the city had to offer. But what was on offer here was truly unique.

The café was situated on the shore of a small boat basin, giving the customer the impression of being on small peninsula in the lake. From his or her table, the customer could see the mountains of Congo on the other side of the lake. If it were close to sundown, the customer could also see the lights of fishing vessels twinkling as they began their night's search for riches. And as the sun set, the hippos from the lake began to move, swimming and farting right by the café as the customer downed a beer or chomped on a ham sandwich. It was a special place. While it was only midafternoon and too early for the real show, they enjoyed the serenity and lulling rapture of the great lake.

After sustaining body and spirit, they continued along the lakeshore to a small bay where the Greek fleet was anchored. If one did not know better, one could think one was on the shore of Milos or Paros, with the same ornate vessels at anchor.

The Greeks had come to this area in large numbers between World War I and World War II, when there was a change in the colonial rule from German to Belgian. The Belgians had welcomed the Greeks as traders and service providers. A large community developed, with their own Orthodox cathedral—by design, slightly smaller than the Catholic cathedral—as well as Greek groceries, delis, and restaurants. In addition, there was a Greek fishery where Mediterranean technologies and gear were adapted to the lake's pelagic fishes.

The Greek community reached its zenith at over a thousand strong after Independence. Now, this population was dominated by individuals of the second and third generations, but in much small numbers, many having returned to Europe due to prevailing political and economic difficulties.

The fishers, with their larger mother ship and smaller light and net boats, fished at night when there was not a full moon. The small light boats had powerful gas lamps that attracted fish. As the fish came into the lights, the net boat would deploy a large purse seine that would be pulled in by the mother ship, hopefully capturing a variety of prey.

It was late afternoon when Jean-Baptiste and Brother Mike reached the fishing harbor and the crews were preparing to go out for the night. They contacted one of the captains, explaining they had come from the Brothers of Piety to get their usual supply of fish. They then discussed with the captain what exactly would go into the order; how many of each size and species of fish and how these would be packaged. It was agreed they should come back the day after tomorrow and, with luck, they would have their fish. Brother Mike knew if they had the pickup loaded by 7:00 a.m., they would be back at the Abbey in time for Vespers.

Brother Mike and Jean-Baptiste found themselves in a rare situation with 36 hours of their own time, no scheduled prayers (they would of course pray), no work, and no other duties. One of the most precious gifts of all: their own time!

☙ ☙ ☙

The Great Lakes area was unfortunately not, as many perhaps thought, a remote safe haven far from a madding world. Quite to the contrary, in its own often-veiled way, it had been, and continued to be at the core of ethnic problems in Central Africa. The plight of local people honestly went back centuries when, as through much of Africa, different peoples migrated to different places.

Those who most probably had the right to call themselves the indigenous people were now a small, small minority; the population was numerically dominated by agrarian stocks who had come from the West, while the traditional society in recent memory had been politically dominated by a second exogenous stock of pastoralists coming from the North. The northern ethnicity was a warrior group that quickly assumed power, often in a most heavy-handed and dictatorial fashion.

By the time of the arrival of the White Fathers in the mid-nineteenth century, the Great Lakes area included a number of kingdoms, the Mwami (or King) being of the northern ethnic group. These feudal states saw the pastoralists as the nobles and the farmers as the serfs. While the lines were blurred, this bipolar structure, with a minority dominating a majority (in general, the people from the West outnumbering the people from the North by 4 to 1, and the indigenous folk by more than 20 to 1), was prone to strife. This instability led to considerable demographic fluidity, as those feeling as though they were the mistreated and marginalized majority attempted to move to other neighboring areas where they would be free of the domineering pastoralists.

This unrest had led to various experiments at Independence. Some newly formed countries were majority rule and others were still controlled by the minority. These population dynamics and their time-honed frictions also led to various periods of out-and-out confrontation, with these contests often bloody, even atrocious.

The net result of this history was that ethnicity was very important. While ethnic groups did intermarry, there were still very clear feelings and stereotypes of each group that were often magnified by frequent (but not always true) observations that the physiognomies of the two major groups epitomized their standing: the patrician Nilotic pastoralist and the servile Bantu peasant.

The interethnic antagonism was a simmering pot that boiled over at recurrent intervals. However, the green hills of Africa were often far from the global political spotlight. Similar pots boiling over in Vietnam or Czechoslovakia took the front page and the evening news. News from Central Africa, regardless of how brutal, simply took a long time to filter out to the wider world. Under the shadow of what could be seen as international apathy, people strove either to keep the old ways or to implant the new.

Brother Mike knew the situation well. He understood the sensitivities and tried to see all sides of the issues. The monastic life was often seen as divorced from the politics of the everyday, but Brother Mike knew one could not live in these green hills without understanding the context. The past was the future. The history of these hills impregnated every thought and deed. To navigate the maze, you needed to understand the lay of the land.

ĕ ĕ ĕ

The tale of this land, romanticized in a popular film of the 1950s and forgotten during the terrors of the 1970s, was the tale of its people and the story within which Brother Mike hoped to achieve his life's aims and his personal aspirations. Without understanding the story, one was faced with a lock without a key.

Brother Mike was digging into all these thoughts as he tried to imagine how he could use his unaccustomed free time. By the time he and Jean-Baptiste had returned to the city center, the sun had set and they decided to go to the veranda of the Palace Hotel, an old colonial relic, for a drink as they decided how to use their time until they got their load of fish.

This castle-like hotel dated to pre-Independence. Albeit once a jewel in the city's center, it was now tarnished and drab in comparison to the shiny new metal and glass hotels that had been built by international conglomerates. These gleaming hotels catered to large international meetings organized by large international promoters with big budgets, as well as to staff from large international organizations with big wallets. They offered all the pleasures, if indeed this could be an apt term, of being in a hotel in Brussels—every room, bed, breakfast, and dinner the same blasé content that was intended to encourage in clients a feeling of detachment from really being in the heart of Africa.

The Palace had been and was different. Under its faded exterior, it still was a fixture with charm, with personality. It was perhaps for this reason that most of the clientele were long-term guests; reportedly, most expatriates

engaged in trafficking any of a multitude of items. The city's modern international airport gave entrepreneurs access to the world's markets while the
porous borders offered access to the riches of the Congo and beyond. It was
rumored that whatever one sought, it could be found at the Palace.

However, the hotel's relationship to perhaps the darker side of international commerce aside, it was a splendid location for the casual visitor to
taste the city. The veranda was a semicircle fronting one of the city's busiest
roundabouts. It was raised well above street level offering the customer an
excellent view of the goings-on. In addition to the extramural sights, the
large surface of the tiled porch offered many nooks and crannies that were
filled not only with the residents doing their business, but also with a cross
section of lovely ladies, butterflies of the night as a friend of Brother Mike's
had once called them, also doing their business. These women, sporting an
impressive array of clothing ranging from the finest of the Champs-Elysées
to the best *pagnes* from Kinshasa with the head-ties piled high and proud,
were impressive in their elegance and style.

For those, like Brother Mike and Jean-Baptiste, who only consumed
the wares on display with their eyes, there was also an excellent kitchen
serving local fish, *steak au poivre*, Belgian endive, and the finest *frites* in this
part of the universe, prepared following an authentic Belgian recipe.

Unfortunately for Brother Mike, after his midafternoon meal, he had
no appetite for the delicacies offered on the terrace. He was sipping a cognac
while Jean Baptist worked on his second frothing beer. From their earlier
exchanges, Brother Mike knew Jean-Baptiste's maternal grandparents actually lived in the city and he was curious as to how Jean-Baptiste would plan
to invest his gift of free time.

As though Jean-Baptiste had read his mind, he offered, "Since we've
got a full day ahead of us, and my grandparents live here, I think I'll go by
and see them tonight. If they're agreeable, I'll spend my time with them as I
don't know when I'll get down here again."

Seeing this as a signal of a temporary parting, to wrap up the day,
Brother Mike ordered two coffees. These highlands produced some of the
finest Arabica coffee in the world, but it was cloaked in the shroud of these
hidden lands and not widely known. This unawareness, however, a blessing
in disguise as the coffee's lack of wider market recognition meant that the
top grades were available locally at very reasonable prices; other countries
with greater export markets often sent the good stuff outside for premium
prices and offered the locals only the lesser varieties.

As they enjoyed the full-bodied brew, Brother Mike took a long look
around the terrace—people laughing, drinking, searching for riches, searching for love. Living in a place that was teetering as it tried hard to establish

itself on strong legs; a place tied to the past and trying to break into the future. A place that reflected so much the young people like Jean-Baptiste. His gaze swung full circle and landed on his colleague, "When was the last time you saw your grandparents?"

Staring into the heavens, Jean-Baptiste seemed to pick a star, "It's been more than ten years."

"So close, yet so far," intoned Brother Mike.

"Yes indeed," Jean-Baptiste replied as if trying to visualize the decade that had passed, and why in fact had he not seen them for such a long time. "Seems like not that long ago I spent at least part of my school holidays with them every year. Then, I guess, I grew up."

"Well, I imagine your mother gets down here more often," added Brother Mike.

This seemingly innocent rejoinder appeared to push Jean-Baptiste closer to the stars and his gaze hardened just a wee bit, "Not really. Father's business affairs keep him more than busy and he relies on mother to take care of the home, family, kids—everything for which he doesn't have time. As you know, he's a minority businessman in an area where lots of people have no love for the minority. He has to watch his step carefully, always walking on eggshells. This leaves little left over for family or whatever. It's not easy to maintain the traditional family ties and support while being a prosperous businessman.

"With all his activities, father is seen by the broader extended family as the success of his generation. This may be seen as an honorific accolade, but in reality, it is a sign of assumed responsibility; the entire family sees father as their helping hand, they assume he must take up responsibilities for the whole family, assist them as it is only he who has the means to assist.

"If he were to do all that is assumed he should do, he would have no less than 20 nieces and nephews living with him, while he would be supporting businesses for four brothers. He has done well, but not that well. As it is, there are five family members over and beyond our nuclear family under his roof, being taken care of by mother. This is already a sacrifice and I understand he cannot do all that is expected. But others do not understand so well and there is ill feeling that he is selfish; keeping everything for himself, when it was the whole family acting together that helped him get to where he is. Like they say in Nigeria: 'There's a national cake and everyone should get a slice.' Dealing with these family matters could be a full-time job. Father may have reacted severely, but he has, in his mind for his own survival, cut his family contacts to a bare minimum. This decision includes not only himself but his wife and children.

"That's a long explanation of why my grandparents don't get many visits these days; not from my mother nor from me. I need to take advantage of the moment."

Brother Mike was in no position to oppose Jean-Baptiste's plans for staying with his grandparents, so he wished him well. Confidentially, he thought the young man would more likely seek some female companionship this evening and then call upon his family tomorrow. Being away from his monastic home offered anonymity. Brother Mike himself seriously considered looking for some brief friendship, realizing this city offered many hidden pleasures of which he could partake with little fear of discovery or retribution. And it was not a moral aversion to such friendships, as he had time and again demonstrated, that kept him from sampling the delights of the city. He simply felt very tired. It was as though, all of a sudden, his thoughts had congealed into a great weight that was perched on his head. His bed at the guesthouse was calling much more loudly than the cabarets beginning to fill with the ladies of the evening as the night's song filled with the cicadas' calls.

In spite of his fatigue, he felt the need to visit the Cathedral for prayer before retiring to his nearby room. Entering the tabernacle, he felt as though he was entering a long train tunnel, the light from the other end just barely visible. He could feel more than see the high arches overhead, as the only illumination at this hour came from the sanctuary lamp in the ambry of the chancel.

He walked down the center aisle like moth drawn to a flame or, he thought, like those little fish in the lake drawn to the fishermen's lamps. In his mind's eye he could imagine the hall full for a Sunday mass, women sitting on the left side and men on the right, as was still the tradition. At the front right pew he genuflected, entering and kneeling on the *prie-dieu* pad. After an Our Father, eyes closed, he let his mind free to roam the furthermost corners of the tabernacle. This was the House of The Lord. This was his house. This was his chosen hearth. Unlike Jean-Baptiste, it was not a place filled with family members and family obligations. It was not a place filled with a ladder to climb or promotions to seek. It was humble. It was simple. It was his choice. He had left all that was family and country far behind. In many ways, his home was his prized and well-worn kit bag. Wherever he went, he carried his bag and he carried his God. That was enough.

Brother Mike knew he was a true believer. He was a religious man. His problem (not seen through his eyes, but those of others) was that he did not see this lifestyle, these values, these beliefs, as being inherently contrary to seeking modest worldly comfort or fleeting friendships with the gentler sex. These were not mutually exclusive. His soul was God's. The fruit of his labors was for God. His mind was devoted to seeking God's wisdom and understanding His Greatness. But where in all this was it impossible to enjoy a sip of fine cognac, savor an excellent meal, laugh with a good woman, or have a few coins to jingle in his pocket?

He was pondering this when he sensed another presence. He stood, opening his eyes, to find a monk about his age standing in the aisle.

"Good evening, I am Brother Mike from the Brothers of Piety—just visiting."

"I am Brother Pius", replied the other in a deep baritone.

"Ahh, the pious Brother Pius", Brother Mike ascribed in an attempt at levity he did not feel.

"Well, be that as it may," the baritone boomed, recognizing the sibling community from the other side of the border, "how can I be of service to my brother from the North?"

The ice was broken, so Brother Mike provided a one-minute summary of their trip for fish, introducing Jean-Baptiste *in absentia*. He concluded, "I have come to the sanctuary of the chantry to contemplate the forces that move our lives. I know that sounds very august, almost arrogant or pompous, but it's really simple. I am a simple person from simple stock who should be tending a field or a flock of sheep in Belgium—not be a representative of our Savior here in Central Africa. Whatever winds of fate, or divine forces of destiny, have led me to where I am—today I am in your hands, Brother Pius."

"Brother Mike," Brother Pius replied, "you are indeed immersed in very weighty thoughts, thoughts that generate the mortar that allows us to build our own religious home to honor God. I had best leave you with these thoughts. But I will be in the *boukarou* in the garden in the back of the church if you should wish to chat with an earthly fellow after your discourse with our Father."

Brother Mike returned to his knees, closed his eyes and sought answers—sought redemption.

Sometime later he left the Cathedral and thought he might just pass through the garden even though he imagined Brother Pius had long left, hearing the call of his own bed. Yet, as he approached the dark silhouette of the *boukarou*, he saw the stocky shadow of Brother Pius. As he drew closer, he saw Brother Pius was seated at a table garnished with what appeared to be a bottle and two glasses.

When Brother Mike reached the rough-hewn table and seated himself on one of the benches around its periphery, he noticed the bottle was a bottle of wine and that it was a good Italian vintage and not the cheaper French or Belgian wines more often found in religious communities.

After being complemented on his good taste in drink, Brother Pius confided what Brother Mike had surmised, that he was like the wine, of Italian roots. However, as it turned out, he was more practically African. His family originated from Bressanone, also called Brixen, in northern Italy, only 45 km from Brenner Pass separating Italy from Austria. An ancient Catholic City with a cathedral dating to 1039 and once a bishop who was a pope for 23 days. Three-quarters of the populist was of German origin.

In the mid-1800s his grandfather had gone to work for the railroad company to work as a young civil engineer on the line to Innsbruck, a project undertaken by the Austrian Empire. Although well qualified for the job, work was not easy for an Italian working in a German environment. His grandfather was always given the most difficult assignments, but never the promotions. When the final segment of the *Brennerhbahn* (Brenner Railway) was completed, he could have continued working for the Imperial Railway Company, moving to a new site deeper in Austria. But his dissatisfaction with his working conditions led him to look for other opportunities far and wide. He found what he was looking for perhaps a bit further away than he had first imagined. The German Colony of Tanganyika was starting the Usambara Railway and they were looking for well-seasoned builders, a category his grandfather could now claim after two decades of working for the Austrians. Thus, the family moved to Tanga, Tanganyika, to work on a new railway in a new country. Unfortunately, the public railroad did not make much headway and his grandfather changed to work on narrow-gauge rail lines serving the sisal plantations of the area.

When the war broke out, while the family was not affected to any large degree, life in the populated centers of a German colony was uncertain at best. Thus, his grandfather, now past middle age, moved the family west to Kigoma, well out of the way of any international brouhaha the European politicians could brew-up. Kigoma was the end of the line for the railway coming from Dar es Salaam, connecting this lake port with its big sister on the shores of the Indian Ocean—just about as far away from conflict as one could get. But Brother Pius' grandfather had miscalculated and Kigoma turned out to be an epicenter of several battles between December 1915 and February 1916 when the Belgians and British fought to take control of the lake away from the Germans. The allies successfully brought two small attack boats to Albertville (Congo) via South Africa and engaged the two larger German warships controlling the basin. The Anglo-Belgian forces took full control of the lake by mid-1916, two years before the end of the war, returning the region's people to a more stable life.

Kigoma was an important port for lake traffic, with ferries heading north to Bujumbura and south to Mpulungu. By the time the family settled

there, Brother Pius' grandfather was well along in years and his father was
the breadwinner. Following perhaps just a bit in his own father's footsteps,
Brother Pius' father had opened a garage with his brother. Shortly after the
war ended, grandfather died and Brother Pius' uncle moved across the lake
to Kalemie in Congo, chasing the proverbial riches said to await any who
would undertake the challenges of living in such an inhospitable climate.

Brother Pius kept close contacts with his cousins across the lake. While
they did not become wealthy beyond imagination, they did well with their
coffee farm and enjoyed a prosperous life. In Kigoma, the garage business
was perhaps less affluent, but there was plenty to do and Brother Pius had
started preparing to enter his father's trade as soon as he finished secondary
school. But the Fates are hard to predict and one summer while passing
his holidays in Kalemie with his cousins, he met a priest visiting from the
Kinshasa Seminary.

The priest was a good salesman and was soon filling Brother Pius' head
with tales not of religious ardor, but of a lifestyle surrounded by servants,
fine food and drink, and plush quarters; days filled with reading and lively
discussion and not toiling in a garage under a crusty Bedford truck or rickety Mercedes van. It was an easy sale for the easy life. As soon as he could
make the necessary arrangements, Brother Pius, or the soon-to-be Brother
Pius, reported to the Grand Seminary of John 23rd under the watchful eye
of the Cathedral of Notre Dame of the Congo.

And it was in this way, years later, Brother Pius found himself seated
across the table from Brother Mike. His story told, it was as though the night
was now a void, what was next?

The telling had been an act in and of itself; an act that had prompted
the emptying of more than half the wine bottle. In the aftermath, the two
brothers sat in silence, savoring the last of the wine and watching a fishing
owl slowly climb overhead as it made its way to the lakeshore. As the owl
banked toward the north shore, Brother Pius rose, thanked Brother Mike
for his company, and disappeared into the shadows, as invisible going as he
had been coming.

Brother Mike remained a while in the quite and obscurity of the
boukarou, staring into the underside of the thatched roof, wondering what
critters were stalking their prey as he gazed unseeingly. His mind, however,
quickly left the geckos or centipedes that may have been combing the thatch,
and centered on Brother Pius and Jean-Baptiste. Two completely different
individuals, yet two individuals, probably among many, who had chosen
the monastic life for the personal comfort it offered and not the spiritual
or societal well-being. He felt this was a relevant, even a significant train of

thought he wanted to follow. But he was just too tired. His bed called too loudly. He followed his confrère into the darkness.

ẽ ẽ ẽ

The next morning, as a soft sunrise gave a glow to the city by the lake, Brother Mike went back to the Cathedral for his morning prayers and then set about business, the first bit of which was breakfast. He had decided not to drive his old truck around. Although he knew the city relatively well, he was in truth a stranger and did not want to have his heretofore successful buying trip sabotaged by some sort of accident or run in with the local police who were known for always finding an infraction that could only be erased with a bottle of beer or a 200 franc note. Going on foot seemed the best choice. Not far from the central market there was Greek bakery and delicatessen where he could get a cup of freshly brewed local coffee and a piping hot croissant.

As he sat at his small table enjoying the buttery richness of the pastry and the tartness of the coffee, which he took with no sugar, he watched the parade of early clients file into the neat and seemingly well-run establishment. Those entering for their hot-out-of-the-oven delicacies represented a cross section of the city: a black limousine with CD plates dropped off an obvious embassy worker to get something special for the boss's breakfast; couples coming from the recently closed night clubs were looking for something that might make the start of the day more bearable; businessmen with nice Peugeots jumped out, leaving the motor running, as they bought baguettes or *pain au chocolate* for the family waiting at home or the mistress waiting for a visit on the way to the office; fishermen from the lake, still encrusted with the night's grime, entered looking for something really good to eat and hopefully drive away the never-ending smell of fish; kids on the way to school stopped for an authorized or otherwise snack; and houseboys from the rich neighborhoods jostled with workers from the ghettos as metal trays of hot goods emerged from the ovens.

Brother Mike's attention was particularly drawn to a diminutive nun appearing to be of Indian origin. It was not that she was small or possibly Indian that was of interest, it was that she was in the bakery at all. All convents of which Brother Mike was aware had fine kitchens, producing their own baked goods of a wide variety and high quality. Thus, what was the good sister doing here where the products were good, but probably could not rival those of a fine French-Inspired convent kitchen?

As the good sister left the queue with a cup of coffee and a small brioche, she arched her neck, looking for a table—amusing Brother Mike as she resembled a crowned crane as she tried to survey the premises from a disadvantaged vantage point. He rose to his feet and signaled with his arm that she should join him. This she did, happy to have a seat in the small space that seemed to be attracting more people than flies.

"Good morning, Sister. I am Brother Mike from the Brothers of Piety to the north. Can I offer you a place at my table?"

"Good morning kind Brother Mike. I am Sister Sujitha and most happy to accept your generous hospitality."

Brother Mike noticed that her head bobbed as she spoke and he assumed she was from the Kerala region of India where such a habit was common.

Being ever the straight-talker, Brother Mike enquired, "I am curious Sister, as I know well the quality of most convent kitchens, what is it that brings you out to sample public fare?"

Sister Sujitha took a long drink of coffee, hers heavily laced with milk and sugar, and a small morsel of brioche, exhaled and said, "Brother Mike, my story requires more time to tell than my cup needs to be drained."

"Ah, it is by chance that I have an abundance of time and of curiosity as well. I am waiting until tomorrow to procure fish for our Abbey, so my time is yours if you would like to recount your tale?"

Whereupon, Sister Sujitha told Brother Mike how she was on her way to Kirungu in the Congo, the former Baudouinville. She was going to help care for members of the Church in this community located on a plateau above the lake. Indeed, this Catholic community is the same as that tended by the White Fathers when they established their first mission in 1893. She was waiting for the evening ferry to take her to Moba Port from whence it was a short drive inland to the town and the church.

This area was very remote, the Marungu Highlands reaching to over 2,400 m providing the backdrop for the town. By virtue of this remoteness, this area had been like a magnet to those wishing to escape, fleeing whatever internal or external forces that prompted them to enter into one of the most secluded parts of the continent.

During the ebbs and flows of power shifts in the lake basin, as colonial and ethnic influence and wealth changed with the times, there was inevitably a group that was not on the winning side; a group for whom those now in control could have great animosity. For those on the wrong side of the equation, the only option for survival could be to disappear, and Kirungu and the Highlands were good places to disappear. Groups or people wishing to fade away were able to set up cliques that controlled any of a variety of activities in this faraway part of the Congo that was not even acknowledged by the central government—oft-times these interlopers dominated and disrupted the lives of villagers who had lived along the lakeshore for generations. These disparate factions, in many instances including various ousted political groups, added to the confusion that was brought in by those from the outside wishing to melt away. When the, at times whimsical, local traditional leaders were inserted into the mix, there arose a very volatile atmosphere making life for the most vulnerable very difficult.

Once one left the town centers, there were no real services—no rule of law. It was a true natural order where the fittest ruled and the weakest tried to survive. The Church was attempting to help those in need through ministrations of faith, clinics, and schooling. But, as always, resources were thin. Sister Sujitha represented the Missionaries of Mercy, founded by Mother Teresina in 1949. The Missionaries of Mercy targeted the poorest of the poor and they had surely found their mark in Kirungu. The extreme difficulties in doing anything made some wonder if they would be able to achieve anything at all. Thus, she was a one-person fact-finding mission to see if they really could hope to achieve some positive results on the lakeside or if they should be focusing their efforts elsewhere.

As predicted, Sister Sujitha's cup was now empty and her plate cleaned of even the tiniest brioche crumbs. Brother Mike offered a refill, but she politely excused herself to make some needed purchases of supplies to carry with her to the congregation at Kirungu.

After she left, Brother Mike reflected back on his thoughts of last evening: the twists and turns of life, monks looking for personal comfort, and a nun going into the most inhospitable of situations for no personal gain, only to help those in need.

Since he was close to the big market, Brother Mike decided on a stroll to settle his mind and spirit. Things in the *marché* were already awash in a tide of humanity. Transient vendors had set up on the margins while inside the walled-off marketplace he could hear the cacophony as all sorts of people undertook all sorts of transactions, all at the top of their lungs.

He skirted the market itself, avoiding the hubbub and scramble, and, sidestepping the great smoldering heap of putrefying offal that the market generated each day, walked through the adjacent area filled with shops and stalls that seemed to concentrate on selling hardware, car parts, and farming equipment. Here the ruckus was considerably less tumultuous and he was able to amble about at his own pace without having to jostle for position. He continued on in a random fashion, thinking about life as his feet felt their way. Unaware of the passing of time, he was awakened from his trace by the cawing of a pied crow on a high eucalyptus branch. He focused on the present and realized he had meandered into an up-scale residential district on the slopes of the hill behind the city center. Looking at his watch, he saw the morning was coming to an end. He decided to complement the croissant with a nice beer and sandwich on the terrace of the Palace Hotel.

It was a good hour later before he strolled onto the terrace, already busy with a variety of merchants and hawkers selling variety of wares from lithesome lasses peddling solace to a high-power entrepreneur trying to seal a deal with an equivocating civil servant. One whole corner was occupied by a band of loud and disheveled WTs—world travelers. Brother Mike spied their olive drab Unimog parked down the street. These people, generally Europeans, paid extravagant sums of money to ride across parts of Africa in the open air back of any of various sorts of heavy-duty trucks, alternately camping and staying in cheap hotels, then returning to their homes and describing to their mates over bridge or billiards how they had "done" Africa.

Brother Mike chose a table as far from the noisy travelers as possible, and ordered a beer, a ham sandwich (on fresh baguette), and *frites*. He was forewarned by the waiter that the travelers had flooded the kitchen and orders were slow in coming. He assured the attendant, attired in white shirt and dark tie, that he had all the time in the world.

This slowdown in service did not affect the bar and Brother Mike was able to consume several pints, his long walk having whetted his thirst. As he was rising to use the loo, he accidentally bumped into another client apparently headed in the same direction.

"Sorry," said Brother Mike as he turned back to see with whom he had collided in his haste. He was greeted by a sunny smile set off by a red beard and a head of long red hair—all of this atop of person of at least 20 stone.

"Now don't ya worry," was the gleeful reply accompanied by an extended paw that would make a black bear proud. "My name's Dan, what's yours?"

"I am Brother Mike and I am, with some urgency, on my way to the loo."

"Well Brother Mike, I was heading that way too. How's about we drain off the excess together and come back and I'll buy you a fresh pint?"

"Agreed."

When they were reseated at Brother Mike's table, Dan pronounced, "I'm an American. Where ya from?"

Brother Mike did his best to control a small smile. If the accent did not immediately give it away, the sneakers, blue jeans and T-shirt had him pegged as a Yankee long before he had made his admonition. But the world was full of them. "I am originally Belgian," replied Brother Mike.

"'Originally'? Is that like, ya know, you've changed? What are ya now, Norwegian?"

"Oh no. I am still officially Belgian and travel on a Belgian passport. It's just that I am a monk and have been living in a monastery to the north of here for years."

"A monk! Wow a monk! You're, ya know, the first monk I've ever met. A monk? Why'd ya become a monk? You in trouble or someth'n?"

"Oh no, my young friend, nothing like that. My home is very Catholic. Every family likes to have at least one member go into God's service. I found my own service to God as working in His name in an abbey to help those unfortunate who need a helping hand."

"Uh-huh. So what do ya do?"

"Oh, lots of things. Our community provides help in many ways spiritual, intellectual, and corporal. We are a brave and diverse group helping those so in need. My own responsibilities are more in the line of helping my fellow brothers accomplish their tasks. I make sure the clinic has medicine, the school books, and the cafeteria food."

"Uh-huh. So you're like, ya know, a religious delivery boy?"

"Well, not really. But enough about me. What brings you to the sunlit terrace at the Palace Hotel?"

"Me huh? Well like I said ya know, I'm American. I was in the Peace Corps, ya know, in West Africa. I did my, ya know, two years for better or worse; not really sure, ya know, how it all came about. But when the time was up, ya know, I was out. Wasn't in no hurry to get back to Pennsylvania, ya know, so I just sort'a headed south and east to see what I could see. No plan, no itinerary, ya know. Just hopscotching from point to point. Not at all, ya know, like those WTs down there; someone always holding their hand. No siree! I took public transport, ya know; buses, bush taxis, boats, trains, *matatus*, *trotros*, mammy wagons, and even coffee and cocoa trucks. Slept in a field, in someone's bed, or in a car; it didn't matter. Like that Roman guy, ya know, I came and I saw—no idea if I conquered."

"*Ujasiri*, as they say in Kiswahili. *Du courage.*"

"Oh yeah. Ya know, I can handle French fine now," as if to demonstrate, he ordered two more pints.

"But from that rough road to this terrace, there are still some holes in the story I think?"

"Oh yeah. Well, ya know, cutting out all those months of moseying from this place to that, I ended up here and was, ya know, fixing to take the ferry to the south end of the lake. In fact, it was at this very terrace where, as I was waiting, ya know, for the time to reach, I was contacted by this guy—Belgian like you. He said he had, ya know, some of his personal effects up in Bukavu, but with all the goings-on he had, ya know, left in kinda a hurry and had to, ya know, leave these things with his friend. Said he was, ya know, worried about his safety, being kinda old and all, but if I, a strapping young man as he called me, would, ya know, be willing to go and get his stuff, he'd pay me $500.

"Now this didn't, ya know, smell quite right. But $500 is $500, ya know, and I was near broke after all my time on the road. I figured, ya know, what's the worse that could happen. I could get stuck in Bukavu, but I was, ya know, damn near stuck here so why not go for it? So I did."

"Well, I see," inserted Brother Mike, "that you did apparently make it out alright."

"Oh yeah. No problem at all. I think this guy was, ya know, worried about the customs dudes. But I had that cooked. *Bonbons*."

"*Bonbons*?" asked Brother Mike.

"Yeah *bonbons*. You know, those hard candies they sell all over the place. Well I learned long ago, ya know, that if you've always got a handful in your britches pocket, when people start, ya know, asking too many questions you just reach in and start handing out *bonbons* and the temperature changes immediately. No one is, ya know, interested in you any longer. They're just, ya know, interested in *bonbons*.

"So I had my pockets filled with, ya know, Bukavu's best *bonbons* and when I, ya know, went across I left nearly a kilo of those sweets with those nice guys manning the border crossing. No problem"

"*Bonbons*!" sighed Brother Mike.

"So anyhow, this guy, ya know, he was so happy about what I did for him, ya know, that he asked me if I could, ya know, do some other odd jobs for him. Now that was some time back and, ya know, I'm still doing odd jobs and he's put me up, ya know, in a nice room in this very hotel."

Brother Mike eyed him with as penetrating gaze as he could muster.

"Yeah, I know now this guy is, ya know, a kind of under-the-table businessman. Now you're a religious guy, I need to say it straight: he's, ya know, a smuggler. I guess that makes me the smuggler's helper. Just over there, across the lake, ya know, Congo is full of riches. There's, ya know, malachite, gold, ivory, and precious gems. And, ya know, it's just a hop, skip, and a jump over to here and, ya know, that shiny new airport just waiting to get these things to buyers in the Middle East, Europe, or Asia.

"I'm just, ya know, really one link in a very long chain. But speaking of which, ya know, I do have my little, ya know, space on the side."

He reached into his jean's pocket and removed not a *bonbon* but beautiful emerald, "See this here? It's almost 8 karats. Was in a box, ya know, we got that came up the river and across at Kisangani. I had to go, ya know, inland to get it so I figured, ya know, if I liberated a few pieces, who'd know?

"But now I need to get to South Africa, ya know, and meet my brother. We haven't seen each other for 15 years, ya know, and he's gonna be there for some reason or other. I gotta sell part of my insurance, ya know, to go and see him, otherwise, ya know, don't know when we might meet up. How'd you like, ya know, to be the proud owner of this great gem?"

"Now what's a monk going to do with an emerald?" asked Brother Mike.

"Give it, ya know, to someone you love."

"I am a monk."

"Uh-huh. Don't you, you know, love people?"

"I am a monk. My love is for people as God's children."

"Uh-huh. So how about it? Make you, ya know, a real deal."

The "deal" part struck a note in Brother Mike. After all, he was a businessman and had many areas of interest where there could be a way to find a handsome profit for a fine emerald. His mind began thinking of potential customers when he asked, "Ok, just to help you out in your time of need, and remembering that I am a religious man, what would you be looking for?"

They went back and forth, Dan realizing that he had met his match in Brother Mike, a surprise he would not soon forget. They drained their beers when Brother Mike's nearly forgotten sandwich arrived. Dan stood to leave, extending his hand to Brother Mike. Dan felt something hit his palm and realized this was Brother Mike's way of agreeing to their last price. He shifted the bills to his left hand, reached into his right pocket and put his right hand on Brother Mike's napkin as if to wish him *bon appetit*.

When Dan got upstairs in his room, he saw five crisp one hundred dollar bills when he opened his left hand. This would take him south in luxury.

Brother Mike, for his part, felt a lump under his napkin, picked up the folded linen, dabbed his face and then put the whole thing in his trouser pocket. His ham sandwich tasted wonderful.

It was getting to midafternoon and Brother Mike thought he would take a taxi to the landing where he could double check with the skipper before they went out for the night's fishing. It was nice and breezy on the lakeshore, people running to and fro to get the fleet out to deep water as soon as possible. Brother Mike saw the captain inspecting some lamps on light boats and approached with a big smile and outstretched hand.

"Good afternoon Captain, how did you make out last night?"

"Ah Brother," replied to skipper as he turned to see who was inquiring, "we did fine. Got some really nice fish that are already boxed up and waiting for you. If we have even half the luck tonight, I'll be able to go through and get you all you want—and I mean fish of the finest quality. I'm sure when you see the results tomorrow you'll want to add a bit of coin for the crew's superb efforts."

"Indeed, this is good news and we are always happy to compensate extraordinary efforts. We'll be here at sunrise tomorrow to settle up and get on the road with our bounty; or should I say your bounty?"

The shook hands again in parting, the coarse sand crunched under Brother Mike's shoes as he walked briskly back to the taxi, like walking on peanut shells in a bar, he thought.

Jean-Baptiste had given him the name of a small beauty parlor run by his cousin, Charisse; a place to leave word for him if need-be. Brother Mike gave the driver the address, not a street number as most places did not have official mailing addresses, but a reference point—in this case, across from the Joker Bar.

They returned along the lake to the city center then continued into what the locals called the *Cité*, what others might call the ghetto, the inner city, or the slums. Here the roads were a conglomerate of clay, rocks, and rubbish. The open gutters running along both sides carried things best not described. Buildings seemed to have been built in an *ad hoc* fashion—some residences, some businesses. All were cement block with cheap metal roofing sheets, most with metal "burglar bars" on the windows, and a few with a metal antitheft door as well. Some businesses were well lit with gay signs, while others hung in the shadows like orphans. There were food sellers, general stores, electric repair stores, clothing stores, bars, dance halls, beauty parlors—all interspersed with clusters of homes, most small single-family units, but some larger, shared by several families. Among the clients of these varied businesses there were gaggles of children playing and sometimes doing more intimate things in the oozing drains.

As promised, across from the Joker Bar, a massive multicolor joker image from a deck of cards emblazoned on the wall by the area's budding artist, was the Belle Femme beauty parlor with a signboard outside showing all sorts of hairstyles and braids that could be done by the skillful staff. Brother Mike took paper and pencil from his ever-present holdall and wrote a quick note to Jean-Baptiste. He then entered the parlor and it reminded him immediately of entering unannounced in a classroom at the Abbey when the teacher was absent: the appearance of complete pandemonium. But here there was apparently some order in disorder. It was hard to tell who was doing the hair and who was getting their hair done. Little teams of women were everywhere, preening as they prepared for an evening of entertainment or a weekend of festivity. There were some beautician chairs complete with washbasins and blow-dryers, these occupied by ladies, surrounded by a flock of young girls like someone in a dentist's chair. On random chairs and stools about the room and flowing out into a patio-like arrangement in the back, there were women seated as other women delicately and precisely braided their hair, some like the Eiffel Tower and others the more well-known cornrow.

There was really no recourse. Brother Mike knew nothing else to do, so he belted out as loudly as he could, "Charisse!"

It took three shouts before a young lady in a long Batik dress poked her head around the corner from the outside patio. Brother Mike introduced himself, confirming Charisse was Jean-Baptiste's cousin, and underscoring, as he gave her the small note, that this was urgent. Thanking her, he took his leave and returned to the taxi, asking the drive to drop him of at The Circle.

He had proposed to Jean-Baptiste they meet this evening at The Circle to confirm their plans for the morrow. He was uncertain where Jean-Baptiste really was and of how long it would take him to get the missive. But The Circle was an enjoyable spot. He could savor his beer slowly as he crunched on the little deep fried sardines from the lake with a light flouring of *pili pili*. He could relax, look across the lake, and listen to the hippos. He had waited for people in far less agreeable circumstances.

Brother Mike felt lucky as he was seated at a table in an outer row, only a few meters from the water and with a clear and unimpeded view of the lake, its surface now carrying a growing number of twinkling lights as the fishermen set out for their evening chase. Brother Mike was buying his fish from the Greeks who operated a large commercial fleet, the methods and practices introduced with them from Hellenic lands far to the north. There were, however, scores if not hundreds of smaller artisanal fishers. These smaller-scale operators would often use one or two canoes. Brother Mike knew from previous visits to the lakeside that these canoes could be traditional dug-outs, but were most often more substantial craft better able to handle the often rough, and at times dangerous waters of the big lake. International development agencies had introduced steel boats some time ago, but this had been a dismal failure. The latest batch of visiting experts were now in the process of trying to replace the steel design with fiberglass. However, there were also craft from local boatbuilders made of wooden planks and quite seaworthy.

Regardless of the boat design or size, the fishing practices were the same and everyone competed for the same stocks. Right now these were exported as far away as Dar es Salaam, and the fisheries were already pro-ducing smaller and smaller catches as the pressure grew. Brother Mike won-dered how many more times he might make the trip to the lake before the supply completely dried up?

Brother Mike was on his third beer, his mind bobbing up and down with the men on the lake, when he heard the chair beside him scratch as it was pulled across the uneven floor. Looking up, he saw Jean-Baptiste.

"Well, young man, how's the family?" he asked after they had shaken hands and exchanged their more formal salutations.

"All are well, thanks to God," replied the younger man with a big smile.

"And the grandparents? Hope they are doing well for their age."

"All are fine. Concerned about the continuously bubbling pot of politi-cal turmoil, angry about rising prices, and complaining about the younger generation. Therefore, all is normal."

Feeling Jean-Baptiste did not want to pursue the topic of his private life, Brother Mike shifted gears, "I've just come from the beach, the fish will be ready tomorrow at sunrise as we had hoped."

"Good," imparted Jean-Baptiste. "In anticipation of this, I have taken a room at the guest house for the night so we can be together and get to the landing on time."

This was exactly what Brother Mike had hoped. "Fine, that will work well. I suggest we take in one last look at the nighttime lake over a nice beer and then we can go to the Palace. I saw their special today is *Capitan Grillé*, so we can get a good plate of fresh-out-of-the-lake fish before we head to bed."

They took a taxi from The Circle that dropped them near the Cathedral where Brother Mike had parked his faithful old pickup in a secure location. They then took the pickup to the nearest petrol station to fill the tank, check the oil, kick the tires, and make sure it was ready for the morning trip north, loaded with fish.

With all in readiness, they set off on foot under the stars to enjoy a few more free hours on the terrace of the Palace before returning to the Abbey and its more regimented lifestyle.

The terrace was full but they managed to find a nice table. The WTs had moved on so service was back to normal. Brother Mike saw Dan on the other side of the veranda but only greeted him casually, as he was engrossed in earnest conversation with a young beauty who looked like she might have had some Sudanese roots.

The grilled fish was excellent as were, as usual, the *frites*. They even topped this off with a *mousse au chocolate* followed by an apéritif. Brother

Mike was reunited with his old friend cognac, and the burning of the amber liquid following the coolness of the mousse was sublime.

The remainder of the trip went better than could have been expected. The fish were ready as promised at sunrise and of the highest quality. Brother Mike was happy to give the skipper a substantial tip for the crew, wondering if any of them would ever see a franc of it. The run up the precipice to reach the highlands was accomplished, even if begrudgingly, by the old pickup now carrying much more weight than it was accustomed. Moving under the sign of the Church, the border crossing further north was executed with ease, with no duties or inspection. They arrived at the Abbey well before Vespers, having time to unload the truck, have one of the helpers wash down all the gunk that had accumulated in the bed, and then go and wash themselves down before going to the chapel.

As he disrobed, eager to climb into his welcoming old bed, Brother Mike felt an unaccustomed lump in his trouser pocket. Reaching in, he withdrew a shimmering green stone. He had already forgotten his recent transactions with Dan. He was now the proud owner of one of God's precious gems—an emerald. What would he, a monk on a hill, do with an emerald? He was not sure, but he knew he would think of something. He wrapped his prize stone in a small piece of parchment and put in the drawer of his bedside table next to his Bible.

6

ON THE DRIVE BACK from the Lake to the Abbey, Brother Mike and Jean-Baptiste had searched near and far for topics to make lively conversation and pass the time. They had generally avoided personal matters until they had crossed the frontier and were not far from the Abbey. Brother Mike then felt he needed a few minutes of serious time with the young man. The arrangements for him to pursue sculpture surreptitiously were tenuous at best and Brother Mike was not sure if he had a fallback plan. Thereupon, he adroitly and indirectly opened the subject with his passenger.

Brother Mike was surprised to learn that Jean-Baptiste himself had been thinking similar thoughts. He said this change of milieu had allowed him to put things in better perspective and he felt he really had a talent for art—a God-given talent that would be a sin to ignore or abuse. He felt this was his true calling from his Savior. He realized his father would be unhappy, but he had spoken with his grandparents who, although from the other side of the family, promised to intervene on his behalf.

With these thoughts in mind, on their free day, Jean-Baptiste had not been in search of pleasures of the flesh, but had been at the Congo Embassy. He had spoken to several people who had encouraged him and helped him make an application for the *Ecole des Beaux Arts* in Kinshasa. If he were admitted, he would move to Congo and put his religious life on hold until he had fine-tuned his special skills God had given him.

Brother Mike absorbed this news with mixed feelings. Certainly from the point of view of his various affairs (commercial and personal), this was a good thing. He did not want to integrate Jean-Baptiste fully into all his diverse pursuits, and now this was a moot point. But, he did very much like the young man and would miss him when he left.

Well, chalk another one up to "Acts of God."

Brother Mike happily found himself again on the pond bank with his fishing pole. He was impressed yet again at the pleasure old habits brought. Sitting on the dirt holding a piece of cane was definitely not something spectacular. Or, at least in the wider scheme of things, it was not spectacular. But for him, it was spectacular. It fomented a deep inner peace and nurtured a clear mind. Certainly, he thought, this was all done through God's Goodness. However, the magic mixture of a pond and a fish helped. Were not fishermen among Jesus' favorites? He was certainly not a fisherman like those on the big lake, dozens of whom lost their lives as they trolled the unpredictable depths. Nonetheless, he may have been a fisherman of sorts. When he wove nets like a spider spinning a web in some of the business affairs, he often felt he did trap the uninitiated in the latticeworks he knit. But was that more personal dynamics than fishing? He did not know. Yet, it was here on the pond bank where he was surely a fisherman, even if a very modest fisherman.

Brother Mike exhaled deeply. The symphonic rattle of the banana leaves mixed with the scent of eucalyptus added to the feeling of being grounded in Mother Earth as his grip on the pole loosened and he forced his mind to return from those analytical chambers where he sought human ways to interpret God's Transcending Truths, forcing his thoughts to take up the immediate challenges of now. It would take him a day to catch up after his absence. The Tanganyika fish needed to be entered into the inventory and then divided among the various kitchens, with the choicest morsels, of course, for the Abbey and the rest rationed among the clinic, school, and public kitchens. He had to prepare a series of receipts for his travel expenses and he had to see what, if anything of importance, had happened in his absence. He also had to get in touch with Philip. It had only been a few days, but it seemed like weeks and he was anxious to confirm his upcoming participation in the ogling on the terrace of the Crane and his seat at the card table.

His mind was again refocused when he heard a soft splash from the pond. As he looked across the calm water, after a few minutes he saw a small almost snake-like head pop up above the green background of the pond's surface. From one of his colleagues, he knew this was a local grebe, a miniature variety with great webbed feet. It was capable of great underwater speed, easily entrapping many unsuspecting juvenile bream as they leisurely selected from the abundance of foods offered by the fertile pond. With the instantaneous snap of the grebe's razor sharp beak, one second you're there, the next you're not. He knew he could dwell on that phenomena of life for quite some time in the intoxicating theater that was the fishpond, but his duties beckoned to him from up on the hill. Reality was a bitch.

ꙮ ꙮ ꙮ

Brother Mike was mentally prepared to set about his tasks with his normal efficiency as he somewhat reluctantly walked back up the hill. However, as soon as he reached the Abbey compound, he was vigorously hailed by Brother Mark. "The Abbot wants to see your now," his colleague nearly yelled.

Changing course, Brother Mike set off for the Abbot's office. Knocking, entering, and going through the formalities, he sensed the Abbot was a bit uneasy. Seated across the large desk from his leader, he prepared for bad news, even though he couldn't imagine its origin.

"My dear Brother, you are from Ghent, isn't it?" the Abbot enquired.

Knowing full well the Abbot knew full well that he was from the Ghent area, he acknowledged this fact with a slight nod.

"There's a bit of a problem," the Abbot continued. "Yesterday the Rector of the University contacted me. There's this one Belgian instructor, a certain Rolf, who teaches chemistry through support from the Belgian Government. Well, this fellow is creating all kinds of disorder, both in his public and private lives. The Rector is concerned it will reflect badly on the University. He wants to make a strong complaint to the Belgian Government. But this would reflect badly on all of us. I have, therefore, convinced him to hold back a while and allow us to seek God's assistance in resolving this issue. Since you're nearly his brother in terms of geography, I thought it would be good for you to seek him out and assess the problem. We would all hope he can, with God's Grace, find a way to get back on the right track. Your help will be greatly appreciated. Let me know if you need anything from my office."

That was it: short and to the point. A new assignment for Brother Mike and not, like most, one he relished. But he was the man for all seasons and these were his orders so this was what he must do.

After getting things at the monastery set up to move forward during yet another absence, he set off in his pickup over the bumpy road to town. His first stop was to try to see Philip. It was midafternoon and he took a chance that Philip might be at home. This was indeed the case, Philip just opening his first beer, having closed a little early. After warm greetings and confirmation that the poker game was still on, Brother Mike set to his task. "Philip, by chance do you know Rolf who teaches chemistry at the University as part of the Belgian project?"

"A little," Philip replied. "Not well at all, but we've crossed paths at mussel feeds at the Crane or other get-togethers that tend to regroup the local Belgian crowd. What do you want to know?"

Avoiding opening up the entire subject at this juncture, Brother Mike decided to try and be discrete—not one of his strong points. "Well, the Abbot just asked me to call on him to see if he could benefit from some spiritual comfort."

Ever the say-it-like-it-is man, Philip retorted, "That's a raft of crap you've just sailed by me—doubletalk I'd guess, for somehow he's got his tit in a wringer. Not surprised though. While I don't know him well, you don't need to know him to know of his reputation—it's all booze and women. And he's married. Wife's named Jenean. She's also from Ghent. They've a little girl about five named Mary. I reckon they came here about five years ago when the project supporting the University expanded. They're in this same neighborhood, but at the other end."

Brother Mike changed the subject as it seemed he had learned all he could about his quarry. He joined his friend in a beer and recounted just the high points of his trip to the lake before asking for his leave.

Back in his pickup, Brother Mike debated his next move. He could try and get some more background information from others in the Belgian and University communities, or he could go head-on into the ring to engage the bout. Ultimately, he decided on this latter course and drove to Rolf's house, not far away, as Philip had said. He parked on the street, the house hidden behind a cypress hedge with a rickety gate offering passage to the other side. Traversing the hedge, he found himself in an unkempt yard filled with children's toys of all sorts. He also heard shouts, unclear whether of joy or sorrow, from the back of the house, so he walked around the side and found himself in another unkempt garden, the centerpiece of which was an inflatable wading pool in which children frolicked—four black and one white. Scanning further across the garden, in the shade of a flamboyant tree he saw three reclining chairs occupied by three adults—one white man, one white woman, and one black woman—all in swimming suits. The ground around the chairs was littered with overflowing ashtrays, empty bottles of beer, at least two mostly empty whisky bottles, and a variety of newspapers and magazines.

As he seemed to be unnoticed by all, Brother Mike made great show of booming a "Good afternoon!"

With this salutation reverberating off the walls, both the children and the adults were brought to attention and for a few seconds there was complete silence. Quickly the children decided this was nothing of importance and began squealing and splashing again. The adults, however, put their glasses and reading material down, the ladies pulled the straps up on the tops of their two-pieces—two ladies, thought Brother Mike, who should not really be wearing two-pieces—and all three looked quizzically at their greeter.

Brother Mike broke the kind of trance that had developed between them by announcing, "I am Brother Mike from the Brothers of Piety. We are calling," Brother Mike made it up as he went along, "on members of the Belgian community to see how this community can be more engaged in the work of our Abbey. Our monastic community has been divided among a number of emissaries such that we each contact those who come from our same region in Belgium in sort of a geographic brotherhood. I believe like myself you come from Ghent?"

There was still a long silence from the adults who then, almost as one, took long and deep swallows from their glasses, which they retrieved from the parched grass under their chairs. Finally Rolf stood up saying, "Brother, welcome. Sorry to be so disheveled. This is the playtime for the kids and we're enjoying it with some adult relaxation as well." He motioned to another canvas chair leaning against the tree, "Please pull up a chair."

Brother Mike duly seated himself and accepted a glass of beer offered by Rolf, not really sure where the glass had come from.

"To your health!" Rolf offered. He continued, "Both my wife Jenean and I come from Ghent and this is our friend Ladawa from Bukavu. Over there, like floundering fish, are our children."

Brother Mike stood and greeted each of the ladies individually, regaining his seat and his drink. He thought he would try a little fishing. "Our community, linked through the Church to a much larger network, is active in many ways in the town. Are you familiar with our projects?"

Rolf admitted with no regret that none of them were churchgoers, nor were they active in much beyond the day-to-day responsibilities of teaching at the University and managing a family. It was very close to a dismissal.

Brother Mike still planned on hooking a fish. "Oh, I do understand," he replied. "Life out here is not easy and everything is very time consuming. Nonetheless, as you are a chemistry instructor, I thought maybe we could talk about whether or not you thought you might be able to have some free time to help with the science curriculum at the monastery school?"

"Well," said Rolf, massaging his long chin. "Right now is not a good time, and I really don't think I'd ever have time to really do justice to your work. But as a fellow product of Ghent, maybe we could meet sometime later to see what could be done?"

"Excellent," chimed in Brother Mike. "How about meeting for a drink on the terrace of the Crane tomorrow afternoon about teatime?"

It was agreed and Brother Mike retraced his steps to his pickup, feeling somehow better sitting there than in the canvas chair under the flamboyant tree.

The next day, Brother Mike was seated on the terrace well before the appointed hour to gather his thoughts and watch the arrival of his target. Rolf showed up twenty minutes late, disheveled and smelling of hooch.

Brother Mike lost no time. "My friend Rolf, a good afternoon to you, can I offer you a lovely cold beer?"

"A double whiskey'd suite me better, oh those students! Oh yeah, good afternoon to you Brother."

A fresh beer for Brother Mike and the whiskey for Rolf were ordered and delivered as the two made small talk about the weather, the disrepair of the town's secondary roads, and the threats of pending electricity cuts due to increases in prices of petrol products—all topics well suited to the Crane's terrace.

Savoring his beer, Brother Mike jumped in, "Rolf, my friend, I must be honest. While it is true we would be interested in your inputs in the curriculum for the monastery's school, my main mission is on another topic. As you may know," Brother Mike was now warming to the tale he was spinning, "the Church has an impressive network across the country: monasteries, convents, parishes—all in all, encompassing every corner of the landscape and touching the lives of most of the inhabitants. As you also may know, the political situation is far from ideal. Some would say it is volatile. We need to have safeguards for the Belgian community. To this end, our Church Leaders are in discussion with the Belgian Embassy to see how the Church's web can be effectively used as a safety net for our citizens. At the initial stages, for this to work, we need to establish some sort of workable arrangement among ourselves, the Belgians, and then inform government of this arrangement so they will not find out about it later and cry espionage. You know, that has happened before.

"So here we are, the Church and the Embassy preparing a security plan and then crafting an appropriate notice to government of this activity. Seems logical enough even if not straightforward. But what do you think happened?

"The government pounced on this opening to comment on its views of the roles of the Belgian inputs, both sectarian and secular. As you know, the government is mounting a campaign of a new nationalism, sort of a future-through-the-past movement. Trying to resuscitate many of the old ways. Favoring local languages over French. Promoting traditional styles of dress over modern fashions. Playing down new technologies while emphasizing old values.

"In this campaign, they want to minimize the models of what they see as contrary behavior. People behaving in a way contrary to their new old model are not seen in a good light. And, for us to really succeed with our security plan, we do not need the light of government shining on our community. We would rather they agree we move forward and that we keep our work in the shadows."

Brother Mike could see his elaborate tale was losing Rolf who was far more interested in a second double whiskey than his discourse. Slapping the table to refocus the discussion, he continued in a loud voice, "So dear Rolf, as you can clearly see, we have a situation."

Rolf clearly did see there was a situation and he corrected it by ordering another whiskey. He then pulled up his socks, so to speak, eyed Brother Mike, and stated as strongly as he could, "What's this all about?"

"Rolf, my friend," Brother Mike softened, "it's about you."

Rolf diverted his eyes, finished his drink, signaled the waiter for another, then stared at his lap, his right hand shaking slightly.

"Rolf," Brother Mike continued, impressed by his ability to spin such a complex yarn to address such a simple matter. "This falls under that much thought about but little talked about chapter—pleasures of the flesh. It is not my place to stand in judgment, God will do that. But through my position, I have been asked to discuss with certain members of the Belgian community behavior that might be deemed by our hosts as inappropriate, especially given their stance on modern lifestyles. Behavior that might jeopardize larger arrangements between the two governments.

"Your life is your own to lead. But when it impacts on the larger community, it is hoped a kind word might help subdue some of the more blatant aspects. In short, as can be seen from your consumption during our present discussion, without mincing words, you drink a lot. I too drink. But the quantity you consume, often in public, has led to concerns about your academic abilities as well as your overall health.

"You have apparently also adopted a rather unusual social structure for your home with, in effect, two wives. You are certainly aware of the history of polygamy in this country and how the Church has encouraged the leaders to adopt a monogamous culture. Now, when an international expert comes to the country and pursues a polygamous life, how do you think this looks?

"My task," concluded Brother Mike, "is not to scold you or even try to change you, it is simply to inform you that these issues have reached sensitive ears and unfortunate action could be taken if some changes are not observed. I don't think any of us want to go home in disgrace."

Rolf had already finished his last drink and was scanning the veranda for the waiter. Seeing no one, he exhaled deeply, looked Brother Mike squarely in the eye and replied in a stern, if quiet voice, "Thanks for the chat Brother Mike. Seems I can't get served here so, if you'll excuse me, I'm going to get one for the road, or as they say here, 'one to raise my spear,' and then head to my office to grade exams."

Rolf rose, shook Brother Mike's hand and made his way to the interior in a kind of zig-zag fashion. Brother Mike finished his now warm beer and wondered if all his marvelous, and quite plausible telling of tales had been a waste of time. Had Rolf uncovered his ploy? Did Rolf really not care? Well, enough for the moment. He had his instructions from the Abbot and had carried them out to the letter. It was time to report back and find out the next move from those master chess players who pulled the strings in the background.

ě ě ě

When Brother Mike did report back, the Abbot requested he put the Rolf issue on hold for a while to see if any of Brother Mike's good advice had sunk in. In the meantime, he should go about his regular duties.

A week later, Brother Mike was just thinking about visiting his spot on the pond bank when he was summoned again to the Abbot's office. The protocols having been observed, Brother Mike found himself seated, facing an unhappy looking head of the monastery.

"Brother Mike," the Abbot started slowly, "you can take the Rolf matter off your calendar. He was medically evacuated last night to the capital and will be flown immediately back to Belgium, with no real chance of returning here. Apparently he developed serious DTs last night and began chasing his little girl with a broom. Jenean ran to the neighbors who thankfully were home and together they subdued Rolf and held him while someone went for the police.

"He is gone now. I am told the Congolese part of his family has also gone, returning to Bukavu. Jeanine and her daughter are packing and will soon be returning to Belgium, though I have no idea if they will still be living with Rolf.

"It seems, from what reports I've heard, that Rolf actually did try to stop drinking. Indeed, it was this abrupt turning off of the tap that led to his tremors. Now some might say he was bullied into this action. Some might say he was intimidated by a higher force. I hope no one says these things. We need to try to help this particular episode close quietly. I will do what I can.

"In the meantime," the Abbot slowed the pace of his discourse even further, as if fatigued by his own inspiration, "inasmuch as you did such a good job with the fish, I need you to focus on potatoes. As you most probably know, we have been receiving our potatoes for some time from a northern businessman who buys from the farmers and transports the produce here to our larders.

"This gentleman has been consistently rising the price, blaming increasing fuel costs. But he has now proposed a major price hike that really makes us question if we can continue to do business with him.

"I believe we can do much better dealing directly with the farmers. I want you to check this out. Kindly prepare to travel to the North tomorrow."

7

BELGIANS LOVE THEIR *FRITES*, considering them their national dish. They persistently argue with their neighbors, the Dutch, as to who has the best recipe, the Belgians taking great pride in the selection of the right potato, the use of the right oils, and employing the right techniques—almost a science in and of itself. The Belgian contingent at the Abbey consumed five times more potatoes than any other segment of the monastery's population. Potatoes were important.

The northern part of the country was where potatoes were grown. The mountainous area had rich volcanic soils and produced abundant harvests. While the quality was excellent when taken out of the field, poor storage facilities and a very humid environment made spoilage and crop deterioration real problems. If, as the monks did, you wanted top quality potatoes, you had to get them soon after they were unearthed.

All this Brother Mike understood. Going straight to the farmers made good sense. But farmers here, as elsewhere around the country, were smallholders. They produced small surpluses for the market and were generally not organized into cooperatives where larger quantities could be procured. Hence, going straight to the farmers could well prove to be a good idea that was hard to put into practice—yet another of so many good ideas, he thought, that perhaps were difficult, but not impossible with God's Help, to bring about.

He decided he needed first-hand experience. He would go to the North to buy a pickup-load of potatoes, the process of doing so providing considerable insight as to how to move forward to put more permanent and affordable procurement arrangements in place, with the undoubtable result, the gratitude of the Abbot and the whole community. It was a win-win: goodwill from his confrères and good *frites* for his discerning palate.

The trip involved about five hours of travel, but the time was quite variable due to construction on the road. The first part of the journey—to the nation's capital, located 145 km to the north, smack-dab in the middle of the country—was routine. From there, however, it would involve climbing the Congo–Nile Divide, the confluence of these two massive river systems, one emptying into the Mediterranean and the other into the Atlantic. To begin the ascent, he crossed the Nyabugogo River at the capital, leaving the bedrock of the highlands. Already at an elevation of 1400 m, the road climbed to 2000 m, winding between the 2400 m peaks and then following the Mukungwa River to the regional capital of the North, which sat at 1800 m with the volcanic peaks forming the horizon touching 4000 m. This portion of the road, from the Nyabugogo to the Mukungwa, was being re-worked and was unpredictable.

The government had initiated a program to improve the country's major highways, heretofore they scarcely warranted this title as they were, at best, single-lane tracks. The major contractor (or perhaps better said, bene-factor) for these works was China. Across the country there were camps, closely resembling WWII concentration camps, where hundreds of Chinese workers were billeted. The common rumor was that these Chinese were ac-tually prisoners doing forced labor. As far as Brother Mike knew, this was never proven. Nonetheless, in spite of their impressive inventory of high-quality road building equipment, it was amazing how much of the work was done by manual labor.

Brother Mike wished Jean-Baptiste could have accompanied him on this trip. However, the young man had just received his admission into the *Ecole des Beaux Arts* and he was busy preparing his own trip to a much farther destination and of a much longer duration.

All was going well and Brother Mike had passed the 2000 m mark and was descending to the Mukungwa Valley when he felt the vehicle begin pulling to the right. He pulled over on the shoulder and walked around the truck. As he had feared, the front right tire looked low, but maybe, just maybe, there was enough air to carry him to the city.

This time luck was not on his side, or at least not completely. After about fifteen minutes the pickup felt definitely lopsided and upon inspec-tion the tire proved to be nearly devoid of air. However, on the positive side, just a few hundred yards in front of him was a muddy track leading to a Chinese camp, visible in the valley below, about two kilometers from his present position. Going slowly, he should be able to make the camp gate.

Although the pathway to the camp was heavily rutted from daily heavy traffic, and the old pickup engine had to work to pull its weight at such a slow speed, Brother Mike did make it to the barbed-wire-topped gate, where he parked off the road and went up to the entry to see if he could find a helping hand. Changing the big pickup tires was already a rigorous job, but doing this in the mud significantly compounded the matter.

As he neared the gate, he saw a group of about five workers coming through the fence and approached them. "Good afternoon gentlemen, I am Brother Mike from the Brothers of Piety, any chance you lads giving me a hand with my tire? I've had a puncture."

The men stared vacantly at him, two dragging heavily on their cigarettes, seemingly unable to see him through the smoke and the other three looking as though they were peering into fog.

"I say gentlemen," Brother Mike changed from French to English, "any way to get bit of help?"

No glimmer of acknowledgment in the five pairs of eyes.

In desperation, Brother Mike tried repeating a single Kiswahili word "*Matata, matata, matata!*" But this had exactly the same effect—none.

Unbeknownst to Brother Mike, another pair of men from the camp were witnessing his efforts. They probably could have interceded sooner, but there was little entertainment here in the middle of nowhere, so they took what pleasures they could find, even if it was just some old white man getting flustered at trying to talk with their workers. But the fun was over.

The two men ambled to the gate. As they approached, the other five men scurried off. Seeing them coming, Brother Mike offered greetings in French and English in quick succession. He was most gratified to receive a reply in English.

Brother Mike explained who he was and showed the two men the now completely flat tire. One of the two men turned around and called something. The five men returned, obviously not having scurried very far.

When the five-man-team had returned to the pickup, the elder of the two English-speaking Chinese gave them instructions; apparently telling them to change the tire.

"The spare's under the bed," offered Brother Mike, seeing one of the men poking about the bed.

A few minutes later his Samaritan returned with news, "No good. They check spare. It OK. You no want go with no spare. No good. We fix your tire."

Brother Mike mentally arranged the puzzle of words, understanding they did not want him traveling alone with no spare so they were going to fix the damaged tire. He suspected that such a camp had a comprehensive garage and work on a tire would be a simple matter.

Brother Mike and his new best friends watched as the team of off-duty road builders jacked the pickup up, removed the tire, and rolled it through the gate in the direction of the back of the compound. He began following his tire when one of the English speakers indicated he should follow them and leave the tire work to the crew that had been assigned to the job.

He was led down an alleyway between parallel rows of barrack-like buildings. While these truly looked like WWII barracks from afar, close up there was no real resemblance. Although they were painted a similar olive drab, on close inspection they were totally constructed out of cheap corrugated roofing sheets. There were seven rooms per block, these fronted by a small porch that ran the full length of the building. There were two faucets at each end of the porch and Brother Mike guessed this was their supply of water. Walking by an open door, the door too made of roofing sheets, he could see that the inside was simply cardboard attached to the wooden studs that held the roofing sheets. The building was in fact a metal-cardboard sandwich.

The room he glimpsed would not even qualify as a dormitory. There were four sets of bunk beds and on the far wall a small set of eight cubbyholes, apparently for personal effects. There were no comforts and, he thought, only the barest of necessities.

His guides led him further down the alleyway to where it rose slightly as the valley bottom reached the base of the hills. Here the accommodation looked the same from the outside. However, when they motioned him to enter one of the rooms set out like beads on a string, he immediately noticed a different configuration—all were not equal. While the room was the same size and construction, there were but two single beds, a coffee table and four easy chairs occupying a good part of the space, a small paraffin refrigerator in one corner with an electronic kettle atop.

Brother Mike accepted the offer from one of his hosts to sit in one of the chairs, which looked more comfortable than it was, while the second resident of the room, with great practice, hit a switch on the kettle to boil water for tea.

The pot boiled surprisingly quickly and soon Brother Mike was sipping very hot tea, trying to decipher his hosts' presentation. It was obvious that guests were few and far between. They enjoyed both demonstrating hospitality and explaining their lives as though they realized rumors of a Chinese invasion were rampant and they hoped to set the record straight.

The two men took turns in telling their tale with great animation. Brother Mike did not need to feign interest, as he was truly intrigued by these people who had come so far to live with so little and to work so hard—an asceticism, he noted, exceeding by far the reported frugality and abstemiousness of many religious communities.

While the state of the main workforce, prisoner or no, remained a mystery, Brother Mike did learn that his hosts were both graduates of technical secondary schools who had a sort of engineering/construction specialization. They made it clear that recruitment was through a tough competitive process and they were very happy to have been chosen. Although they were far from any urban areas, the free space, fresh air, and clean water were great attractions. The work was hard, but, through a few sacrifices in the present, they would hope to have a future that would offer higher-paying jobs with better working conditions—maybe, mused Brother Mike, a different twist in *laissez-faire* free market forces.

As it was, they lived like a Chinese island in a strange land. They had their own gardens to grow their own vegetables—many brought from China. They had their own chicken coops and pigsties. They had communal kitchens with several huge woks that turned out voluminous quantities of Chinese dishes. They smoked Chinese cigarettes. They listened to Chinese music. And, of course, their interpersonal contacts were with other Chinese people.

Brother Mike mentally compared the situation at this Chinese work camp with those at the Abbey—there were many similarities. The monks, however, in general came to spend a lifetime and couched their presence under the category of religious service. The Chinese came for months or years, and lived under rougher conditions in the hopes of ultimate economic and social advancement at home. Two sides of the same coin?, wondered Brother Mike.

His thoughts were interrupted by someone knocking, as it were, on the flimsy metal door. When he looked up, he recognized one of the team of five charged with repairing his puncture. There was a loud and rapid exchange of Mandarin. Then, somewhat abashedly, one of the hosts, Brother Mike still knew no one's name, said to him, "So sorry. Problem. Worker break nut."

There was a follow-up discussion led by Brother Mike that revealed that, when the men were putting the wheel back on the pickup, they were using a pneumatic wrench and broke off two of the bolts when over-tightening the nuts. They assured Brother Mike they had a complete workshop and would be able to remove the broken bolts and replace them. However, this required they go and look for their storekeeper who was off the premises at the moment. He had the key to the storeroom where the replacement bolts could be found. The bottom line was that the work would not be finished before dark and it was, in their opinion, best that Brother Mike spend the night in the camp.

While not welcome news, traveling alone was challenging enough without adding a night drive in the mountains with a tire that may not have been repaired as well as one might hope. Hence, he accepted their offer and was led to a similar room in a block about midway along the chain of beads that housed hundreds.

This room, identical to all others, was obviously a guest room and quite possibly a VIP guest room as it had but one almost-double bed, a chiffonier of local origin, and a stand with a porcelain washbasin with a bucket on the floor to carry water from the outside tap. There were even curtains of a sort, sewn of coarse sacking, but adequate to block out the outside and any curious eyes.

Brother Mike was unsure of what the evening would have in store, so he prepared for all inevitabilities. He removed his shoes and knelt beside the bed to say his prayers, being especially thankful for the kindness offered by his hosts, certainly as part of God's greater plan. He then fetched water, cold and clear, from the tap on the porch. After filling the basin and removing his clothes to his waist, he washed off the grime of the day. He shook out his shirts before re-donning them, went to his ever-present holdall and got his flask of cognac, letting this golden liquid slowly slide down his throat as he lay semi-reclined on the bed in his stocking feet.

Shortly after sunset his two guardians knocked softly on his door and accompanied him to a large communal dining room that was redolent with the smell of hot oil and sautéed garlic. The hall was divided by a cardboard partition, one side with dozens of long tables with equally long benches at their margins. The other side of the divider had a score or more of tables accommodating eight to twelve people each, these with straight-backed chairs, probably made in the camp of local materials.

Through a door in the back, he could see a great kitchen with the bubbling woks and heaps of vegetable on counters, with teams clothed in what were once white aprons hovering over everything. This scene somehow reminded Brother Mike of flies hovering over offal, a thought he tried hard to drive from his mind.

Hot tea was served in an enameled mug and soon thereafter a sister enameled plate was placed before him, piping hot, filled with rice and vegetables, smelling magnificent. Brother Mike bowed his head to offer a prayer of thanksgiving. This solicited stares from those seated around the table, so he said his prayer softly to himself. He then tucked in and the food tasted as good as it smelled. The images of flies vanished.

While observing those with whom he shared the table, he noted that the meal was really a question of refueling, like taking his truck to the petrol station—something that you had to do. There was little chitchat or socializing. It reminded Brother Mike of what he had heard of the customs of the local people. For decades, as it had been reported to him, really since the beginning of their history, food was seen as an unpleasant necessity. Meals were often taken in seclusion or, if there was a larger group, the men and women went to separate places to eat in some privacy before returning to fraternize. It was only with the 20th century's almost forced introduction of the "modern world" that eating assumed a new and more epicurean con-text—and this only for some segments of the population.

Brother Mike was mulling over these thoughts and enjoying the spicy dish when he realized all the other diners were again looking at him. Taking in the scene, he understood—all the others had already finished their meals and they were waiting for Brother Mike to do the same so they could vacate the table. Obviously, given the size of the camp, people ate in waves and the next wave was probably anxious to refuel.

Finishing quickly, Brother Mike joined his chaperons, walking out into the cooling night air. Slightly to the side there was a large paddock and it was here, Brother Mike inferred, that the camp staff really socialized, most of them over cigarettes. Scattered all about there were little huddles of men accentuated by the red glow of their cigarettes; the air filled with a cacopho-ny of human voice, almost chant-like, as each now joined his "brother" from the same village or region in China, speaking in their dialect and recalling images of home to help lessen their homesickness and feelings of isolation.

Brother Mike and his companions meandered across the paddock, almost like people going to the fair, walking among stalls that were really miniature human communities. They circled back and Brother Mike found himself unexpectedly, but to his relief, at the door of his room.

One of his protectors announced, "Truck fixed. Sorry for delay. To-morrow at 0600 we come to go eat then you go."

Brother Mike, a bit ashamed he knew no one's name, thanked his hosts, shook their hands, and went into his room where he quickly found his cognac for a few calming drinks before saying his prayers and getting into the surprisingly comfortable bed. Maybe it was just the fatigue.

The morning came all too quickly, further sleep was impossible given the great commotion that rose to meet the sun as the camp awoke. Brother Mike knelt and said his morning prayers, then repeated his ablutions of yes-terday, grabbed his holdall, and was ready for whatever should present itself.

The pickup handled well as he continued down to the Mukungwa Valley. He felt in fine form. He had had a good breakfast of rice gruel, vegetables, and tea. The sky was cobalt. The day had had a good start.

As he got closer to the northern regional capital, the difference in the regions became clear. Whereas at the lower elevations such as the Abbey's, valley farmers would be going to market carrying bunches of bananas, balanced on bicycles, pushcarts, or someone's head. Here in the North, farmers were heading to the capital's big market with gunnysacks filled with potatoes lashed to bicycles or pushcarts or perched on someone's head.

As he approached the city, the narrow road became more and more packed with people going to the city to sell produce, buy necessities, seek medical care, look for administrative support, visit a friend, or simply to have a taste of city life. There were bicycles, wheelbarrows, motorcycles, pushcarts, people herding cattle, goats, and pigs. There was a family of four on a Suzuki 100, a wife balancing on the handlebars of her husband's bicycle, a mother on foot with a baby on her back, another at her side, and perhaps another waiting to appear. There was a father with his young son hoisted high on his shoulders. There was an old man carried in a stretcher by four stout youth from his clan, undoubtedly heading to the hospital. There were also city taxis, long haul taxis, buses, and private vehicles. It was a labyrinth that demanded Brother Mike's full attention to navigate.

It had been several years since Brother Mike had been here and the city had grown and metamorphosed considerably. Nonetheless, he had a rough idea of his destination. He passed the big central market on his left and joined the road heading west to Congo for a short distance before turning right on the road leading to the northern border. Once on this thoroughfare he could see the sharply pointed steeple of the Cathedral on his right. He knew this diocese was quite recent in the bigger picture of Catholicism in Central Africa, having been established by Pope John XXIII in 1960. Yet, young as it was, it had done well. The Diocese ran the Nimbambora Hospital and a teachers' college. Brother Mike recalled reading of the urgent need for additional medical services, as the chief and greatly over-subscribed public facility built in 1939 only assisted as a clinic until 1964 when it finally became a fully-fledged hospital. The relatively recent inclusion of Nimbambora meant the goal of full medical coverage was closer, if still elusive.

The Diocese also maintained a pastoral center for visitors and he headed there first to get a room, a bath, and a change of clothes. Refreshed, he walked the short distance to the Cathedral looking for Father Juvenal, the contact he had been given by the Abbot.

Brother Mike found the Father in the vestry. After perfunctory greetings, Brother Mike enquired if the Father had received any word from the Abbot of the Brothers of Piety? Father Juvenal acknowledged he had indeed received a message that was rather unclear, something about potatoes.

Brother Mike proceeded to explain their potato problem, repeating that the Abbot had instructed him to make new arrangements, with the preference of working directly with farmers. Father Juvenal revealed that, although he had been unsure of the specifics, he had contacted people in the dioceses' eleven parishes, requesting information on potatoes. All the parishes had replied to his enquiry, and six indicated potatoes were in fact a major crop. With this new information, he would now contact the six potato producing areas and ask them to have any farmers interested in supplying potatoes to the Church to come to the city. Furthermore, he suggested they arrange for the assembly room in the Church's shelter, St. Victor House. If all went well, they could assemble the interested parties by tomorrow afternoon. In the interim, he would send someone to the market to reserve the necessary quantity of potatoes, at good local prices, that Brother Mike would take back to the Abbey himself. If all went to plan, Brother Mike could be back on the road south the day after tomorrow.

Brother Mike was impressed with, and grateful to Father Juvenal. He was the kind of guy who could make it anywhere, so Brother Mike wondered why he had joined the Church, but dared not ask. Brother Mike felt Father Juvenal was cut from the same cloth as he—well organized, to the point, and, he hoped, efficient. He now had a workable plan developing. He decided it best to let Father Juvenal get on with the necessary arrangements, as his presence only slowed down the process.

Brother Mike asked Father Juvenal his opinion as to the best hotel in town. Without much forethought, the Father said the Vironga, where there was a really good kitchen. Thus, to thank Father Juvenal for basically making Brother Mike's mission possible, he invited him for dinner at the hotel at eight. Father Juvenal accepted somewhat reluctantly and then emphasized to Brother Mike that he needed to get things moving if they were going be able to keep to their timetable.

Brother Mike now had almost ten hours to kill. A walkabout seemed like the best way to start off, so he headed back toward the central market. The streets were a variegated throng at this time of day. There were European tourists—some traveling in style, others moving in WT caravans. All were probably here to visit the parks in the volcanoes north of town where there were rare troops of mountain gorillas. There was a wide array of farm and farmer service folks as the area was known not only for potatoes, but also pyrethrum, coffee, and tea. There were large tea estates to the west of town, according to rumors, owned by Colonel Gaddafi, while most of the pyrethrum and coffee was grown by smallholders scattered between the peaks. There were many travelers moving about the streets, as this was a major intersection for voyagers heading to the neighboring countries to the north and west. And then, as a regional capital, there were those with whom Brother Mike shared the byways looking to solve governmental debacles, trying to visit family in prison, going to court, seeing a doctor, or attempting to get their child back in school.

Brother Mike walked through the market, noticing it was not as clean or as well organized as his market in the South, but aside from these slight differences, it was functionally and materially the same. It had the same stalls selling vegetables, fruits, fresh meat, and fish. It had the same booths with all the necessities of home and hearth. It had piles of clothing, new and used, spread over plastic sheets to keep some of the mud away. There were stacks of pots and pans piled high. There were machetes, long-handled hoes, wheelbarrows, and hammers. There were toiletries and home remedies.

As he was in no rush, Brother Mike decided to inspect some of the merchandise on display. He looked at a bath towel, a pair of tennis shoes, an aluminum frying pan, a kerosene lamp, a cross-cut saw, and a set of dinner plates. Everything was made in China. His Chinese friends were certainly here, not only building roads, but also providing most of the ordinary items a typical family used day in and day out, a job heretofore undertaken by a whole subset of local craftsmen and entrepreneurs.

Wondering how long it would be before China ruled the world, Brother Mike exited the market and continued through the surrounding commercial area, walking quickly by a myriad of shops selling anything and everything, most of which, he thought, of course was made in China.

As the sun reached its zenith, and, since it had been hours since he had partaken breakfast with his Chinese hosts, he decided it was time to look for a little sustenance, a light meal so as not to quench his appetite for this evening's menu. Jean-Baptiste had told him, if he had time, to look in at the Good Luck Cafe, so he stopped a passerby, enquiring as to the location of this eatery. It turned out to be very near and within half an hour he was seated at a plywood table with some sort of plastic tablecloth stapled onto its surface. The place was crammed. Many of the clients appeared to be youngish men who ate communally, sitting around a large platter heaped with beans, cassava, cabbage, and potatoes. Each participant, as it were, had a soupspoon and dug into the mountain of boiled food. The combined effect was that the heaps seemed to disappear before Brother Mike's eyes.

Brother Mike knew that beans were the staple throughout the country. In a normal household in the rural areas, the dry beans would be put in a large clay pot with layers of cabbage, cassava, sweet potatoes, and/or Irish potatoes on top. Water would be added, the pot covered, and placed on the fire to cook for a good long time. Brother Mike himself had a great fondness for beans, but in respect to the evening meal he anticipated, he forwent his number one choice and settled on a quarter of grilled chicken with an order of *frites*.

The bird, as Brother Mike knew well when ordering, was scrawny with pitiful little meat, but a good taste of charcoal and seared skin. The fiery *pili pili* sauce helped make it an enjoyable repast, and the big plate of hot *frites* was a wonder. Brother Mike would have thought he would have to be at the Abbey to get *frites* of this truly excellent quality. Perhaps, he thought, the extreme freshness of the potatoes played a big part. They were exceptional and he left, he hoped, with just the right degree of fullness to not spoil his appetite for the much-anticipated evening meal.

Brother Mike let his feet lead him as he had happy thoughts about the great *frites*. It seemed as though they knew where they were going, so he just followed, now thinking about bigger things than *frites*, wondering why people do the things they do? This was an unwieldy subject to ponder while somehow navigating the streets of the city. At one point Brother Mike decided he should put this topic on hold and get his bearings. As he looked around, he realized he was very near Nimbambora Hospital, the hospital maintained by the Church. It made perfect sense to him that he pay a visit.

As he stood in front of the main entrance of the hospital, a man rushed past him carrying another man in his arms, this second man's left leg covered in blood. Brother Mike followed the two inside more out of curiosity than inquiry. The rushing man ran to the first medical person he saw and exclaimed loudly that his friend needed urgent treatment. Amazingly, in spite of the obvious urgency, this agent of the hospital simply pointed to the main desk and walked calmly away.

The man trying to help his friend was exasperated as he ran to the front desk. There were two women, possibly nurses, taking behind the counter. The man first offered a polite "hello," but this solicited no reaction. He then continued at increasing modulation until finally the two ladies stopped their very intense conversation and looked indifferently in his direction without making any effort to get up or help.

By this point, Brother Mike could see, the man was in a high state of aggravation. Brother Mike wondered if he could facilitate things.

He approached the desk, saying to the supposed nurses sitting in the breeze of a fan, "Excuse me ladies, I am Brother Mike of the Brothers of Piety visiting Nimbambora, one of the Church's prime healers. I wonder if you might be able to be of some service to these gentlemen who obviously are in need of your kind attention?"

The older lady, a large heavy-set woman with a scowl on her face that seemed to be permanently etched into her wrinkles, slowly and with great show raised from her chair and approached the counter. She seemed not to see Brother Mike, fixing her eyes on the man now having evident difficultly to continue carrying his friend who was of no small size himself. "Where's your hospital card?"

"Card!" the man nearly screamed. "I don't have a card, I need urgent treatment for my friend who has badly cut his leg while working in the field and is bleeding profusely."

The woman pretended as if she had not heard the man's plea, adding "It's not your card I need, if the man in your arms is to be treated, he must have a hospital card. Where's his card?"

At this, the porter made a holler like a wounded goat and the man in his arms managed to raise his head from his friend's shoulder and feebly say to the uncompromising lady, "Madame, please. I have no card. I am wounded, I need help . . ."

The woman seemed ready to turn the two away and Brother Mike felt he must again intervene. "Madame, kindly get this man in a room where he can receive medical treatment immediately. I am working with Father Juvenal and if there are any problems in this man's admission, I am sure the Father will be able to sort things out."

Both men looked at Brother Mike with intense gratitude while the woman showed that she could do the impossible and her scowl became even deeper and wider. Nonetheless, perhaps due to the mention of Father Juvenal, who Brother Mike knew kept his presence known, the lady did leave the desk and guide the two men further into the interior of the hospital. Brother Mike hoped there would be some care now provided to the injured man. He contemplated the roles of health workers—who was helping whom?

He decided enough was enough, and he certainly had enough on his own plate. For once, looking for the path of the least resistance, he left the hospital posthaste. He then returned to his reverie, strolling slowly, taking in the sounds as the city peaked and began to slow, many of its current residents now preparing to go home—back to the villages, the farms, the shops, the bars, the families, and the clans they had left early this morning. He made a big circle, ending up at the steps of the pastoral center.

Brother Mike went to his room and freshened up, rinsing away the sweat and dirt he had accumulated through his perambulations. He said his prayers, and lay on his bed for a few minutes of rest. He must have dozed off, for he was awakened by a knock at his door. He arose and went to find at the door one of the guest house's jack-of-all-trades boys, the universal and ubiquitous helpers who played such a big part in making things—all sorts of things—run. He was politely informed that Father Juvenal had sent a car for him. He promised he would be down in five minutes and set about getting ready for dinner.

Descending to the foyer, Brother Mike found there was more than a car, there was Father Juvenal who was the driver of the car. They greeted each other warmly and set out to the Vironga.

The hotel restaurant was dark and rather heavy space with varnished hardwood walls, heavy open beams, scarlet velvet curtains, pictures of the volcanoes on the walls, and large wooden tables with captain's chairs and candles with scarlet shades. The clientele seemed to be all European, while the caterers were not.

In spite of the almost Teutonic atmosphere, which didn't exactly buoy up Brother Mike's spirits, the tables were comfortable and the menu seemed more than satisfactory. They ordered a good bottle of French wine, and Father Juvenal had vegetable soup to start while Brother Mike ordered Belgian endive. Father Juvenal then had bream *meunière* and Brother Mike had *entrecôte*, both plates garnished with fresh green beans and *frites*. They topped it all off with *crème brûlée* and cognac. All in all, it was an above average repast.

The conversation started with the practical. Father Juvenal had heard back from the six potato producing parishes. Farmers would be at St. Vincent's at one p.m. While Brother Mike met with the farmers, Father Juvenal had arranged for one of his staff to take Brother Mike's pickup and get it loaded with potatoes for the Abbey. If all went well, Brother Mike should be back on the road south before three p.m.

Quick and to the point, the business was finished. It was time for more personal conversations. Brother Mike was still troubled by his experiences at the hospital this afternoon but decided this was neither the time nor the place to bring it up. So, like approaching the fishpond with stealth so as not to scare away the big bream, he opened the conversation delicately, "My dear Father Juvenal, are you from this area?"

"Indeed," Father Juvenal replied, having nearly finished his soup. "I am from a commune about 30 km to the west of here. My father, like almost everybody's, was a farmer, he and my mother farmed coffee and cassava on our hillside fields, and grew potatoes, Irish and sweet, along with beans in the communal valley. My parents had ten children. Six lived to be teenagers and four have continued to become adults.

"That great big family, at least in your European terms, lived in a three-room home on the hills, like most of the farmers' homes you see today, made of fired brick and tile and balanced precariously on the slopes. We had very little. But we were very happy.

"My family attended the parish church every Sunday and the children, when old enough, went to the parish school. For some unknown reason, I turned out to be a good student and had a chance to go to seminary—a chance for which my family was eternally grateful. My parents were so proud of their son, the priest.

"They have since passed and my oldest brother has taken over their home and fields. My older brother, who falls between the eldest and me, also had to keep living in the old family home for several years until he was able to save enough to build his own home, at which time he could ask his girlfriend to marry. Both my brothers are farmers and, as you know, farmers don't make a lot, so their life is simple, not veering very far from the life of our parents.

"We have a younger sister to complete the sibling group. She is really smart. Not just a lucky kid like me, I mean smart. She is in university and hopes to get a law degree. Imagine, someone like us from the hills being a lawyer. I can almost feel my parents smiling."

Brother Mike felt touched by the candor of Father Juvenal and the honesty of his tale. People from isolated areas being able to get a hand up through the Church's support. He wondered how Father Juvenal would have liked farming.

"Well Father," Brother Mike tried picking up the ball, "you may be one of those rare people who can look at the present, feel the past, and prepare for the future. I imagine your religious life is very different than that of a farmer? And, as we are here to help 'the people,' to a large extent it is the farming families we need to assist. How do you see their future?"

"That, my dear Brother," picked up Father Juvenal, "is a very, very relevant but challenging question. We are on a seesaw. It may be more than a metaphor to think of our communal position as being on the crest of two watersheds, a moral Congo–Nile Divide.

"Our people are proud of their long history, free of the influences of outsiders. You know, we have a saying, 'God may go anywhere during the day, but at night He comes back here to sleep.' We see ourselves as special and we see ourselves as being intrinsically linked to our past.

"This is not necessarily bad. All God's children are special. And, our past has many lessons, good and bad. But if we cannot separate the good from the bad, and learn from both, we are apt to repeat the same terrible acts we have already committed in our past. Can the Church really teach us to love one another?

"I like to hope so. But I am constantly reminded of the realities of today. We have been so long left to our own volition, we are fearful of what the world offers—what the world wants.

"I would think, to try to provide a practical answer to your question, if the Church can really make an impact on educating the youth and healing the ill, we may be able to make inroads into changing things for the better—really looking at some of our past as being terrible lessons of what not to do—affirming our need to live as Christ has taught us."

By this time, they were finishing dessert and thinking about what needed to be done today to be ready for tomorrow—after a cognac, of course.

Brother Mike let the golden liquid slowly slide down his throat. Through hooded eyes he peered intensely at Father Juvenal. He was a fine-looking man. Tall with broad shoulders, close-cropped hair, and intelligent eyes. He had great charisma and knew how to be a charming conversationalist—and also, Brother Mike supposed, a stern master. What was his social life? Did he too have female friends? Did he too see the need to adapt and adopt the prime directives to make life more livable? Brother Mike really wanted answers to these questions, but he knew he did not know Father Juvenal well enough to even open this line of thought.

They exchanged banal chitchat for a few more minutes, each simultaneously exclaiming the hour was late, there was much to do, and it was time to get back to their respective residences.

On the ride back to the center, Brother Mike told Father Juvenal that, since the meeting with the farmers was in the afternoon, he wanted to look up a friend. He would leave the pickup in the parking, the keys at the front desk, so it could be loaded for the southbound trip at the Father's convenience, and he would go about his visit using a taxi.

Brother Mike passed a very quiet and restful night. He awoke early, said his prayers, bathed, dressed for the day, and had a continental breakfast in the main dining area. He then called his friend Louis.

He had first met Louis in primary school. His family fit into one of those categories of 20th-century nomads—his father was always looking for the perfect job, seeking the ever-elusive winning lottery ticket. And, with the postwar mobility across Europe and much of the world, there were many games to play, tickets to buy.

Louis' father had been working in a bank in Béthune, France, at the time of Louis' birth. Louis would tell Brother Mike that his fondest early memories were the hourly tolling of the bells from the Béthune belfry. Although Louis had less clear recollections of the family's early days, the family crossed the border into Belgium when he was eight. They moved about for several years before settling in Brother Mike's parish, thinking they had found their new permanent home. However, after four years, Louis' father either had found a new game to play or was simply bitten by wanderlust, and the family moved back to France, this time, to the south of the country. He continued, however, to write to Brother Mike on a most irregular schedule, keeping his old friend abreast of his family's seemingly never-ending relocations

From the Côte d'Azur to crossing the Mediterranean seemed a logical step and Louis' family then began a long, but perhaps inevitable southern migration from Cape Bon, where in 1941 the 4th Italian Cruiser Division lost a five-minute sea battle with the 4th British Destroyer Flotilla, to the end of the road at the Cape of Good Hope.

When they reached South Africa, Louis was a well-educated young man. In fact, Louis was a well-educated white man who was fluent in French and Flemish, with a good base in English and some Arabic—just the sort of person the country was seeking. With his earlier studies in biology and chemistry at schools spread along the pathway of his youth, he found an entry position in human health research. With the amazing heart transplant effected by Dr. Christiaan Barnard in 1967, much attention was focused on health and money was flowing in to support research in the hope of keeping the spotlight on monumental innovations, while incidentally keeping apartheid in the shadows.

By this time, Louis' father was too old to chase rainbows and his mother far too tired to keep moving. Thanks to Louis' up and coming work, they were able to get a small cottage near the Cape where they spent their remaining days.

Louis stayed single, never really feeling comfortable in the white South African social scene. Nevertheless, with his fluent Flemish, he fit in perfectly with the Afrikaans-speaking community and had as active a social life as he wished.

Throughout the years, he kept his link with Brother Mike—a postcard from here, an aerogramme from there. Not too far back he had written a longer missive, telling his pen pal that he had had enough of the pressures of research, the great rush to get new things out even before they were tried and true, the backstabbing competition for funds and notoriety, and the long, long hours of intricate planning and work, only to have the results hijacked by some know-nothing administrator. No, it was time for a change.

In his work, he had often used primates for experimentation, a fact that had pained him and that he was only able to justify by thinking of the greater human good. But as he became disenchanted, the suffering inflicted on the noble animals seemed harder and harder to accept. Therefore, he joined a group—actually, he had helped found a group—that was going to establish a center to try and rehabilitate lab primates while lobbying against their use in research. They had purchased some land in the north of the country on the Olifants River and he would be leaving the city for the bush—the veldt—in the very near future.

Then, just a few months ago Brother Mike had received a much briefer note. Not to be following in his father's footsteps, but Louis had decided to move yet again. He found the infighting and posturing of his group difficult to tolerate and had accepted an assignment in Central Africa working with a team that was trying to help the mountain gorillas survive. Now, after all these years, he and Brother Mike would once again be in the same country.

Finally, following half a generation of separation that had wrought untold change, Brother Mike would see Louis today. He greeted the opportunity with a mixture of anxiety and joy. Would he be able to reconnect? Were the now misty childhood memories a better souvenir than the present?

They had agreed to meet at the Volcanoes Lodge on the road to the northern border, about 15 km from the city center and halfway to the camp Louis shared with the other primatologists. Brother Mike hired a city taxi for half a day and they left town before 9 a.m.

The road was good and they were going against traffic so they made their destination in about 20 minutes. The lodge was composed of a large main building encircled by a cluster of bungalows, looking for the world like a hen surrounded by her chicks. All the buildings were thatched, with rough-hewn wooden walls and verandas going around at least two sides. The main building's roof was steeply peaked, reminding Brother Mike of a stereotypic witch's hat.

There was a large kidney-shaped parking area in front of this central feature, with a small stone swimming pool off to one side. The whole area had been cut out of the forest and was largely shaded, facilitating the driver's wait in the car.

Brother Mike went up the first flight of stairs to a patio-like area with a dozen small tables covered by parasols and interspersed with a variety of local flowers in large ornate fired clay pots. He continued up a second flight that led to a twin set of oversized glass double doors apparently leading to the lobby, with a wooden veranda extending to the left and right of this central entryway. He was in the process of pushing on one of the big doors when he heard a whistle that brought back memories of his youth.

He looked to his left and right, at first seeing nothing and no one. Then as he took a second look, on the left veranda, back under the shadow of the overhanging thatch, he spied a figure seated at a table and waving his arms.

Brother Mike hurried to the table and as he approached, a large man jumped up and put him in a forceful bear hug. After a hearty embrace, they pushed away from each other and gazed at the workings of the past decades. Brother Mike had no idea what to expect. His visual memories were of a typical brown haired, brown-eyed boy like so many others with whom he had shared primary school. But that was many years ago and time leaves nothing untouched.

Nonetheless, as he examined his childhood friend, he had to conclude the years had been good to him. He had a strong body, good posture, and only a small gut that barely overhung his belt. His skin was clear, as were his eyes. But there were wrinkles where none had been and the lush brown hair was now much thinner and interwoven with gray. Well, thought Brother Mike as he took his seat, I hope he feels I have weathered time as well as he has.

The table was clear of any food or drink and it was still midmorning. Brother Mike was uncertain what Louis had in mind in terms of refreshment. However, his uncertainty was short-lived as, when the waiter miraculously appeared as soon as Brother Mike's backside hit the chair, Louis ordered two beers and two orders of *frites* with fresh mayonnaise. Somehow, this seemed just right for this reunion that had taken so long to happen.

While they waited for their order to arrive and after a few mundane pleasantries, Louis explained his assignment. The mountain gorillas of this part of the continent were rare and endangered. This area was one of the most densely populated of the continent, and many were asking if there was space for both gorillas and men. For the past several years, a team of scientists and general do-gooders had been working to convince the deciders that the gorillas were in fact a wealth yet untapped, a wealth that, once exploited, would show how gorilla and man could cohabit successfully. The core idea was that the gorillas were worth more in their native habitat, alive, than as a trophy or a zoo attraction. Tourists brought money and created jobs. Gorillas would bring tourists, it was that simple.

But it was anything but simple. First, the underlying policies of nationalism and self-imposed isolationism were really not conducive to the development of a still nonexistent tourist industry. There were, moreover, already a few limited tourists coming to see the gorillas in spite of the almost pioneering conditions. Some managed to see the great animals, using privateer guides. Most left unfulfilled and, from the government's point of view, having contributed little toward economic growth. Also, there was pitifully little known about the gorillas. How many were there? Where do they go? How could they be the centerpiece of a tourist industry without destroying their natural behavior?

There was, however, intense international pressure to protect the gorillas. If the country could accomplish this and at the same time have economic and political gains, this would be a win-win. Accordingly, the government had put a moratorium in place to see what could be done and how to do it. Louis' team was the heart of this venture. Most of the members were involved in collecting the most intimate data on the gorilla families. They recorded movements, feeding behavior, sexual behavior, births and deaths, bad times, and good. They were already in their third year and, as these field data sets became available, there were other teams who were analyzing these data to see how one could configure tourism for the benefit of the government and local communities, but not to the detriment of the gorilla families.

The work had been progressing well but they had reached a stage where there was a serious hang-up—a potentially important health issue for both humans and gorillas. Most often, primates were seen as vectors of diseases that affected humans. However, the reverse was equally true. Humans could very possibly be vectors for disease that could affect gorillas. This was Louis' job. He was to assess the risks in both directions, making recommendations as to how to minimize risks if they could not be avoided altogether. The whole project was now awaiting his recommendations before the next steps could be planned in detail.

Brother Mike was rapt as Louis spoke. This was a whole new world to him, and these were subjects of which he had had no previous knowledge, yet subjects he recognized as being of considerable importance on multiple fronts.

Their food and drinks came as Louis had been describing his work. Brother Mike took a big swallow of beer, somehow enjoying the almost sinful feeling of having a lovely cold brew before noon. As it splashed into his stomach, he felt his body embrace it, asking for more. He honored the request, and took another mouthful before picking up a crunchy *frite* and dunking it in the deliciously tart fresh mayonnaise. By the time Louis had concluded, Brother Mike had drained his bottle and cleaned his plate. This pushed Louis to order another round for his friend if he did not want to eat and drink alone.

Brother Mike picked up the discussion, thereby slowing his own consumption, providing Louis with a thumbnail sketch of his activities. But he was immediately aware that he really did nothing, had done nothing, compared to Louis. This awareness was, in and of itself, interesting to Brother Mike. Perhaps because of his religious training, or maybe just because he was the way he was, this imbalance between his accomplishments, at least as he saw them, and those of Louis, was not an issue. While others might feel inadequate when sitting across from a peer who had seemingly done so much more with his life, Brother Mike was frankly happy that Louis had had what appeared to be good and productive life and that he obviously enjoyed what he was doing. For him, just getting back in physical touch with someone from his youth was a generous gift and he was most grateful for having had this chance to see his old grade school chum again.

Brother Mike felt as though he and Louis had a true parallel energy. Louis was, Brother Mike was happy to note, even after all these years, still someone with whom there were the bonds to foster into a real and meaningful friendship. And, if there was one thing that Brother Mike had learned, it was that real friendships were rarities, gems of inestimable value. People spoke so freely of "my friend" this and "my friend" that, but true friendships that could stand the test of time and the rigors of human nature were unique. Brother Mike had hopes that his relationship with Louis could be such a unique bond.

His desire to forge a close relationship notwithstanding, it was time to prepare to say goodbye as he still had to meet with potato farmers. From gorillas to potatoes in one day, not bad!

As they separated, they promised to stay in touch and Brother Mike invited Louis to the Abbey any time he could get away from his mountain adventures. Brother Mike then rejoined his taxi and was soon with Father Juvenal, preparing to welcome a still unknown number of potato farmers.

In fact, the turnout was better than expected. Brother Mike was pleased to see that, in at least three parishes, the farmers had joined together in some sort of a marketing structure to ensure they got the best price for their crops. These larger groups would be perfect suppliers for the Abbey. Through the deft orchestrations of Father Juvenal, they were able to reach an agreement with one of these groups—an agreement resulting in a considerably lower price for the monastery and also, hopefully, in a considerably fresher product reaching the monks' table.

Half an hour ahead of schedule, fully loaded with fresh potatoes, Brother Mike said *au revoir* to Father Juvenal and headed south. The trip was uneventful, although he arrived quite late at the Abbey and had to wake up some people to unload the pickup. It was after midnight when he gratefully found his bed. He slept soundly as someone who had done a good day's work.

8

BROTHER MIKE AWOKE EARLY, still perhaps hearing the rhythm of the road. After prayers, he felt he was due a bit of quiet time and crept away to his favorite spot on the pond bank. It seemed he had only just arrived, and he was centering his thoughts on complex issues of moral responsibility when he felt a tap on his shoulder. Turning, he saw one of the many young men, novitiates, who assisted the Abbot. He often thought of them as his squires, the shield bearers, buzzing around a knight, just as he often thought of the Abbot in his Abbey as a knight in his castle. And, it was, in truth, the Abbot who had sent for him.

Upon complementing him on a job well done with the potatoes, the Abbot, as he was wont to do, cut straight to the chase—true to his knighthood, a tournament jouster with a keen eye. His target was a new mega project funded by one of those multinational organizations with deep pockets, something called, of all things, the Global Project. While the Abbot only had sketchy details, it seemed this project could do just about anything. Its main aim apparently was simply to help rural dwellers. With this in mind, the Abbot wanted Brother Mike to contact the project's leadership and see if there were ways and means to improve the road leading to the Abbey.

They agreed Brother Mike would take the rest of the day off and then go into town by midmorning the next day to follow up on this project, at the very least making appointments to meet with some of the key staff.

Brother Mike gratefully spent the rest of the morning back on the pond bank. He even skipped Midday Prayers and lunch to sit quietly, lulled by the lullaby of the eucalyptus leaves and banana fronds, thinking of the convoluted paths men face when traveling through life. Knowing the right way to go seemed a near impossibility; everything appeared to be based on pure chance or Divine intervention. And, in his business, the latter was the rationale of choice. If we were all His children, then not only did He have a lot of children, but they were each following often tortuous paths. Well, he thought, trying to calm his deep worries that seemed to be surfacing more and more regularly, he was too old, too far down his personal path—and, as they liked to say here, "you can't bend a dried fish."

The next morning Brother Mike started his assignment as he had others before, seeking out Philip to find out about the Global Project. Philip simply seemed to know a little about a lot of things.

Brother Mike found Philip in his clinic. He waited while Philip finished his current patient, then the two stepped outside for a quick chitchat.

After welcoming him back from his safari north, Philip told Brother Mike he had heard of the Global Project, but had few specifics. They had just built new offices south of town, in the Rango neighborhood, not too far from the Migina Valley. They were one of the new highly political monster projects that had massive budgets, huge staffs, and professed to be all things for all people. He thought the man in charge was a certain Bizimana, a local guy who had just returned from studies abroad. To date, as far as Philip could tell, the only thing they had managed to do was pad the payroll with friends and supporters of the various politicians who had helped bring in the financing, be the justification ever so flimsy and diffuse.

Brother Mike followed Philip's directions and was soon bumping down a track apparently leading to the river valley below. He wondered how it could be that a big project that reportedly, among other things, improved roads had such a bad road to its own headquarters?

The road turned to the left, leaving a small wood lot, entering a clearing where there was a large fenced enclosure—three-meter-high, imported chain-link fence that Brother Mike's discerning eye immediately tagged as being very expensive. The hub of this circumscribed space was occupied by a new large building of brick and glass that was certainly a source of pride for someone, but that reminded Brother Mike very much of the Chinese camp where he had so recently spent the night. It was a long narrow building with two dozen doors opening on a wide veranda. It was probably intended to provide some sort of physical segregation to different parts of the project, but it looked for all the world like some sort of hotel, or a Chinese work camp.

This main structure was the backdrop of an expansive gravel parking area in which there were a score of private cars and at least twice that number of brand new Land Cruisers and double cab 4x4 pickups with the Global Project's bright insignia on the doors. The space between this hub and the perimeter fence was occupied by a number of other structures: garage, shop, storerooms, apparently classrooms, and even some chalets that must have been guest rooms.

Brother Mike parked his dusty and well-worn pickup in a corner of the parking lot and quickly mounted the three stairs that took him to the veranda. Here he found each door to have some sort of cryptic sign: Operations, Outreach, Finances, and so on. Walking down the line, he found one saying "Director." He knocked and, hearing nothing, entered. He found himself in a small anteroom with barely enough room for the two desks it held. Each desk was occupied by a very attractive young lady dressed to the nines, a bit of a surprise given the almost rural setting.

Brother Mike addressed the ladies jovially, saying he was from the Brothers of Piety and wished to speak with Director Bizimana. The lackadaisical women reacted as though he were a troublesome mosquito in their ear; knowing it was there, but wishing it were not. They remained silent for several minutes, perhaps thinking he would leave if they said nothing. But, when he remained standing in front of them with a too-large-for-comfort grin on his face, they did ask him to take a seat on one of the three straight-back chairs that were squeezed against the back wall, whereupon one of the two ladies disappeared through an interior door, one of two.

Brother Mike sat uncomfortably on the cheaply made chair, taking in what might best be called the reception area. The two well-dressed ladies sat in what looked to be equally uncomfortable and wobbly chairs in front of matching desks with little of substance on the surface. One lady seemed to have a bit of mail on the corner of her desk and an open woman's magazine occupying the center of her workspace. The other lady had one of those bright red folios for securing documents for the boss's signature on one corner of her desk, an empty "out" tray posed over an overflowing "in" tray on the other corner, with today's newspaper open in between.

The newspaper lady returned through door number one, fixing Brother Mike with her mascaraed eyes, asking him rather abruptly to please be patient, the Director was a very busy man. She then returned to her seat, entering into deep conversation in patois with her workmate. From the giggles and coy expressions, it seemed unlikely they were discussing global development.

Brother Mike tried to say a brief prayer, but found himself gazing up to the ceiling, trying to imagine how many cubic meters of wood were used to support the asbestos roofing sheets a full two meters above the asbestos ceiling squares. It was his habit, when not knowing what else to do, to try and reconstruct the building where he found himself—trying to imagine the blueprints, the material used, the labor employed, and the result obtained. Somehow, he felt these almost *post mortem* examinations helped him better judge the materials he was asked to procure for the Abbey.

He had lost track of time when the magazine lady rose, as if responding to an invisible and inaudible signal, indicating to Brother Mike he could go through to see the Director.

Closing the door behind him, Brother Mike extended his hand, put on a warm smile and, eying the hefty man who rose as he approached, said, "Mr. Bizimana, it is a pleasure."

"Doctor Bizimana", was the reply, with the strong emphasis on the word "doctor."

"Oh, I'm sorry, DOCTOR Bizimana," replied a fully composed Brother Mike. "I appreciate you taking time out of your busy schedule to see me," he continued, seeing the open newspaper in the center of the Director's desk and the partially finished cup of coffee at its side.

The Director gave a "humph" and rather sadly sat down, never having shaken Brother Mike's hand.

"Yes," he said, picking up on Brother Mike's emphasis. "DOCTOR Bizimana, first liberal arts doctoral candidate from Central Africa in Toulouse."

"Congratulations", chimed in Brother Mike with little spirit, hoping to quickly get to the subject that had brought him here, so as not to unduly delay the good Doctor from rejoining his undoubtedly still-to-be-fully-read newspaper.

"Yes," continued the good Doctor, seemingly unaware that Brother Mike had actually come with the intent of discussing something with him. "My exhaustive work is covered in my writing on *Derived Indicators of Poverty in Rural African Populations Dominated by External Economic and Political Forces.*"

"Wonderful", was the half-hearted reply from Brother Mike, thinking to himself that the indicator of poverty was that people were poor.

"Wait, wait, wait", enthused Doctor Bizimana as he pushed a small white button on a metallic device that then gave out a sound like a doorbell.

Within seconds the magazine lady appeared. She regarded her Director demurely, almost curtsying, "Yes Sir?"

Without looking at her, the Doctor instructed, "Go to the storeroom and get a copy of my thesis from the box on the lower shelf."

She left quietly and hurriedly and in her absence Doctor Bizimana glanced at his newspaper as if Brother Mike had accompanied her.

In what seemed like no time at all, the nearly blushing lady reappeared, staring at her boss with puppy dog eyes, she silently placed a thin, bound sheaf of papers with a nondescript gray cover in front of the Director, covering his newspaper to his obvious dislike.

Saying nothing, he motioned her away. After she had disappeared, he took a tortoiseshell fountain pen from a holder on his desk and, with great fanfare, signed the gray cover before handing the document to Brother Mike with two hands as though it were the Holy Bible.

Brother Mike thanked the Director profusely for his kind gift, underscoring how aware he was that this represented a tremendous amount of effort and was, moreover, a work that would be of great benefit to his country.

The Director accepted the praise with a bowed head as though awaiting Communion.

Brother Mike then took the opportunity of a silent and hopefully receptive Director to present his rehearsed exhortation: would the esteemed Director's project by any chance have plans to work on roads near the Abbey of the Brothers of Piety? If the honorable Director was familiar with roads in that part of the commune, he would certainly know they were in very poor state, improving them not only a good service to God's work at the Abbey, but also a great service to the local population that suffered day in and day out in getting about over nearly impassible tracks. Additionally, the Director may have heard that the Abbey was planning on a major expansion in the coming months. The bad condition of the roads increased the risk of added costs since some building materials could not come in through the twisting and potholed road and would need to be offloaded from larger lorries and reloaded onto pickups for ferrying into the Abbey. Clearly the Global Project could extend a great helping hand to all by upgrading the deteriorated road network.

They say first impressions are lasting and, if Brother Mike's first impressions were of any measure, he felt from the onset he was wasting his breath. The disinterested Director was unlikely to take the Abbey's situation into consideration. In truth, it seemed clear that Doctor Bizimana was unlikely to do anything that did not benefit Doctor Bizimana. Nevertheless, when he had finished his allocution, he sat with upright posture and a smile on his face awaiting the great man's reaction.

There was but a moment's pause before the Director picked up his coffee cup, focused on his newspaper saying, "Thank you, we will inform you if we are able to do anything in your area. As you know," he added as either an afterthought or perhaps an excuse, "the project is just starting and there is so much to do with our limited resources. We have many difficult decisions to make before we do anything on the ground. But you will be kept appraised. Good bye."

As Brother Mike withdrew through the anteroom, the ladies were sharing a mirror and putting on fresh lipstick. He offered a muffled good bye for politeness sake and entered the bright sunlight that was bathing the parking area.

When Brother Mike was getting into his lovely old pickup, he spied the two anteroom ladies heading to one of the chalets. He wondered if they had a rendezvous with the Director? Oh yes, he thought, the heavy responsibilities of leadership, as his pickup reluctantly chugged into motion.

Brother Mike thought he would look for Philip before returning to the Abbey. Given the hour, his first thought was to check at his home. When he tapped softly on the sliding glass door, he was a bit surprised to see Angela come to his call. He explained he thought Philip might be home but as he was not, he would try and find him at his clinic.

Angela said she would have nothing of it. Their son was out with Joseph. She had just finished tidying up and preparing Philip's favorite *carbonade* for dinner. She needed a cold beer and she hated to drink alone so, it was Brother Mike's duty to come to her aid and have a beer with her, to prevent her from dying from thirst on the spot.

Brother Mike was taken unawares by this new and welcoming Angela. Although she had never been rude or even indifferent, there had always been a cloak of cool reserve about her that seemed to have fallen off her shoulders this afternoon. Brother Mike felt obliged to comply with her appeal and gratefully accepted the offer of a beer, hoping it would wash away some of the bitter taste that had crept into his mouth after leaving the Global Project's headquarters.

While Angela got the beer from the kitchen, Brother Mike ambled over to Kasuku's cage to say hello. The parrot seemed to recognize him and bowed his head. When Angela appeared with the drinks on a tray, Kasuku turned his back on Brother Mike, proclaiming in his loudest voice, "Asshole!" They all laughed, including Kasuku who had a throaty chuckle.

As Brother Mike enjoyed the refreshing beer, Angela sat in relaxed fashion across from him, her beer bottle sweating on the coffee table as she politely enquired about his family and childhood. He was impressed by the ease with which she probed the conversation with an obvious first-hand knowledge of Belgian customs and geography.

He really had little to say other than recount the worn-out version of his personal drama that he shared for public consumption—the hidden truth somewhat less glowing. Most of his devoutly Catholic family and friends had welcomed his decision, at an early age, to follow Christ. He had been a novitiate like hundreds of others, questioning his path and his ability to follow this path on a daily basis, but somehow completing the journey and becoming a monk. His decision, nevertheless, to enter into a monastery in Africa had been a difficult conclusion for his family to accept, as they had hoped he would have stayed closer to home where they could maintain some degree of contact. As it was, he rarely returned to Belgium and, after decades of absence, even the letters from family were now few and far between. In spite of the faded picture he painted of having strong roots in Ghent, The Brothers of Piety were Brother Mike's family and life.

He quickly turned the tables on Angela, but was much more focused in his questioning: what was it like being married to a Belgian, living a racially mixed life split between Europe and Africa?

Angela was detached and analytical in her reply. Her immediate family notwithstanding, there were many people on all sides who opposed mixed marriages. Many held these views on the grounds that God had not intended the races to mix. Others felt the union was one of singular advantage; either the gold-digger syndrome with the woman taking advantage of, or being solely attracted by the man's wealth by African standards, or the trophy-bride syndrome, with the man taking advantage of, or being solely attracted by the woman's physical beauty, thereby making her unavailable to the local male population. At the end of the day, however, none of this mattered as the opposition was a minority and their marriage was based on love.

With particular candor, nonetheless, she admitted that Philip's family had had a terrible time getting used to their son marrying an African. In fact, for a while they had treated him as though he were dead and she was really still unsure if they completely accepted her. If there had been any soothing of the wounds, it had been because, as grandparents they were enjoying seeing Germain. Still and all, she imagined out loud that if she were a fly on the wall in her in-laws' house after she and her family had visited them, she would hear a lot of negativity about "that damn black woman." But such was life. Some people here also undoubtedly thought of her being married to "that damn white man" as a jailable offense. Her own family was a case in point.

All this aside, Angela was proud of her *matisse* son. She felt that if all the world's groups, tribes, and clans—groups, tribes, and clans that so often do not get along—groups, tribes, and clans that may hate and kill each other—intermarried, if all became one common intermingling gene pool, then just maybe the world would be a better place. Perhaps people would be less anxious to kill their brother or abuse their sister. Perhaps people would offer a helping hand instead of a slap in the face.

Brother Mike was touched and intrigued by the depth of Angela's reflections. He did not want, however, to dishearten their heretofore cheerful conversation with more in-depth examinations of the ills of man, despite the fact that this subject stirred his own soul. Therefore, he deftly changed the subject, asking about her work with her properties. Angela too sensed they were teetering on deep topics that could dispirit their amiable discussion.

She quickly rearranged her thoughts, providing Brother Mike with an al-most frivolous accounting of her landlord work.

As she spoke, Brother Mike marveled at how congruous the human animal was, wherever you found him or her. The grievances of landlords were truly universal; victims of deadbeats, derelicts, and the disrespectful—yet able to make often more than a modest living.

Angela finished, showing the paint stains still on her hands as both badges of honor and signs of the suffering of a property owner. This seemed to signal an end to their respite, Brother Mike shifting his position as if readying his departure. Angela quickly noticed this change, offering a last pint of beer for the road. Brother Mike was in the process of politely insist-ing on departing when she reminded him of the local custom to take one last glass to, as the old folks used to say, "raise the lance." Brother Mike did not mention Rolf's recent recital of this saying. Feigning *naïveté* and in spite of, or perhaps because of the possible double entendre, he felt compelled to acquiesce and enjoyed one final frosty pint before heartily thanking Angela for the hospitality and rejoining his pickup.

Brother Mike decided to brief Philip at a later date, his responsibilities at the Abbey beckoning as he took the main highway north to the monas-tery's cutoff. He felt his truck should be able to get back on autopilot given the number of times it had made this trip. He did, in fact, put his brain on autopilot as he held the wheel and thought about Angela and what an un-usual woman she was. His revelry was shattered as the pickup jerked off the tarmac onto the rough laterite lane that would ultimately bring him home. His teeth rattled as he caromed off the washboard surface. His thoughts, with no small amount of disinclination, shifted to the Global Project and its likely complete indifference to the state of the road. He bet his Chinese friends would be able to make short work of these terrible roads if they were put to the task.

Pulling into the Abbey, he decided to go straight to the Abbot's offices before getting ready for Vespers to update him as to the meeting with the project and the unlikelihood that the roads would receive any much-needed care any time in the near future.

9

BROTHER MIKE WAS HAPPY to plan on returning to his accustomed routine. The fish and potato trips had been interesting, but he was content to pick up his considerable portfolio at the Abbey and concentrate on that and that alone. In so doing, he felt he was getting back into the rhythm of the brotherhood—back on track. He was now regular with his prayers and his common meals with his confrères. He had his hands in a dozen mini projects at the monastery, was dealing with logistics both for his immediate community and his special friends in the community at large. He shared drinks with Philip on Saturdays and they played cards on Wednesdays.

Christmas season arrived again, to Brother Mike its approach was all too soon—it seemed they had just finished Lent. The Abbey was all aflutter with this special time of the year. The chapel was decked out in greenery. The monks set up their *crèche* in the open space in front of the chapel, each figure painstakingly carved by different members of the community. The butcher shop prepared choice Christmas meats while the bakery prepared sumptuous Christmas strudels and puddings. The schools went on Christmas vacation, while the brothers prepared gifts for all the children in the orphanage.

The past summer dry season had been particularly severe, followed by little if any precipitation from September through November. The streams were down to a trickle, the hillside pastures brown, and the all-important cows now heavily grazing in the valley bottoms. Many families were suffering as the stores from the last harvest were getting all the more meager. It was the hungry season. It was a time of dust and heat. But just as the Big Day approached there was a lovely rain. These much-appreciated irregular events were called the "cow rains" by the locals. But by whatever name, all agreed this was God's Hand blessing the birth of His Son and christening the land of His People.

The weeks following the heady days of Christmas were somehow hollow, everyone wanting to keep the holiday spirit alive, the energy ignited, the good feelings fed. But the chapel returned to its normal drabness, with the crèche lovingly wrapped and stored for next year, the bakery producing the same old baguettes and the butchery back to meat with or without bones. The short-lived great times were gone, at least until Easter.

But this was a time to get a lot of work done. Brother Mike was busier than ever, trying to keep ahead of what he felt to be his routine duties of the moment. He rarely ever had free minutes to visit his prized spot at the fishpond. While he did not miss his rendezvous with Philip, he was working long hours just to keep afloat. Then the Abbot announced he was ready to implement his plans for the expansion of the Abbey.

For more than seven years, the Abbey had been asking for special funds from the Church to expand and improve its facilities. They had always been told to be patient. When things broke down, new students or patients came, or the ailing resources were otherwise stressed, the Church advised the Abbot to be patient. Patience is said to be a virtue and finally this had been proven so by an almost lavish allocation by the Church for a major upgrading of the Abbey.

This news was, of course, met with great joy from all. However, as all began to realize the implications, this joy was quickly tempered with reality. Much of the oversight and monitoring work was expected to be accomplished by the Abbey's residents. This meant all were required to do more, a lot more.

ཥ ཥ ཥ

Work was piling up as the Abbey started to implement expansion activities; these requiring considerably more materials and supplies as well as necessitating a larger labor force for whom there were also additional requirements. This meant Brother Mike had two or three extra containers to clear a month, while still maintaining the orders for replenishing routine supplies, arranging for storage and inventory of all goods at the monastery, and helping his friends in town whenever and however he could. Furthermore, since he was known as the go-to person for arranging things, he was, much to his displeasure, additionally asked (required was more like it) to obtain all the necessary permits and authorizations to undertake the expansion—adding on to the orphanage, schools, and health center, expanding the workshops, and building new housing.

Much of the required administrative paper work to cover the large job site was taken care of at the provincial capital, but some of the approvals required endorsement of offices at the national capital. Thus, in spite of his dislike for large cities, Brother Mike found himself making regular trips to the country's capital.

Although he had assiduously tried to avoid the big urban centers, through the years he had had to unavoidably spend considerable time scurrying about the capital's byways as well as ferreting out the secrets of its offices and services. In so doing, he had his personal routine for this city, much as he had a routine for all his actions. He always stayed at the guest house behind the Cathedral where he took his morning and evening meals. However, at midday he liked to go to a small café in the center of the city that prepared, according to his palate, an excellent bream thermidor. When accompanied by a glass of good French wine, it was a worthy repast—one not to be missed.

True to his habits, his first afternoon in the city, after a lovely plate of bream topped off with a creamy and rich tarragon and wine sauce, he set about calling on the various offices needing to validate the Abbey's expansion plans. He had allocated two days for the assignment, as it was often hard to—as they said in the civil service—find the officers "on seat." He made good progress before the close of business, deciding to stop for a much-needed cold beer to refresh his overused throat after so much discussion. He had just taken a seat at a sidewalk bistro when he felt his forehead breakout in a sweat, he then felt like someone was choking him, his breath nearly shut off. He tried to call to the waiter for help, but slipped silently to the ground, clutching his neck.

Fortunately other customers cried out as they saw him slumping into a heap on sidewalk. Because of the commotion, the manager came running, and seeing the cause of the disruption, he immediately called the police who were able to get to the centrally located pub in just a few minutes. Noting the object of concern being an apparently passed-out white man, they promptly called their superior and an ambulance—both arriving at the same time. Whether through good training or good luck, Brother Mike arrived in the central hospital's emergency room less than half an hour after collapsing. His breathing was more a series of shallow rasps. His face was badly swollen. He could not speak. He could not tell them anything about his problem. He could only gasp and look afraid. It was frightful for all concerned. The intern receiving new patients immediately realized things could rapidly get out of control and he quickly called the senior medical officer who, it turned out, had recently transferred here from the provincial hospital in Brother Mike's area. While he did not know the Brother personally, he had seen him around and knew more or less what he did and with whom he was affiliated. But this knowledge did little to help Brother Mike now. Luckily, and

Brother Mike was to wonder later if it were just luck, the doctor recognized the symptoms of a classic allergic reaction and he quickly gave Brother Mike several powerful fast-acting antihistamine injections as well as something to calm him, relaxing his muscles.

After several hours of observation, Brother Mike's condition began to improve. His swelling slowly began to go down. His breathing deepened. And, although he could still not speak, he could contrive a short cacophony of sounds to try and communicate.

In spite of his inability to communicate well verbally, his mind was in overdrive. He had seen his death. He had seen, felt, and experienced his life being extinguished as his throat closed. His present state of living, after the certainty of death, brought about a feeling of euphoria. He had seen death and escaped.

Was this supposed to happen? Was this God's will? Of course, it must be.

Was this because of his religious following? Was this a miracle? It well could be.

His mind whirled about like a child's spinning multicolored top, almost randomly moving from place to place. He was in a hospital. People were looking after his wellbeing. Then he began to laugh, silently but vigorously. The thought of people looking after him made him recall, for some unknown reason, the stories he had been told about the kings of this area. Every time the king had a bowel movement, members of his entourage would scrupulously examine the stool to ensure the king was in good health. Were people scrupulously examining his stool? He hoped so.

Then more laughter seemed to rack his brain as he thought of the king's stool. Here one was referring to the king's feces. But, had he been in West Africa, the king's stool would be the seat upon which the king sat, a symbol of his authority and power. Stools and stools. He was lucky to be alive. The shock overcame him like a wave when he played on the beaches of Oostduinkerke-Bad as a child: cold yet warm, harsh yet soft. Then there was nothingness.

The presiding physician came to see Brother Mike, waking him just before midnight. Despite the one-way communication, he expressed his guarded satisfaction at the course of treatment for the allergy, but highlighted his concern. The central hospital had few private rooms and these were all already full and overflowing. He was worried that if Brother Mike were assigned to a general ward, he might even contract something more virulent than his current condition. He felt Brother Mike should look for alternate accommodation, but something where he could be closely monitored for the next 24 to 48 hours since these strong allergic reactions were tricky things that could get worse as quickly as they could get better. He then smiled broadly and said to Brother Mike, "I think I have a solution."

He motioned to the nurse who excused herself for moment and then returned with someone in hand. It turned out that that someone was Angela. Brother Mike was astonished, but could only make some gurgling noises. Angela noticed his questioning gaze and decided to put him at ease, "I was here visiting the doctor's wife. You know he used to practice with Philip and now I stop by to see them whenever I am in town. As it turns out, I am here to arrange for supplies for my houses, but have to wait several days for everything to be assembled. My sister has a home here where I stay when I am in the city. There is plenty of room and I would be happy to look after you until you get back on your feet."

There it was, an arrangement that fit all the requirements and made everyone happy. An act of God or serendipity?

Angela's sister had a neat and homey residence in what appeared to be a middle class area about five kilometers from the city center. Like many such cities, the capital was a patchwork of business, government, and residential neighborhoods. The majority of government offices were clustered around the plaza where all public celebrations were held. The plaza was on a plateau just below the summit of one of the hills that made up the city; the President's Residence occupied the highest peak. Brother Mike would later wonder if here the Head of State too felt closer to God?

Wrapping about the government area, like a fur collar around a woman's shapely neck, was the commercial area that included both the large open-air market and the innumerable shops, boutiques, and stores. These flowed from the plateau and wound around the gentle slopes that slipped closer to the steeper part of the gradient. Then on the steep ground, where the land fell away at a sharp angle, where refuse and rain would rush to the valley below, there were the ghettoes for the barely employed, the unemployed, and the unemployable.

Interspersed through these landmarks and pieces of the urban quilt were other residential areas: those closer to the Residence and those on the surrounding hilltops being for the rich and powerful, and those on more neutral ground for the small but growing middle class.

It was to this neutral area that Angela took Brother Mike, to a neighborhood with both electricity and running water—a neighborhood, though somewhat aslant, not so tilted as to affect the lives of the residents.

As they entered, Brother Mike expected to meet a sister and perhaps other family members. To his surprise, no one seemed to be home. Upon his enquiry, Angela explained (an explanation she had to repeat several days later, as Brother Mike's head felt like mush). In fact, she had no sister. This home had been for one of her brothers, a home he shared with a wife and son. But, after her unacceptable marriages to a Congolese and then a white man—a *mazungu*—her father had barred her from the family and she had had little contact with her brother or his family. Nevertheless, through common friends, she understood her brother was quite a Lothario, unable to avoid chasing any of the fairer sex. His wife had thought she could support this often-blatant behavior; paying the price for the good education her son could have by being part of a well-to-do family by playing the role of the tolerant wife. Ultimately, she could no longer countenance the growing indignities. Yet, for a good Catholic family, divorce was out of the question. As always when in a bind, their father, sly old fox that he was, had come up with a solution to avoid as much family embarrassment as possible and continue the external appearances of an up-and-coming *nouveau rich* patriarchy. The wife and son would move to Belgium where the boy could have an even better education. He would rent a flat for her there and she could keep the house in the capital as a base when she and her child came home for school holidays. Angela's sister-in-law could not have asked for more. Consequently, the house sat vacant most of the year, Angela using it as a base, unbeknownst to her father, whenever her affairs brought her to the capital for an extended stay. The enemy of my enemy is my friend. Angela and her sister-in-law were now very close.

The house itself was somehow reminiscent of the house Angela shared with Philip in the provincial capital: a three-bedroom bungalow, the small bedrooms accentuated with a roomy living-dining area that abutted on a compact but adequate kitchen.

Angela helped Brother Mike with his holdall and overnight bag, getting him settled in one of the smaller bedrooms that, from the accoutrements, was likely the son's room. Brother Mike was a little wobbly. The tranquilizers and antihistamines made his head feel like it was full of cotton wool. His vision was a bit blurred and his speech, still limited and slurred. At least he could manage to get out two or three words, but these were hoarse whispers and his throat felt like it had grown to the size of an elephant's, albeit the swelling was all but gone.

By the time he got settled in the room, it was time to take his medications and these put him nearly immediately into a deep sleep. Thanks to the chemicals surging through his bloodstream, he remained asleep or in a fuzzy semi-sleep state for an extended period. He had no idea for how long.

Angela would appear through the haze with something to drink and then give him his pills to swallow. She would slip away into the shadows and then she would reappear again, water glass and pills in hand.

Angela, for her part, showed she was an able nurse. She followed the doctor's orders exactly. By the second day, when the dosage of all the medications began to reduce, Brother Mike began to return from his trip to Never-Never Land. By the third day, he was able sit in the living room and listen to Angela retell the tales she had recounted when they had arrived, his drugged brain having retained little of the first go-around.

Angela had been giving him fruit juice and broth to drink. He had now spent several days without solid food in his stomach—a period adequate to dissolve a few of the extra pounds he carried. Also, a period long enough to generate a substantial appetite once his throat felt well enough to be able to swallow real food.

Angela sensed an appetite was returning. She went to the market and got the necessary ingredients to make a savory *carbonade* with *frites* and sautéed vegetables; good and nourishing. Brother Mike read the newspaper and some magazines Angela had also purchased for him while she cooked in the kitchen, filling the house with wonderful aromas that made the saliva flow.

When the meal was simmering and the *frites* had been deep fried for the first go, Brother Mike went to his holdall, retrieving his Courvoisier and pouring each a stout serving.

They sat in the parlor, sipping the warming liquid and complimenting themselves on how well they had handled this crisis, and how badly it could have turned out if things had happened differently. It was comfortable. It was intimate.

When the food was ready, Brother Mike helped Angela set the table. As they were moving between the kitchen and the dining area, they bumped into each other as they rounded the kitchen counter in different directions. Brother Mike clearly felt Angela's breasts beneath her cotton dress. He held the contact just a few seconds too long.

The food tasted as good as it had smelled, the first real meal Brother Mike had had in some time. The hearty *carbonade* accentuated by an equally hearty red wine. While they enjoyed their meal, the conversation was sporadic and abstract—the weather, the harvest, the new road west. It was as though they were avoiding saying what they wanted to say, hiding behind shields of the trivial and the inconsequential, while the serious subject at hand remained behind the veil.

As they were clearing the table, Brother Mike bumped into Angela again at the same place in the same way, this time strategically planned. This time, he did not pull away from her breasts, but applied more pressure as he looked into her eyes.

Angela's initial reaction was to look away. But, then she turned back and held his gaze, slowly her arm encircled his waist and she pulled him to her as she felt electricity building from the tips of her toes to the tips of her ears.

Brother Mike embraced her with all his strength and then, with his left hand, lifted her chin and kissed her deeply on the lips. *Alea iacta est* (the die is cast).

Lust? Carnal craving? Near-death aftershock? Lechery? Alcohol-induced aphrodisiac? Depravity? Original sin? Concupiscence? Insanity?

All these words flashed through Brother Mike's mind early the next morning. As the sun rose, filtering its rays through the curtains, and he found himself in bed next to a still sleeping Angela, he was ridden by guilt, regret, and shame. His close friend's wife! Her husband's close friend! This was not what was intended. Friendships with a lady were in no way meant to mean sleeping with your friend's spouse. There were many ladies with whom Brother Mike had been and could still be friends: nuns, nurses, widows, spinsters, and others. There were numerous options and opportunities. It was not, and should not be, could not be condoned to rollick with married women, especially your friend's wife.

Brother Mike thought maybe this was a figment of his imagination, a remnant of the strong medications he had been taking. He closed his eyes tightly, shook his head and then opened them again, only to see Angela beginning to stir as she awoke.

Then, in a flash, just as the words had flashed through his mind, when Angela turned her naked body toward him, all thoughts of shame and impropriety vanished. He took her in his arms, felt her heat meld with his, and his thoughts were only of holding her forever, loving her forever, being intertwined with her forever.

The sun was much higher in the sky when Brother Mike and Angela left the bedroom to prepare some coffee and baguettes with fresh local butter to quench their growing craving for food, as their hunger for other more sensual fulfillment began to dampen slightly. They ate in silence. Each balancing the fundamental questions: Why? Why not?

There really was nothing to say. What had happened had happened. Things happen. Angela was in no way considering leaving her husband. She loved Philip and their son. He was a good husband. She had lived an open and carefree life before their marriage, with many liaisons and some serious relationships. But this was the first extramarital adventure she had embarked upon and she had great misgivings. But it was what it was.

Brother Mike was less able to be pragmatic, less fatalistic. He was a man of God. He had broken the Commandments. He had sinned. He was wracked by anguish. Yet, strangely, he was warmed by an afterglow of loving that seemed to almost outshine his sin. He knew not what to do.

He had, of course, his own moral code. He had his own interpretation of the limits that defined his role, as he saw himself, as a man of God. He felt enjoying, others might say succumbing to, corporeal pleasures was simply a part of his God-given earthly existence. But he had never been so tormented. He had previously always been able to justify his actions. How could he do so now?

ě ě ě

As it turned out, there was nothing that had to be done immediately. This was their last day together. Angela's supplies were ready to pick up and she would soon be *en route* home with her stores. Brother Mike had also been released by the doctors. He would check on the documents he had left at various offices. He hoped these would now be ready to be picked up since they had been at their respective destinations for some time. Once they were in hand, he too would head south. It was Thursday. In two days' time he would meet Philip at the Crane. How would he be able to look upon his friend now? How could life continue as it had been?

In spite of Brother Mike's anguish, reality was knocking. He had to heed its call and collect the documents the monastery needed to move forward on its expansion plans. After all and above all, he had been—and still was—on the Abbot's business.

It was time to get on with life. It was time to take care of business. It was time to leave this refuge where he may have just avoided his final departure, replacing it with another seemingly almost as dire situation.

Before opening the door, he hugged Angela fiercely, stared intensely into her eyes, kissed her almost violently, then opened the door and left in search of a taxi to take him to his pickup parked in the guest house lot. Walking along the weather-beaten residential byways, taxis harder to find as the midday rush approached, he felt as though he were separated from his surroundings by a bubble—his vision distorted, his feet heavy as if covered with foam.

Nonetheless, once behind the wheel of his comforting pickup, he commenced a circuitous journey through various government buildings, collecting the documents that had been in his charge. To his own surprise, he was able to assemble the entire portfolio without delay and was soon southbound, crossing the Nyabugogo River.

In less than two hours he was pulling up the hill to the Abbey. The trip was a blur in his mind. He had forced all thoughts of his night's indiscretions out of his head for fear of becoming so fixated on his dilemma that he would cause an accident on the crowded highway. He continued to push these thoughts out as he locked the car and took the dossier to the Abbot's office. He met several of the monastery's employees and confrères as he mounted the stairs and traversed the hallways. They all welcomed him back, hoping his health was restored. He wondered what they would think if they knew how he had spent last night?

Fortunately, the Abbot was out and Brother Mike left all the papers with one of his squires. The young man also wished him well, but Brother Mike knew this did not mean wishing him well in bed with his friend's wife, even if the young man's own hormones were rushing through his veins.

The day was waning and Brother Mike needed to prepare for Vespers. Thereafter, he was sullen through supper, despite receiving many well wishes and cordialities. Brother Mike was fearful of the darkness and silence of his bed. He was worried his guilt would overcome him and his mind would crack. He was worried he would have visions of Angela and his body be filled with longing. He was worried he would have visions of Philip, his brain filled with remorse and fearful of retribution.

As it turned out, Brother Mike's body and brain were both seriously fatigued with the events of the past days and he fell into a sound sleep as soon as his head hit his pillow. He awoke in time for Vigils, almost unaware of the burden he carried. Almost. For a moment he thought it had all been a dream. He had never left the Abbey. But this only lasted a minute. He quickly returned to the present, knowing he had indeed committed a most grievous sin.

Yet, the world, for better or worse, was still there. The Abbey's bell still tolled. He went to the chapel. He went to the dining hall. He went to check on his projects. Then he even went to his best-liked spot on the pond bank. Being in the solitude he shared only with the bream, the tadpoles, and the dragonflies, he thought he would find some solace for his soul. He thought he would be able to concentrate on his sin, understand better his sinning, and know what steps to take to absolve himself of his sin. But these understandings never came. Indeed, he was scarcely even able to think of Angela and his—their—horrendous deed. It seemed his brain was building a shell around this event, preventing access to this subject that was so in need of reflection, pushing it to one of those hidden recesses where it would ferment for however long was necessary.

Deflecting, his mind easily went over the plans for the expansion, the waybills for incoming shipments, and even the menus of the refectory. Here his brain was sharp and on point. But this great weight he carried, this self-inflicted wound, went unattended.

Unable to find internal consolation, he went to confession, divulging his sins—professing his sins in his obtuse way. He prayed, asking for God's help. He performed an examination of Conscience. He declared he had broken God's Commandments. He conceded he was remorseful, all too aware of the error of his ways. He affirmed his need of absolution, reaffirming his love of, and service to God. He sought the Rite of the Sacrament of Reconciliation and said Acts of Contrition, expressing his sorrow, performing penance.

But, the weight was still there. He could feel its pressure, but its pain was less acute as the shell thickened and hardened around it. From a constant and persistent burden, it slowly metamorphosed into a period of sharp pain of remembering. Then, as he dove more and more deeply into his work, even these episodes of profound pain and sadness became less frequent and more bearable. It truly amazed him. Was this what people referred to as recuperative powers? Within less than a week he had to virtually force himself to pull up the pain to feel the remorse that he had thought would plague his every moment. It was now like other distant remembrances, an act he seemingly was no longer even sure he himself had committed.

After his return to the Abbey, he had begged off his normal Saturday meeting with Philip. He excused himself because of all the catch-up he had to do given the time he had lost due to his illness and the on-going renovations of the monastery. Philip had been very understanding. Brother Mike knew the situation would have been greatly different had he really known the reason for his absence: he could not look Philip in the eye.

Nevertheless, with the tricks of the brain, by the time poker day rolled around, Brother Mike felt seeing Philip face-to-face would no longer be an impossibility. Quite to the contrary, he felt a deep friendship for his drinking and poker partner and was looking forward to seeing him. His tryst with his friend's wife seemed now some fictional adventure of which he had read, not some carnal act that he had initiated. He did not know if it was a self-defense mechanism or escapism, but whatever it was, he was happy to embrace it. Whatever soothed his pain. Whatever diminished his shame. Whatever made tomorrow a good day to be alive. Whatever worked was welcome.

10

BROTHER MIKE SEAMLESSLY RE-ENTERED into his established routine. The Abbey's ambitious renovation project required a large part of his time, including regular trips back to the country's capital. He was able to carve out some personal time, keeping most of his Saturday rendezvous with Philip as well as most of his Wednesday card games.

He tried to get to the fishpond every few days to recharge his batteries—to take stock, feel the good earth beneath his feet, and the breeze in his face. He now felt he carried a sort of passion-fruit-sized hardened sphere in his body, a globe of shame and guilt that was sealed off from his essence. An orb he sometimes felt in the recesses of his brain or in his chest where it made his breathing labored. Sometimes he would feel this hardened ball, this lump in his throat where it would seem to strangle him. This brought back memories of his recent near strangulation that would make him break out in a cold sweat. But this choking was not caused by none-too-fresh bream thermidor, as had been the first case. This squeezing, this suffocation was his own doing, his choice.

He marveled at the irony that he thought of this corruption in his body as being like "passion fruit." It was in truth the fruit of his unfettered passion. It was a result of his sin. And while he very much felt its presence in his body, it became just another anomaly to be accepted like a scar or a permanently deformed joint: the baggage of life. Or was this simply rationalization? It was, after all, the fruit of sin.

When he would leave the fishpond to walk back up the hill to the Abbey, its silhouette like a stately castle of times gone by, he would see the tiny cemetery for the brothers on the small rise slightly below the monastery's main level. Here his brothers had been buried over the years, most preferring to pass eternity here rather than returning to the homes of their birth. He imagined he too would one day rest in cemetery knoll, in the shadow of the Abbey, far from Ghent, but he hoped closer to God.

❦ ❦ ❦

He was really surprised at his relationship with Philip. He still thought of him as a special friend. He still greatly enjoyed his company. And, although he now always felt the pressure of this ball of shame, he felt no compulsion to divulge the truth to his friend. He felt no need to settle accounts, to be honest. He only felt the desire to maintain the *status quo*, to keep the friendship as it had been. More to the point, he was able to look Philip straight in the eye and let his own sincere friendship shine through.

He was not only a sinner but also a hypocrite, a cheat, and a liar. And, somehow, he was able to live with these misdeeds. Or maybe he was able to live in spite of these misdeeds.

Lent and Easter came and went. The added responsibilities of this jubilant season added to the demands on his time, making the days long and the nights short.

As the workload rebalanced after the Celebration of the Resurrection, he was happy to get back to the card games that allowed his mind to concentrate on the totally mundane for a few hours.

He often broke even during these matches, but today he was on a winning streak. He seemed to be able to do no wrong and the cards loved him, but those seated around the table had other very different feelings toward his exceptional luck. When the game broke up, he was accused of using holy forces to win all those jackpots. With due deference to divine possibilities, he underscored his own personal mastery of the game, an attestation supported by no one else.

As he was just preparing to exit through the sliding glass door, Angela appeared from the back of the house and greeted each of the men. As she had done for the others, when she reached Brother Mike, she kissed him on each cheek and wished him a good afternoon. But, unlike with the others, she pressed a small piece of paper into his hand as he left.

When he got in his pickup, he opened the fragment, reading, "I'll be at my Sister's for three days in a week's time".

❦ ❦ ❦

This was a shockwave. Angela. Angela. Angela. He had thought their affair had been an act of the moment, a union dictated by unique circumstances, a once-only indiscretion. A happenstance. Something into which he had inadvertently stumbled. Something caused by bad bream thermidor. A fleeting flirtation, now forgotten.

This now was an invitation to a planned and calculated sin. Knowingly, with premeditation, cheating on his friend, committing adultery against God's Rules. This was going far too far.

To make matters worse, he knew sadly he could commit this sin. He could succumb. Once the door was opened, it was hard to close.

To his great discomfort, to his shame, he realized he did not want to close it.

He began thinking of Angela. Thinking of their days, their hours together. He may not have become obsessed, but he was more than a little infatuated.

He would again do the unthinkable.

It was not even necessary to make any changes to his schedule. He, in fact, had new documents to take to the capital and was already planning on spending a night there during the period highlighted by Angela. But he told her nothing. He made no reply. He sent no secret note.

Still, when he had delivered his documents to the various government offices, when, as usual, by mid-afternoon he had parked his pickup at the guest house, in spite of himself—or so he rationalized—he took a motorcycle taxi to Angela's sister-in-law's bungalow. He told himself this was just to look. He told himself this was just idle curiosity. He would not even get off the bike when he reached the destination. This was, he explained to himself, just checking up.

When the motorcycle reached the house, however, Brother Mike did disembark and knocked on the door. When Angela answered the door, he did take her in his arms and hug her tightly to his chest. When she closed the door, he did kiss her hotly as she guided him to the bedroom.

Then, it was early evening and they were sipping Courvoisier. Brother Mike could no longer hold back. He had to know. He had to try and understand. If he was to be damned to Purgatory, he needed to know why.

"My dear," he started shakily, drained both physically and emotionally, "why are we doing this? Do you hate Philip so? You know this is a sin. Why are we damning ourselves?"

"Dear Michael," she always called him Michael, "we are doing it because we can. I do not hate Philip. I love Philip. And, I love you too. Not as I love Philip, but I love you."

This only added fuel to Brother Mike's utter frustration, "But why? We know it's wrong."

"Is love wrong?" she asked. "Is it wrong to enjoy the moment, not knowing what will happen tomorrow, not knowing what will happen in five minutes? You could have died from spoiled food. Is it not good, even in God's eyes, to live life to its fullest?"

Brother Mike tried to keep this on a personal and not theological level, "But Philip is my friend. Philip is your husband. What would he think of us?"

"Michael," she smiled, "I am and will always be Philip's wife. Sadly, he is very preoccupied these days. He is taking correspondence courses with the Catholic University of Leuven in some new technologies they want to introduce here. Additionally, his infirm mother has taken a turn for the worse and is not expected to live much longer. Philip calls her on the phone from his office every day. When you add in his normal practice, the poor man is totally overwhelmed. But this will pass."

"So," interjected Brother Mike, "I am a stop-gap?"

"No, Michael, you're a friend."

Brother Mike felt his own words coming back to bite him. It was clear that he and Angela saw their relationship differently. For her it was a simple, almost natural, encounter with a friend that did not challenge her marriage. For him it was sin. But for both it was physically gratifying. Pleasure and affection for two individuals who, at that moment in time, needed, or felt they needed each other.

"Michael," she said with a twinkle in her eye, "you think too much and do too little, come with me."

She led Brother Mike back to the bedroom where they stayed until the sun rose.

This was not the caring and nursing that had accompanied their first coupling. This was pure and unadulterated gratification. This was carnality.

Obviously, Angela accepted it for what it was, wanting no more, seeking no less.

Brother Mike found himself entering the void. Was this in reality any different than any other of his female friends? Was this any different than Sister Alice or any others? Was this not a different slice of the same pie? Was this not just normal human behavior? As long as no one got hurt, where was the problem?

He tried valiantly to convince himself that this was as ordinary and innocuous as having dinner or going to the cinema with a lady friend, be he a monk or not. But, when you scraped off all the icing, it was simply sin—wickedness.

But Brother Mike now knew that his agonizing today would soon be somehow miraculously transformed and ensconced into his sphere, his globe, his orb. This passion-fruit–size lump of scar tissue that would forever be part of his body and spirit, but that would precariously reside in an unused dark corner of his brain, his soul, until again activated by his inability to control his urges and his desires.

Brother Mike's early morning torment was cut short as Angela brought fresh coffee and croissants to the bed. They ate hungrily among the rumpled sheets, saying little. She then said she had to leave early to pick up some paint for one of her properties. However, with that crooked smile and a glint in her eyes, she added that, since she had a long list of still-to-arrive supplies for several places she was renovating, she would be back here for the night in three weeks. She then hurriedly dressed, gave him a big slobbery kiss and told him to put the key under the flowerpot on the right side of the front door when he left. Then she was gone.

The next several months were a jumble. The work at the monastery was at its peak. Things were going on everywhere. Brother Mike thought it must have looked very much like an ants' nest from on high.

He managed to keep most of his dates with Philip for drinks and cards. He managed also to find time for his fishing, just much less than he would have liked. He also managed to have three more rendezvous with Angela as she finished her renovations and he completed all the documentation for the new and expanded Abbey and facilities.

He had a chronic dose of guilt that emanated from his orb deep in his brain. This was not affected by confession, prayer, or introspection. It was a tiny burning ember of sin that sprang into flames when he saw Angela.

During their meetings, he was like a man near death from thirst who will drink anything, even if he knows it will make him very ill, but will save his life. It was not that these unions were so exceptional or magical. Physically, they were pleasing, but not so different from those relationships he had had with other female friends. Yes, emotionally he felt closer to her than many of the others. But in and of itself, this did not seem to be an adequate justification for his wrongdoing.

In the end it seemed he, a religious man, a man of God, was terribly attracted by sin. The continuation of the liaison could no longer be ascribed to a weak moment of loss of control stimulated by drink or fatigue. Intentional planned sinning was a dire act that must, in some way, be the motive itself for the shameful acts.

Gratefully, as he impotently tried to tackle his misdeeds and confront his sin, the opportunities ceased to be readily available. The monastery's renovation program was completed and inaugurated. Brother Mike's regular travel north stopped and he returned to his typical duties. With tremendous thankfulness, he saw his life return to its humdrum routine.

Then, leaving the chapel after Vespers on the day honoring Saint Peter Claver, Brother Mike was stunned to see Angela waiting for him. They exchanged sedate greetings and she led him to the parking lot where to his surprise, she took him to an old pickup that closely resembled his own. She motioned for him to get into the passenger side.

Closing the door behind him, Brother Mike observed, "I had no idea, my dear, that you had a beat-up old contraption like mine." Noting the distracted look on her face, he added, "My pick-up, I mean."

"Michael," she captured his eyes like an owl fixating on a field mouse, "we're not here to compare means of transport, I'm pregnant."

It was a blow to his midriff that caused a great involuntary expulsion of the air from his lungs. His heart palpitated and the little ember in his brain throbbed like a chrysalis ready to burst.

She let him regain his composure with several minutes of silence and added a feeble, "I'm sorry."

Brother Mike hyperventilated a few times then with difficulty asked, "Are you sure I am the father?"

"No," was the simple answer.

"What's to be done?" he struggled to grasp the full ramification of her news.

"Nothing."

"Nothing?" he sputtered in disbelief.

"Yes, nothing," she calmly repeated, "the baby is due around March next year and we will see what we will see. As you are the one with the direct line to God, you can ask His help and guidance."

There was really nothing more to be said. He felt a kiss inappropriate on the Abbey grounds, so offered a rather tepid hug and then left the pickup to go to the dining hall, hearing her start the vehicle and drive off into the darkness.

Brother Mike often felt he was a robot. Somehow, he knew not how, he went through his ordinary daily life, his daily prayers, his daily tasks, his daily meals, even his daily chats with those he met; he did it all as he had always done it. But he felt in no way ordinary. Now it felt mechanical, almost unreal.

While his body was doing what it happily and customarily did, his mind floated like a balloon in the wind; sometimes a slight breeze, sometimes a terrifying hurricane. It bounced about in a sea of nothingness, seeking direction, finding none.

Nonetheless, the shock of possibly fathering a child slowly subsided. The aftermath of this trauma was a new layer of scar tissue on that ever-present orb in his brain. It was now denser, heavier, but still most often out of the way, crouching in the murkiness of his sin.

Brother Mike began to see himself as the mythical characters of Sisyphus or the Daughters of Danaïdes who were punished in perpetuity for their sins, one being required to continually roll a stone up a hill and the others to carry water in a sieve. His reparation was to be in constant mental anguish—at times a dull throb, at times a heart-piercing stab. While those pushing stones or carrying water saw their castigation the same, day in and day out, Brother Mike strangely felt lucky that his pain was ever-changing—a constant reminder, but not a barrier to daily life.

His pain would subside and then he would see Angela or Philip and it would erupt with a vengeance. It could be like a vise closing on his brain, his nerves screaming, his eyes tightly closed against the convulsion. But, even when he had internal pangs, he was able to mask these with a degree of good will that surprised him. He was able to affably and honestly greet Angela and Philip at their various meetings. He was able to share a drink with Philip, play a game of poker, talk about local politics, do all he had always done, with, as far as he knew, no sign of his on-going distress.

However, in the darkness of his room, as he fitfully tried to find peace in sleep, the walls of the Abbey seemed to press in on him—the silence of the night transforming into the humming of a hundred wasps in his ears. As the walls closed in on him, the hums became but a single word, "Why, why, why?"

He began holding his Bible to his chest to drive out the noise, to fend off the encroaching walls. Then, one night, by accident, behind his Bible, he again found his emerald at the back of the drawer. Was this a sign? It could be.

He placed the beautiful green stone under his pillow, hoping, almost praying if it were allowed, that the green fire from this precious work of God's art would burn away his sins—heal his soul.

From that night on, he placed the emerald beneath his head, at times nearly feeling as though the stone were purging him of his ill deeds—giving him the strength he needed to follow his road to serve his Lord.

11

IT WAS JUST AFTER All Saints, in principle the peak of the short rainy season. But this year, as seemed often to be the case of late, the rains had been paltry and in hamlets across the hilltops there was growing concern about having adequate pasturage for the cattle.

The drier-than-normal conditions did make some things easier. It was easier to clean up all the mess after the extensive renovations and expansion at the Abbey. It was also easier to venture into the hinterland, as the tracks that quickly became impassible with sticky clay-rich mud were still open.

So it was that as their game was winding-up, Philip proposed to the group, to break up the typical end-of-the-year slump, they do something adventurous and go camping for a couple of days in Nyungwe Forest. He explained the poor rains would make the weekend most agreeable, with no deluges, few mosquitoes, and relatively trouble-free roads. This was, he continued, prompted by a visit from the University of Liège by Professor Klein, a noted entomologist—in fact, a lepidopterist. The Professor served as a visiting faculty member at the local university, profiting from his biannual visits to search for rare butterflies in the forest. Thus far, he had found two heretofore unknown species.

Philip added that Robert Klein was "quite a guy." Although in his early 60s, he could scurry over the hills and through the ravines all day seeking his beautiful flying wonders. At the end of a day romping through the vines and briars, he would consume voluminous quantities of his favored Scotch before heading to the sack with his nubile young assistant of the moment, ladies to whom he referred as his flowers of the night.

As Philip paused, Kasuku chuckled then added, "asshole."

Philip wrapped up his plan, indicating the good Professor was giving classes on the local bugs, beetles, and other crawling and flying six-legged creatures for the next ten days, so he proposed a safari to the forest in a fortnight. Philip had even arranged with one of his colleagues at the University to borrow his VW bus so all six of the explorers could travel in one vehicle.

Karl and Antonio expressed their fervent enthusiasm. Karl offered to bring extra rations of drinks and Antonio offered not only the food, but to cook it once they'd set up camp. While he hoped he put on a brave face, Brother Mike was less exuberant, chiefly due to his discomfort around Philip. Even so, to avoid raising any questions, he too, if blandly, supported the outing, promising to bring meats and bakery goods from the Abbey.

In accepting, Brother Mike added, "We're four, the Prof is five, but you've arranged for six—who's the sixth?"

"The Gentleman's current *inamorata*, of course," Philip concluded with a smile.

Slowly, facing his misgivings, Brother Mike accepted he should, realized he must make the forest trip. He needed to maintain an air of normalcy, regardless of how he felt. And, despite his reservations, he found himself looking forward to some time in one of the natural wonders of his world— Nyungwe Forest.

At the appointed day and time, they all met in a parking lot on campus where each could leave his personal vehicle. As they climbed into the now crowded VW bus, the card players were impressed with their first views of Robert Klein: he was clean-shaven, well-coiffed, looking considerably younger than his six-plus decades. And, the players were aghast at his assistant.

Noticing the attraction, nearly fawning, focused on his buxom aide, with typical gusto, the Professor introduced his adjunct, Sally; offering she was a graduate student at the University of Nairobi. As this school was a sister institution with Liège, Professor Klein was an advisor to several Nairobi students including Sally.

Sally was tall and slender with a complexion like polished obsidian. She wore tight jeans, a royal purple tunic, with long tresses falling elegantly over her shoulders. When she smiled in greeting to the erstwhile gamblers, she lit up the interior of the minibus and took the men's breath away.

Thus, with a deep breath, they were off on their adventure.

The laterite road took them east through one of the poorer parts of the country before reaching the protected forest. Small farms, looking so fragile that a strong wind could send them skittering down the hillside, were precariously clinging to steep, stony slopes with the occasional cassava or coffee plots. The forest reserve itself, reaching elevations of 3,000 m, was a rare slice of Afromontane rainforest covering over 900 km². The heart of the forest, a jungly intersection where one road continued west to Lake Kivu and another headed south to the border, was 80 km from their starting point.

While conditions were dry and traffic was sparse, the potholed and washboard road would scarcely tolerate speeds over 70 km/hr. With stops for beer and to heed the calls of nature, it was nearly midday before they reached the junction at the forest's core, deciding to take the less traveled southern fork in search of a campsite.

They had traveled less then 10 km in a southward direction when they came upon a small clearing surrounded by numerous flowering shrubs that Professor Klein announced was a perfect place for finding butterflies and also a damn good spot to spend the night.

As they piled out of the minibus, Karl and Philip disappeared behind the vehicle and for the first time Bother Mike noticed there was a baggage rack on top, neatly enveloped in a wrapping of tough dun-colored canvas.

Philip reappeared, perched on the rack's rail, reminding Brother Mike of Kasuku in their home. Philip carefully untied the canvas, handing down to Karl a wide variety of boxes, sacks, and other items.

Miraculously before his eyes, Brother Mike witnessed a small encampment spring forth in the clearing: three two-man tents, complete with sleeping bags, a folding table with six folding stools, and a kerosene cooker and variety of cooking implements. The camp was ready to go before Professor Klein had put on his boots and fitted the handle into his butterfly net.

The good Professor then opened a small metal trunk that had been among the items on the roof, removing a variety of jars and other paraphernalia used in killing and mounting the object of his hunt. Once these were carefully arranged to his satisfaction, he grabbed a leather shoulder bag that had also been in the trunk, picked up his net, grabbed Sally by the hand, and disappeared into the underbrush.

The four men perked up their ears and heard the couple moving through the forest, like a deer slowly escaping from its stalker. The noise from the butterfly chasers faded and, when there was nothing but the shrill double whistle from a nearby cuckoo strike, Karl reached into one of the boxes, pulling out a bottle of whiskey. Seeing this, Antonio went to the box of utensils and found four glasses.

With brimming goblets, they sat around the table. Philip produced a deck of cards and the game was on. Antonio must have supplied an industrial quantity of whisky Brother Mike thought, as the glasses were refilled more quickly than the cards were dealt.

Antonio went back to the stores and returned with bowls of groundnuts, sliced baguettes from the morning's ovens, along with a plate of meats and cheeses. The players eyed these treats with unrestrained appetites as the whiskey helped the saliva flow.

Darkness falls quickly in the tall story forest and it was soon dusky under the trees' canopy. The players folded their hands, but kept their drinks close at hand. They listened again with perked ears for the return of the hunters, but the woods were silent except for the swoosh of bat wings, as these creatures of the night took to the air.

They were just beginning to worry seriously, and didn't know what to do. They were unable to seek help, unable to know where to look for their campmates, unable to do anything but wait. Then they heard the snapping of twigs and soon the thuds of heavy boots on the ground. As the light was waning, the Professor and Sally exited from the bush with smiles on their faces and Sally's tunic a bit askew.

Seeing their compatriots sitting about the table, Karl now lighting a lamp at its center, the Professor bound over, expounding, "Look at these lovelies—say can one of you chaps get me a glass with some whiskey?"

He opened his leather shoulder bag and with great delicacy removed more than a score of glassine envelopes, each with a carefully preserved butterfly. "We had a great chase!" he stressed as he accepted a brimming chalice from Antonio. "There are wonderful, wonderful specimens here—I reckon the dryness has concentrated them around damp areas—a sight to behold. In fact, I suspect maybe one of those we caught may be a new species. And, Sally's miraculous with the net—a real forest nymph." He then took a gigantic swallow of the honey-colored liquid in his tumbler.

Sally, sitting on a log just at the limit of the lamp's light, smiled at the mention of her skills, her bright white teeth gleaming like pearls outlined by her silky sable complexion.

Antonio busied himself with the evening meal. Sally joined him in the makeshift kitchen encircling the kerosene cooker. The Professor refilled his glass, taking a seat at the table, assuming his role of the head of the classroom, began a monologue about the forest's flora and fauna including its populations of chimpanzees and colobus monkeys. Every few minutes he would pause for a deep breath and a deeper swallow of whiskey.

Although Brother Mike felt he was soon reaching his upper limit, Karl and Philip tried to keep pace with the good Professor and soon the pile of empty bottles was frightening; the Professor asked Sally to move the "cadavers" further out into the forest where they would not be constantly reminded of their consumption.

The whisky was replaced with red wine for the dinner, which was promptly consumed by the ravenous group of explorers. When the dishes were cleared, Sally excused herself, saying the rigors of the hunt had tired her and she was retiring early to her tent.

The men broke the seal on a fresh whisky bottle and brought out the cards. As Philip dealt, the Professor, with a bit of a vaporish look to his eyes, pronounced from nowhere, "Glad there's no God damned Walloons here!"

The venom of the Professor's declaration was blatant and ferocious, slightly shocking to Brother Mike's sensitivities as many of his confrères found their origins in Wallonia. Whether to calm the tempest, or to support the spirit of nationalism, Philip raised his glass and with great solemnity almost chanted, "To the Flemish, to Flanders."

Five glasses clinked and were drained as all saluted the tribal rift that was at the core of much of Belgium's political angst. Philip and the Professor joined in a somewhat-slurry improvised version of *De Vlaamse Leeuw*, the Flemish nationalist battle anthem dating back to the 1800s when there was strong anti-French sentiment in Belgium that metamorphosed into strong feelings against Francophones in general—in more recent years, these being the French speakers of Wallonia.

The Professor, the popular educator, the highbrow scholar, at least when in his cups, and almost certainly subconsciously, was a rabid proponent of tribal hegemony. His impromptu and self-assured zealous bigotry pushed at weathered doors many wished would remain tightly shut.

Brother Mike, as well as Karl and Antonio, seemed relieved when, with equal aplomb and spontaneity, the Professor stood up unexpectedly, and a bit unsteadily, announcing it was time for bed.

The remaining foursome watched him teeter toward the small tent where they assumed Sally was ready with a welcome embrace, though whether or not he was in any state to reciprocate, was a question of some dispute among the tarrying players.

Brother Mike was in some ways happy to see the group thinning out. The weight of his relationship with Angela had not, as he had hoped, been lessened by the foray to the forest. He had been battling in his own mind, the Flemish battles aside, whether or not to use this isolated occasion to open this tender subject with his friend—a friend he had horribly wronged.

He was pulled from one side to the other: yes, it was the right thing to do and this was a good place to bare his soul; no, there was no reason to open a door when no one was knocking. Yes. No. He was tied in knots. He had no idea what to do, but the whisky had given him courage, hopefully not false courage, and he was leaning to the "yes" side of his internal struggle.

Then Brother Mike's dilemma was overtaken, once again, by events. Philip, in the style of the Professor, suddenly stood up and announced he too was off to sleep. Karl apparently saw an opportunity to escape further alcohol-induced damage and quickly was on his feet saying he'd share the tent with Philip.

This left Brother Mike and Antonio to decide whether or not to finish off the bottle before putting everything ship-shape and then tucking themselves into the last snug two-man enclosure—this, appropriately, reminding Brother Mike of what a butterfly larva must feel like when furled up in its cocoon.

Brother Mike discretely let Antonio get settled, saying he needed to devote some time before sleep to his prayers. When he finally got down on all fours and crawled into his tent, he could hear loud alcoholic snores coming from Philip and Karl's tent while there were some coos and mews coming from the Professor's nighttime enclosure. He took off his shirt and pants and then scooted into the sleeping bag, and only the high levels of fatigue and drink allowed him to quickly fall into a sound sleep on the hard ground.

Habits are strange things and, in spite of all, Brother Mike was up and dressed early in time for his Vigil prayers; feeling closer to Divine Power in this copse, one of God's masterpieces. In addition to the usual morning invocations, as he was wont to do over recent months, he asked His Lord for guidance in addressing what he called, between God and himself, "the Angela problem." Today, he was hoping just maybe the holiness of the site, surrounded by God's Mysteries, would bring him into special communion with his Maker. But, regardless of his sublime surroundings, as always, he received no Divine intervention. Once again, besmirched and riven, he picked up his great weight of guilt to carry through another day.

The other explorers appeared in slow succession, like a family of mice slowly emerging from their hole in the wall. The last to surface were the Professor and Sally, as was expected. The aging pedagogue materialized first with bloodshot eyes and tousled hair. Sally showed up a good thirty minutes later, looking bright eyed, freshly coifed, and groomed. She greeted all with a dazzling smile and a hearty, "*Jambo, habari za asubuhi.*"

Day two followed more or less the template of day one. The Professor and Sally disappeared soon after breakfast, their shoulder bags plump with tidbits to munch as they chased the most special of the special flying tapestries that inhabited this magic forest.

The non-insect–hunting group sat around the table a while, drinking coffee and wondering who would make the first move to dose the java with a big shot of cognac—Brother Mike's refreshment of choice, as they all knew.

Professing they did not come all this way just to drink and play cards, which they did anyway every Wednesday, Karl and Antonio declared they all should go on their own safari. While admonishing the other players for not savoring the forest as it should be experienced, it was suggested that they look for those elusive primates the Professor had highlighted in last night's lecture. Philip expressed deep concerns about getting lost within five hundred meters of camp and spending the next week wandering aimlessly in the dense undergrowth until they died of famine, pestilence, or were eaten by some beast.

Brother Mike, believing himself to be more of a spectator to these discussions, felt Philip's reaction was a true reflection of his comfort zone. Doctor Philip was in his realm when working inside someone's eye, sitting in a sterile chamber with clean and well-known surroundings. The Afromontane forest was not his milieu of preference, not by a long shot. Likewise, the bank of the Abbey's fishpond was about as much of the natural world to which Brother Mike wished to be exposed for any extended period.

For all that, in the spirit of brotherly love, Brother Mike poured cognac into the four mugs of aromatic Arabica that each was sipping, suggesting perhaps the best choice for the morning outing, now that afternoon was approaching, was just to walk along the road, which was really a path, as the ruts, be they ever so overgrown, would always lead them back to their camp.

It took one more mug of laced coffee before consensus was reached. The group then stocked up on edibles for the hike and, as agreed, headed along the southern road that, if they continued through the day and night, would take then to the border crossing.

Antonio had a camera hanging about his neck and was keen on taking snaps of all the forest sights, changing rolls of film before they had walked an hour. Karl had binoculars about his collar and was intent on seeing as many wildwood birds as possible, with the hope lingering in the back of his mind that he might even see a chimp through his prism.

Brother Mike and Philip let the two would-be naturalists take the lead, walking at a more leisurely pace, stopping to appreciate an exquisite flower, a multihued stone, or a strangely formed leaf. With their stop-and-go gait, they typically were at least ten minutes behind the cameraman and his ornithologist sidekick.

Seeing the rhythm of their canter, Brother Mike entertained the idea that this would be an ideal time to broach the subject of Angela with Philip. On several occasions he swallowed hard, steadied his nerves, and called Philip's name. But as soon as Philip turned and held him in his gaze, Brother Mike's fortitude melted and he quickly invented a new topic for some platitudinous chatter, leaving untouched the weighty topic that so overloaded his soul.

Under the canopy of the labyrinth, it was difficult to track the sun's arch across what Brother Mike assumed was a blue sky overlaying the verdant, nearly impenetrable mass of vegetation that was the Nyungwe. But the thicket seemed to absorb time like the humus soils sucked up the torrential mountain rains. Brother Mike looked at his wristwatch, realizing they had been walking for over two hours. It was time to think about turning back to camp as there was still the evening meal to prepare and the sunlight, filtered as it was, disappeared early in the *terra incognita* where they found themselves.

He called Philip's attention to the lateness of the hour and they agreed they should sprint ahead to overtake Antonio and Karl, getting them turned around as quickly as possible. The task proved much easier than anticipated as Antonio had shot his last roll of film and Karl's eyes were red and sore after peering for so long through his lenses.

Before reversing course, however, the group sat on some fern-incrusted stumps, emptying their pockets of all consumables, including emptying Karl's silver hip flask of whiskey. They munched and sampled, marveling yet once again at the majesty that flowed about them, before following their own steps back to camp. The return was slower since all had already had more exercise than they were accustomed. But on the return, they walked four abreast, almost militaristically, with an air of having accomplished an important task and now in a hurry to start the next one—for all knew, next up was a teatime game of cards accompanied by social imbibing.

The phalanx of poker enthusiasts reached camp at the same time as an effervescent Professor and Sally came forth from the forest in the opposite direction—a convergence the whole group greeted with great camaraderie symbolized by the opening of more of the seemingly endless supply of whiskey bottles that must have made their way into the camp supplies from Antonio's storeroom.

It was a near perfect rerun of the previous evening: the excellent meal prepared by Antonio was accompanied by voluminous, what Philip called "industrial quantities" of whiskey. It was, in turn, followed by an animated game during which the Professor again railed against the despicable Walloons. However, in spite of the good Professor's haranguing about the need for national exclusivity and cultural purity, after the day's long walk, all headed to their sleeping bags at an early hour. Brother Mike's slumber was not even inhibited by the wheezing and snorting emanating from his poker adversaries nor by the whispers and purrs from the Professor's tent.

Just before sunrise, as Brother Mike was preparing for Vigils, there was a shrill cry that echoed across the camp, stirring all tents into motion. When the blurry-eyed campers assembled near the table at the camp's center, they spied, according to Karl's keen eye, a Cassin's hawk eagle on an overhanging branch, apparently contentedly tearing a mouse limb from limb. Karl, the residing *de facto* bird expert, reckoned the mouse had come to scavenge tidbits from the evening meal and the shrieking bird of prey had pounced, scooping up its breakfast as it brought the camp population to attention.

With reveille having been sounded by the neighborhood raptor, the one-time explorers decided to break camp and leave with the intention of getting back to town by teatime to have a lovely cold beer and some crunchy *frites* on the terrace of the Crane.

When the roof rack was reloaded, including a trove of empty bottles, they piled into the VW; the Professor riding shotgun, Brother Mike and Antonio in the middle seat with Karl and Sally sharing the back over the axel where they were tossed and turned as the vehicle made its way back to the main road.

Even at the low speeds required to maneuver through the twists and curves of the trail, the forest swept by Brother Mike's window like a slow motion 1940s 16 mm Kodachrome film, or like someone pulling away a curtain at a church bazaar to reveal some special prize behind. The brocade of all shades of green moved in a hypnotic fashion, in some way freeing Brother Mike's mind to rise from the ricocheting minibus, plunging it into this sea of lime and jade. He felt his very essence pulled by tides and pummeled by blue-green waves. It was as though he had a great tumor that the forces of nature were trying to rip by the roots from his body to restore him to good health. Like the hawk eagle wrestling the mouse's intestines from its abdomen, he felt these powers could wrench the corruption from his body, from his soul, rendering him whole again.

Kaleidoscopic sheets of color passed in front of his window, now with dizzying speed like staring into a vortex, causing vertigo. The colors accelerated and merged into many shades of gray. He then felt the speed of the vehicle slow even as the gray membranes moved more and more quickly. He tore his eyes away from the side window, forcing himself to focus through the windshield and, to his astonishment, saw the terrace of the Crane in front of him.

As the old VW bus came to a halt before the hotel, the passengers sprang from its innards like pups coming from their lair after a riotous rain. They shook themselves. They stretched, flexed, and breathed deeply. Brother Mike watched the four men hop up the three short steps to a sunny table where they would quench their thirst. He looked back for Sally, but she was nowhere to be seen. She had vanished into the crowded street. Brother Mike realized she probably chose not to be seen with a group of white men at a bar, the obvious conclusion to all being that she was a hooker. As a student, such misidentification could have serious ramifications. Moreover, regardless of the nature of her relationship, the fact that she, a young black woman in whatever capacity, was sleeping with an older white man, if publicly aired, would lead to but one conclusion—she was sluttish, morally bankrupt, and seeking easy income on her back.

In some perverse way, Brother Mike was happy that his thoughts had shifted from his own burden to that of others. He joined the group of ex-foresters and speedily downed the frothing glass of beer Philip offered before taking his seat and turning his attention to another pint to accompany the hot *frites* and fresh mayonnaise. In the warm afternoon sun, with a mild breeze in his face, Brother Mike felt perchance, just perchance, life was not so bad after all.

12

BROTHER MIKE HAD BEEN rather surprised when the Abbot had been so supportive of his trip to the forest—much more enthusiastic, in fact, than Brother Mike himself. Returning after only two nights away and being quickly summoned to his superior's office, the eagerness of the Abbot's actions was now clearer to understand: Brother Mike, as the Abbot almost gleefully informed him, had a new assistant.

With Jean-Baptist's departure, the Abbot had repeatedly attempted to open a discussion of a replacement. All the same, Brother Mike averted these efforts with ease, always raising one reason or another to postpone the discussion to a later date.

Unable to resolve the issue through a frontal attack, the Abbot had used the few days of Brother Mike's absence in the forest to get a new assistant, Fostan, installed. The young novitiate, a member of the minority ethnic group, although ethnicity was intended not to play, and did not play, a role in the selection process. This young man just happened to be available when needed and he was at that very moment waiting for the good Brother in his office, having already been designated as Brother Mike's new *aide de camp*.

It seemed nearly more than Brother Mike could absorb in his present state. He had returned the night before, in time for Vespers, but feeling more than some slight effects from several hours of partaking chilled amber brew with his card-playing colleagues on the Crane's terrace. He had awoken for Vigils with a roaring headache and a bad temper. Now, after Lauds, breakfast, and his instructions from his Abbot, he had gone to his office to meet this tall and slender young man who was unfortunately waiting at his door.

Once again, unable to escape the inevitable, he found himself sitting across his disheveled desk from a novitiate with a masked expression, who was telling him he was, as per the Abbot's orders, here to help Brother Mike with all his duties around the monastery. Brother Mike, while not overly shocked, was still hung over and, to say the least, displeased.

But, he was nothing if not pragmatic. The Abbot had played his cards well and it was now up to Brother Mike, as he had done with Jean-Baptiste, to find a formula that would minimize the intrusion of this young man without raising hackles or warning flags. At the same time, he sensed this novitiate was not at all like Jean-Baptiste. Jean-Baptiste had had ambitions that were open secrets. By helping him achieve these, Brother Mike had helped them both do what they wanted to do.

This opaque person, Fostan, from the onset gave no impression that he was wanting or even willing to share any of his personal life. He was stoic. He was unsmiling. He made Brother Mike feel he was with a much older man.

Brother Mike decided to cast a line and see if he caught anything, "Fostan, lad, now that you're here, how do you find things here at the Abbey?"

"OK," the young man replied with no change in his unexpressive face.

"I am always so happy when the good Abbot assigns a young newcomer to our group here," Brother Mike bent the truth just a wee bit. "As I am sure our Father told you, we here are in charge of logistics; we try and make sure everyone has what they need when they need it."

"OK," Fostan replied with complete indifference.

"A lot of what we do involves people who are not at the Abbey—our suppliers, our partners, and even other religious communities. Is there some special goal you have? Some special interests? Some areas where you would like to work and to learn?"

"No," the tight-lipped youngster answered.

Brother Mike realized he was gaining no ground and changed tack, "Where is your home? Are you from around here?"

"The North," was the muted acknowledgement.

"Wonderful. I was with Father Juvenal not too long ago, was he your priest?"

"No," was the taciturn rejoinder.

Brother Mike saw he was wasting his time. He looked out his open door and saw François, one of the employees who helped in the storeroom.

"François," Brother Mike called, "please, can you take young Fostan, who has come to join us, and give him a tour. Kindly show him around, introduce him to our colleagues, and go over all the tasks scheduled for those working in the storeroom until the end of the week."

When François entered the office, Brother Mike noticed Fostan's scarcely hidden aversion—he instantly disliked the other man. In fact, Fostan opened his mouth as if to intercede on his own behalf, perhaps to change the arrangements. But he quickly clamped it shut and, with a look of deep distaste, followed François without another word, not even a good-bye to his would-be mentor.

Alone as he liked it, Brother Mike knew he had to somehow get a handle on this youngster, Fostan. He decided the best place to start was Farther Juvenal, taking up pen and paper, he wrote to the priest to see if he had any light to shine on his newest riddle.

In the meantime, Brother Mike had to get geared up for the upcoming Christmas season. At the same time, he needed to keep his new helper close to the Abby until he had a better idea of what really motivated this taciturn young man. For the moment, he could hand off Fostan to various workers in his group until after the holidays; if asked, he would explain to the Abbot that he was ensuring the young man had a solid foundation in the behind-the-scenes working of the monastery as encapsulated in the responsibilities of Brother Mike and his team.

He hoped to keep Fostan at arm's length in regard to the businessmen with whom he dealt, only deciding at a later date if he really needed to bring the novitiate fully into the fold in regard to his special working arrangements. He was, therefore, startled when the next day François informed him that Fostan had rather rudely insisted on going immediately into town with the storeroom crew on their regular trip to the market to pick up produce.

The picture grew less clear as Brother Mike further questioned François, discovering that Fostan, once in town, for some reason did not continue to the market with the Abbey workers, but asked to be dropped off at the church where they again picked him up two hours later, up before returning to the monastery.

Brother Mike decided not to confront Fostan directly at this time, but instead, the next time he himself went into town, he stopped by to see Father Daniel, priest of the church where Fostan had been dropped off. Brother Mike and Father Daniel had known each other for many years and had cultivated an informal and easy relationship, although they did not see each other frequently.

Brother Mike found Father Daniel in the sacristy. After friendly chit-chat about the rain, or lack thereof, and the Abbot's appetite, Brother Mike got to the point, "Daniel, I've a new assistant, or apprentice, or sidekick—I don't know."

Father Daniel's thick caterpillar-like eyebrows peaked, but he said nothing, knowing more about Brother Mike's activities and proclivities than Brother Mike knew he knew.

"The chap's—the novitiate's, I should say—name is Fostan. I don't know if you know him? He is originally from the North."

"Fostan," Father Daniel repeated as if chanting his name to the sky. "I can't say a face comes to mind."

"Well, "Brother Mike explained, "I've come to you because, soon after he was assigned got my group, he came into town with some of the guys to get supplies, but asked to be left here at your church rather than going to the market with the rest of the crew."

"Hmmm. When was that?"

"The day before yesterday."

"OK. I remember now. Moses who sells meat in the market had asked me if he could use the Parish Center that day. I had heard the mayor wanted to put some new sanitary measures in place and the butchers were against it, as it would add a lot to their costs. I had thought he was asking to use the room for a meeting of the butchery folks. Then to my surprise, as I was passing the hall early in the afternoon of that day, I heard a great ruckus that sounded more like a football match than a bunch of angry butchers. I peeked into the room and saw no one I recognized from the market. The place was filled with twenty or thirty young college-age kids all yelling.

"I had first thought it was in fact about football, but then, as I listened to a bit of the shouting, I realized it was politics. This was a group of young men nearly screaming about doing away with the ethnic homogeneity that has been the centerpiece of the present government. They wanted effectively to turn back the clock. But instead of the old Nilotic monarchy, they wanted a mutation—an oligarchy where the minority Nilotic Northerners controlled the state.

"Although they supported this doctrine with a joyous and raucous celebration akin to fans at a football match, they were deadly serious. Tribal hegemony. And, it was indeed a deadly topic: a Pandora's box, if you ask me, best kept closed."

Brother Mike was nearly speechless, "Amazing! I never would have thought that such things were underfoot, let alone that someone from our community would be involved. I know there is a lot of talk about 'democracy' and 'multipartism'. People see the winds blowing for a change from the one-party form of leadership—maybe trying to Europeanize political systems. But look what happens in Europe. Looks what happens in Belgium."

"Sorry," injected Father Daniel, sensing a need to extricate himself from what could turn into a lengthy and entangled debate, "I really can't say much more. These guys stayed here hanging around for several hours, judging by the volume, all hyped up about their subject. But I know nothing about who they represent, what they hope to do, or even how much tangible impact they might be able to have."

"Sadly," added Brother Mike, "I fear the answers to your questions will come with time. For now, I have what I came for. I understand better what motivates Fostan and will now have to see what remedial action, if any, is needed."

They concluded their discussion by looking to their motherland and lamenting the recent uncalled-for decline of Royal Sporting Club Anderlecht, the team founded in 1908 that had won the 1975–1976 European Cup and one of Belgium's hometown football favorites—the usual observations of men no longer of middle age, that things are no longer like they used to be.

Brother Mike returned to the Abbey, promptly making an appointment to see the Abbot and, no longer waiting for a reply to his query to Father Juvenal, inform him of the possible political activism that preoccupied the novitiate Fostan. He then went to his spot on the pond bank, trying to collect his thoughts.

13

"Zanzibar!"

Angela had nearly screamed it out, whether in frustration or surprise, he did not know.

After hearing of her pregnancy and then the ominous developments in regard to local politics coupled with the possibility of all descending into chaos as each sought to put in place his or her own political system that provided the biggest advantages for his or her special interests, Brother Mike had sent word to Angela they should meet.

Given the circumstances, it was best to meet where the chances of them being seen together were minimized. She was well known—more as her father's daughter than her husband's wife, but also as a businesswoman in her own right. He had chosen the University's arboretum in the early morning. He had made the excuse to the Abbot that one of their main produce suppliers had fallen seriously ill, was in hospital, and had asked to see Brother Mike. The man was indeed in hospital, but with a broken wrist after falling off the back of a Mercedes truck, reportedly in a drunken stupor from too much banana beer. Nonetheless, the risks of discovery were low and if Brother Mike was ever asked why he thought a broken wrist was a serious life-threatening injury, he would just say he had unfortunately been misinformed.

He had, for the first time in a long time, given Angela a great hug and long kiss when they had met among the acacia trees. He had then unceremoniously blurted out the fact that he had found the solution to their situation: they should run away together to Zanzibar.

"Angela," he explained, "things here might get bad. There seems to be political upheaval not too far off, as all are jockeying for position under this new emblem of democracy. We could cross the border, head east and be lost among the coastal peoples. We could just close this door and open a new one for the new life you are carrying."

"Michael," she said with a bit of sting, "that's just nonsense. First, we don't know the baby is yours, as I've already told you. Then, I'm not leaving my family. In many ways, I do love you and your unique outlook on life. We have had some good times and I like to think you have enriched my life. But my love for you is not the love of a wife for a husband, it is like the love of someone for chocolate. To me, you are like a very good Swiss chocolate, but you are not the man I love—Philip is."

"I was just thinking of the baby," he interposed.

"As I've said, don't worry about the baby," she recalled. "We will take this thing a day at a time. But I am not fleeing my home, running away from the land of my birth. I have built a place for myself here on the ground where I was born and I am not about to throw it all away for someone who is a friend, but not a spouse, nor for fears of political tumult that likely will never happen."

There seemed nothing more to say. Brother Mike tried to provide a suitable exit by concluding, "My dear, that's fine. I was just worried and wanted to share my concerns with you. We will wait and see."

He then hugged her again, a little less enthusiastically than when they had met, and they walked shoulder to shoulder to the gate of the arboretum, whereupon each went his and her own way. Brother Mike drove back to the Abbey, hoping Fostan and his bunch would not succeed in completely turning over the apple cart, and putting the country's delicate political balance into a tailspin.

ẽ ẽ ẽ

Regardless of his political intrigue, Fostan was, as planned by Brother Mike, fully occupied in getting-up-to-speed on his activities relating to the logistics group. While concerned about the newcomer's extramural activities, the Abbot had not wanted to take any immediate action. Brother Mike had Fostan where he wanted him. He could, he felt, return his attention to the growing work precipitated by the coming Christmas season.

The cow rains came, the Nativity was set up, Christmas Eve Mass went off without a hitch and the Christmas Day celebration, to which the Abbot had invited a number of local dignitaries as well as representatives from other religious communities, was also an unmitigated success.

During the celebration, while all were milling about before taking their places at the huge tables piled high with the Abbey's delicacies, Brother Mike was astounded to see Sister Alice coming to greet him through the crowd.

After exchanging complements of the season, with a twinkle in her eyes, Sister Alice asked if Brother Mike would not like to show her where he worked. This was an obvious enticement for a quick tryst, not with an old flame, but with an old acquaintance. Under the circumstances, Brother Mike felt he could not muster any ardor and, as politely as possible, indicated his responsibilities in ensuring the smooth completion of the festivities prevented him from being absent from his current post as informal maître d' of the gala—adding, in spite of himself, that he really did not know if religious communities really had the mandate to have galas at this most holy of times.

Even with the added holiday workload and the near miss with Sister Alice, Brother Mike survived the Christmas festivities and was ready for the more secular New Year celebration, where he hoped he would be able to lose himself in a fog of overindulgence. With some trepidation, he had accepted an invitation from the Crane to attend their annual New Year's bash that assembled virtually everybody—Brother Mike quietly reminding himself that when they thought "everybody," this meant everybody who was anybody in the Belgian community.

New Year's Eve, at least as celebrated locally, thought Brother Mike in an un-monkly way, was totally an inverted, essentially twisted observance for many in his circle of friends and acquaintants. On one side, European tenants, a tiny minority of which he was one, ate and drank to excess—their resolution to continue such overindulgence throughout the year. On the other side, the population as a whole ate and drank sparingly, hoping they would survive the new year. Brother Mike knew frugality was truly in line with his spiritual goals. Sadly, he also knew what he felt his mind needed, possibly his body craved, was a flood of libation to dull his aching soul.

Throughout the last day of the year, he followed his routine. It was only after Vespers that he, with pre-approval of the Abbot, under the pretext that this was essential to maintaining necessary contacts with critical suppliers for the Abbey, got into his old pickup and bounced down the road to town.

Disembarking from the Toyota with a light jacket against the evening chill, Brother Mike found the terrace of the Crane already crammed with revelers, clearly many well ahead of Brother Mike in finding the drink-induced vapors of the changing years. As he strolled through the throng, he was impressed by the festivity mounted by the hotel's owners. In one corner of the veranda there was a large grill stacked with *brochettes* and grilled sausages. Next to this was a table with bowls of hot *frites*. For those with a sweet tooth, there was an accompanying table filled with cakes and puddings. And there was beer. Everywhere there were large buckets of iced beer. The wine or whiskey drinkers were at a bit of a disadvantage, having to pay as they went, but the beer drinkers found themselves in an end-of-the-year heaven with all the brew they could consume. Seeing the possibility for self-abuse, Brother Mike had to remind himself that he had to get back in reasonably good shape for the next day's Vigils.

Prudence notwithstanding, Brother Mike took a dripping bottle from a nearby bucket, nearly three-quarters of a liter per bottle of a throaty blond brew that went down far too easily. Sipping his drink as he floated about the crowd, feeling more like a stranger in a strange land than a convivial merrymaker. Although he had a fundamentally gregarious nature, Brother Mike had a curious yearning to be on the pond bank and not in the mob of *patat vreters* secretly wishing they were in Brussels, Antwerp, or Ghent.

When he drifted across the terrace, Brother Mike spied Philip with a very pregnant Angela on his arm, laughing with a group of, he assumed, University professors, seeming very much at ease and content with the world. He approached, trying to make sure he had a wide, but not too wide, smile, squared shoulders, and a leisurely gate.

As he closed on the group, his eyes caught Angela's and he blurted out in a very, very loud voice, "*Bonne année!*" His momentary self-confidence vanished, he felt as though the world and Philip in particular could see into his soul.

Fortunately, in the din of the revelry, his boisterous greeting was scarcely noticed. Scarcely noticed except by Angela who seemed to have a little gleam in her eye aimed directly at him.

In spite of his tactlessness, he maintained his measured, forward movement, and was soon close enough to wrap an unsuspecting Philip in a New Year's embrace.

"My God Michael, where'd you come from?" Philip sputtered as he shook himself from Brother Mike's overly-enthusiastic clinch.

"*Gelukkig nieuwjaar* and *Bonne année!*" Brother Mike hollered at only slightly fewer decibels than his first regrettable earsplitting outcry, passing through the group shaking hands, including those of Angela. Intentionally, he greeted her last, hopefully seen by others as a sign of respect. Although he held her grip for only a second, it sent electric waves to his very core.

Brother Mike was happy to note that the volume of the crowd was increasing as the buckets of beer were emptied. The racket was approaching the level of bedlam and it really was impossible to carry on any sort of personal conversation. For some reason, the blare made Brother Mike think back to the caterwaul during takeoff of those old DC-3 aircraft with modified Rolls-Royce engines; those old workhorses with which he used to travel during his younger years. Just before the wheels of those venerable craft tore free of Earth's grasp, you felt like you were inside a Mixmaster. That was very much the way he felt now. The only elixir seemed to be to fish another dripping beer from the nearest bucket before the supplies were completely exhausted by the voracious celebrants of Janus.

As he drank his beer too quickly, his mind flashed back to secondary school Latin class and learning of Janus, the god of beginnings. Janus was also the god of war and peace. Interesting, with all their gods, the Romans had one in the same for both war and peace—the doors to his temple kept open during times of war and closed during times of peace. The Abbey's doors were always physically closed but spiritually open to all. Was this sign of war or peace?

An "ooooh" and an "ahhhhhh" from the crowd brought Brother Mike back to the present. He felt more than saw the pack pushing forward. With all eyes focused toward the street, he followed the communal stare and realized there was a humble effort to set off some rather rudimentary fireworks. This somehow made him aware of the passage of time and he looked at his watch only to realize that it was now officially the New Year.

With all attention concentrated elsewhere, he decided this would be a good moment to take his leave. He found Philip and gave him a much gentler hug, whispering New Year's greetings in his ear.

Angela was at Philip's side. He again took her hand, feeling the current resurge, and holding it just a fraction longer, silently wished her well. He was then gone, back on his lumpy pickup seat and *en route* to the Abbey.

14

THE NEW YEAR DID not start well for many. Father Daniel sent Brother Mike a note asking him to stop by the church the next time he was in town. When they met in the coming days, Father Daniel made it clear that their concerns over Fostan were indeed well-founded and that he was, in Father Daniel's opinion, a real threat not only to the Church, but to the stability of the community.

Father Daniel explained that shortly after the holidays, through the intermediary of some local businessmen, the group of northern youth of which Fostan was apparently a member if not a leader, again met in the Parish Center. Father Daniel had stayed in the pantry throughout the gathering and could attest to the acrimony with which the group talked of the current government and those from different regional or ethnic communities. They were clearly and vehemently advocating for a return to the old ways of a small group of the select few dominating the majority. Moreover, they were advocating this be done now and be done at all costs.

What made all this even more worrisome according to Father Daniel was that this group of malcontents was operating openly and had caught the attention of students from the South as well as students from other ethnic groups. There was a definite polarization, with those opposed to the revolutionaries now also organizing.

The day Fostan's group had met in the church, an opposition gathered in the football field across the street. Then, when Fostan and the Northerners left the Center, they retrieved small wooden batons they had hidden in the church's garden and fell upon those assembled across the street, beating any who did not run. It was terrible to see. It was even more terrible when Father Daniel realized it was happening with impunity. For whatever reason, although those fleeing were crying for help, no police came. Fostan's victorious group marched, nearly goose stepping, toward the city center while their antagonists tended their wounds.

Brother Mike took Father Daniel's story back to the Abbot. The monastery's leader was very troubled. He shared with Brother Mike several rumors that local politics were coming to a boil. Under the flag of democracy, many different factions were organizing, as witnessed by Fostan's actions. It was indeed almost as though they were organizing different football teams; each political group had its own colors, jersey, and song. But what might look on the surface like child's play, the Abbot assured Brother Mike, was deadly serious. There were deep and merciless changes being promoted by different groups. The government was having a difficult time keeping things under control. All the while, the international community, only seeing superficial changes, was pushing hard to support what they saw as a wonderful example of African democratization. At the end of the day, it was a horrific national tug-of-war, not with two teams pulling on one rope, but with many teams pulling on the arms of a hydra.

The Abbot had no advice for the wider issues, but for Fostan, he announced he would arrange for him to be transferred to a community in the North where at least he would hopefully be less disruptive being among his own people. This placated Brother Mike's immediate concerns and he was able to go back to work concentrating only on his own numerous affairs without needing to devote effort to an unwanted, and now potentially dangerous, assistant.

While the Abbey found resolution to one small problem that reflected well the crumbling national order, across the country things continued to become further fragmented under the growing wave of multiparty politics. At the University, different student groups were boycotting on different days, such that overall studies had come nearly to a halt. The police had finally awoken and, through Presidential Order (for better or worse), combined forces from the military, set up a growing number of armed checkpoints across the territory.

To those outside the mainstream, it was very much an ordeal of wait-and-see. No one really knew what the morrow would offer.

Ironically, on the Feast of Saint Valentine, Brother Mike received word that his father was deathly ill in Ghent. The letter, mailed over three weeks before in Belgium, had been sent by his older sister, Femke.

Both of Brother Mike's parents were of advanced years and of ill health. Yet, in spite of these concerns, they had managed to stay in the family home where Brother Mike had been born. This had been possible because they were cared for by their first-born, Brother Mike's sister.

Femke belied the Frisian origins of her name, which meant "little girl." She was, to be kind, a large woman: 1.77 m in height and 17.9 stone. She had already outlived her own husband, a hard-working and henpecked accountant, and had seen her own two children go their own ways—one went into the military and the other emigrated to the United States. She was basically on her own, feeling it was now a waste of scarce money and energy to keep the home she and her husband had purchased after so many years of scrimping and sacrifice. Therefore, she had moved in with her parents, back to her childhood home, resisting her parents' pleas to move them to smaller accommodation, and refusing to relocate them to a geriatric center. Femke had taken it as the cause for the remainder of her life to be her parents' shepherd. Living under their roof, she prepared their meals, laundered their clothes, took them outside in their wheelchairs, sat with them when they watched their TV shows. The fact that she was writing her long-forgotten brother meant things had seriously deteriorated and that their father was indeed near the end of his life.

Brother Mike had never thought about the end of his father's life. For Brother Mike, his father was simply there. Although he did not feel particularly close to him, he was a constant. Even though he did not share his father's values or beliefs, he had always known that his father would be there. And now the time was approaching—apparently quickly—when this would all change.

Brother Mike's father had long been a malcontent, in many ways similar to those who were now threatening Brother Mike's peaceful lifestyle. His father had initially been a very active member of the *Vlaams Blok* then the *Vlaams Belang*: political groups that actively and vociferously sought Flemish independence, insisting on strict immigration control where all residents obligatorily adopted Flemish language and customs. It all sounded so familiar now. Tribal hegemony.

This had been years ago, or so it seemed. What of today? In truth, Brother Mike had no idea if his father's politics and priorities had changed. He had no idea at all of what his family in Belgium thought or did. They simply were there and he was here.

Brother Mike sought the Abbot's advice. He had been away from his birthplace a long, long time. Many things, most things, had changed. He had never been a son with strong ties to his family. In fact, his relationships with his sister, such as they were, were generally adversarial as she, among the family members, had been the most strongly opposed to his entering the Church in general and his life in Africa in particular. Femke was the sort of person who was unshakable once she had taken a stance. There was no way she could accept that, in her eyes, her little brother had abandoned the family to become a monk in black Africa.

All this notwithstanding, the Abbot advised Brother Mike he must return to see his father, to say goodbye. It was the right thing to do. He was God's child, but he was his father's son. He needed to see his family. His family needed to see him.

🐚 🐚 🐚

Knowing the Abbot's words revealed the correct path, Brother Mike made the necessary arrangements. He was able to quickly get a seat on a flight to Belgium on compassionate grounds. Within 72 hours of receiving his sister's missive, he was sitting in a window seat of a crowded Sabena flight heading to Brussels. He remembered Philip's joke: SABENA—Such A Bad Experience Never Again. Not too far off the mark. The service was certainly not impeccable and the indifference shown by the crew was memorable, if disappointing.

He stared through the Plexiglass window to the blackness below. He fixated on the nothingness visible from 30,000 feet when moving at over 800 km/hr. Nothingness in spite of the vibrant life that Brother Mike knew existed on the ground as they flew north over the equator—the blackness of the void. Was this what awaited his father?

Brother Mike's father had been born of peasant parents on a vegetable farm in Oudenaarde District of Oost Vlaanderens Provence, south of Ghent. In his early teens he had fled the backbreaking work of the fields, trading this for the backbreaking work in the Port of Ghent. With the expansion of the Ghent–Terneuzen canal in the late 1800s, connecting the city to the Scheldt Estuary in the Netherlands, 32 km away, Ghent had become a major port in Belgium. The movement of goods in and out required the strong backs of many of the city's youth; his father becoming one such youthful stevedore.

Brother Mike remembered his father coming home after dark, barely awake enough to eat a bowl of stew before falling on his bed. When he was not moving the products of the country's industries and farms, he was meeting with his fellow Flemish Nationalists, complaining about the government that produced these products, and calling for a Flemish nation with Flemish values and culture.

Between his insurrectionism and toil, there was little time for a young son. Brother Mike's earliest memories of father–son bonding were of a few rare moments when his father taught him how to bait a hook and catch a good pan-size fish from the Leie and Scheldt Rivers that joined in the city.

Most of his other memories were of a shadowy figure going and coming from the house, but nearly a stranger to the household.

Brother Mike did remember when he had his dog, Rex. He had found Rex as a puppy hiding in a dirty alley on a rainy winter eve. He tried to secrete him in his room, but this was impossible; his mother soon found the pup and all the mess it had caused. However, to his surprise, his mother had not scolded him nor had she thrown the pup out. She had shown him how to make a bed for the dog in the tiny laundry room, which was easy to keep clean. She had then shown him how to housebreak the inquisitive pet, how to feed it, to make sure it had water and exercise; in short, how to raise a dog.

When his father had come home from a party meeting and found a sleeping dog in his laundry room, he had exploded, ordering the animal immediately jettisoned from his already too full house. Uncharacteristically, Brother Mike's mother, a stoic woman who suffered her husband's predilections, stood fast against her husband, insisting their son needed a companion and this pup was about all to which he could look forward.

Rex had stayed and, true to his mother's prediction, become Brother Mike's dearest and most loyal friend.

Brother Mike's mother was a simple woman who had married at a young age, fleeing a penniless and totalitarian father. She had had a baby girl soon after their wedding. However, after that, their hopes of having a big family seemed dashed, her prayers notwithstanding. For a decade those few pregnancies that occurred ended in miscarriages. It seemed they were doomed to be a family of three.

Under those conditions it might be thought the parents doted on their one child, showering her with all she might desire, or at least all that was within their quite limited means. But her father's preoccupations made him a fleeting presence in his daughter's life too, in many ways reinforcing the deep and all-encompassing relationship she ultimately forged with her mother.

Mother and daughter became inseparable from an early age, a team that dealt with all the needs of the family. When the mother would have temporary work, waiting tables at a local restaurant when they needed someone to fill in or finding seasonal jobs around the Christmas holidays, sprucing-up halls that had been used for festivities, the daughter ran the house.

Femke became a hardworking housekeeper. With the constant and insistent prodding of her parents, she barely completed secondary school; and then with very low marks. She seemingly had no aim in life other than to continue with her domestic duties. It had been truly uncanny when, after going to a spring concert in the park near their house, she had stopped at a local pub for a pint and found herself sitting next to a gaunt bespectacled young man who introduced himself as Siebe.

What transpired that evening had never been completely clear to Femke. She had no social skills and no knowledge of how to deal with men—she was unquestionably no flirt. She had never known love nor lust. Nevertheless, by some mysterious channel, that one pint while seated on a stool next to Siebe led to much more, including a much unanticipated pregnancy that prompted a quick and, some might say, ignominious wedding.

Femke prevailed upon Siebe to find a flat close by her parents' house and throughout their marriage, while her husband diligently reviewed the books of some of the city's finest investors, Femke lived a double life. She continued nearly unabated to oversee her parents' home while she tried to establish her own. In many ways, this was an unwinnable situation. She could not, would not, spread herself too thin. She would not, as she felt others wanted her to do, short-change her parents for her husband and their new son. With only so many hours in a day, her own nuclear family suffered the consequences and, much as Brother Mike himself had grown up, Siebe and his son, along with his future daughter, had their own close and loving family group for which Femke was more of a spectator than an actor.

Brother Mike stared into the blackness of the night sky. The hum of the 707 seemed to seamlessly merge with the external oblivion to create a surreal mural that through its emptiness spoke of the human spirit, the family bonds that never were, the loneliness of being but not being, the hollowness of being left out, the hopelessness of being left alone. He would miss the man he never knew, the man who had sired him. But, was this missing what was or what could have been?

Brother Mike dozed off only to be awakened by the grinding sound of landing gear lowering and the pressure in his ears popping as the plane prepared to bring him back, somewhat reluctantly, to the land of his birth. It was just past sunrise on a Brussels' winter morning when he deplaned and headed through the formalities. In another two hours, he got off the train in Ghent with his small suitcase and familiar canvas holdall, and looked for a taxi to take him to the working-class neighborhood where he had grown up. He would now have breakfast with a sister with whom he had been disunited for so, so many years.

As the taxi pulled up, the house looked little changed from decades ago when he had left; not knowing where he was going, but sure he was not going to stay where he was. His finger had barely touched the doorbell when the door opened with the imposing silhouette of his sister filling the portal.

There was no hug. There was no kiss, not even a peck. There was no handshake. There were muted and mumbled "good morning" greetings as if Brother Mike had just returned from the neighborhood grocery store. He was quickly ushered into a straight-backed chair in the kitchen where he was served a mug of hot but acrid coffee to accompany a plate of cold bread, greasy sausage, and a forlorn boiled egg that wobbled on the plate like his tire when it had collapsed on the road north.

Out of duty, Brother Mike did his best to consume the offered food and drink while Femke brought him up to date. Their father was on a respirator in the hospital. He had been suffering from a variety of respiratory illnesses after a lifetime of smoking and inhaling the dust and fumes of thousands of cargo ships. He was sedated but coherent. Their mother was upstairs in their parents' bedroom. She had suffered a third stroke last year and was partially paralyzed. She could hear and understand but she could not speak. She was aware her husband had been taken from their bed to hospital, but did not yet know that the prognosis was so bleak. She, Femke, was concerned that once their mother knew of her husband's condition, she might well have a fourth and fatal stroke.

It was much as Brother Mike had anticipated. The blackness, the emptiness, the hopelessness, the hollowness—they had all settled on the household. Tomorrow was of course a new day, but it did not offer great promise. At best, it offered a choice between a quick or slow trip to an unavoidable and known destination. All that could come to mind was the Swahili wish to travel well: *kusafiri vizuri*.

In the middle of his thoughts about the here and now, Brother Mike realized he had missed his Vigil prayers this morning. His thoughts shifting to his Christian duties, he realized he had not prayed at Vespers yesterday. His routine was changing dramatically and rapidly. He was somehow straddling two worlds, feeling at home and at ease in neither. Then, in the middle of wondering where and who he was, he had a flashback of a pregnant Angela on the Crane terrace. Father, mother, sister, Angela, Abbot, Philip— they began spinning as in a whirlpool—or, he thought, as if in a toilet. That was the correct analogy, his life a toilet. Where was his faith, where was his confidence, where was his courage? In the toilet?

Before his mind was consumed by blackness, he felt a shaking of his shoulder. Not the rib-wrenching shaking his grandmother used to employ to punish him for any of the multitude of errors, in her view, he endlessly committed; a stern yet somehow gentle shaking.

He looked up seeing his sister bringing him back to the reality of the kitchen table.

"You must be very tired after your travels?" she asked quietly, obviously trying to calm a brother who was on the verge of doing she knew not what.

"Yes," was all he could stammer.

"Your old room awaits you. I've put clean sheets on the bed. Go and rest and I'll call you when Mother is up and ready to chat." She was always at her best when giving orders and making arrangements. For a fleeting moment, Brother Mike wondered if his own organizational skills were somehow related to these traits of his sister. This seemed to be a frightening possibility under present conditions.

But the here and now meant he was home. This was not his spiritual home—the place where his spirit, his essence dwelled. However, it was his physical home where he had grown to adulthood.

❧ ❧ ❧

The old house was slightly more spacious than many of its day. It was two stories, constructed of brick. It was a row house, one of hundreds built in the vicinity of the docks. The front door, coming directly from the street, opened to a staircase leading to bedrooms on the first floor. Brother Mike's family had had the luxury of three small bedrooms when many had had to make do with two. The main floor had a small living room, a combination kitchen and dining area, and a compact laundry room. From here, a back door opened into a tiny space that originally contained a coal house and an outside toilet. Over the intervening years the house had been electrified, plumbed, and converted to gas heat. But even with what could be considered as modern amenities, Brother Mike found the house feeling old, almost decrepit. If it had been part of the Abbey's campus, he would have recommended it be torn down immediately with a friendlier structure put in its place.

These thoughts aside, he was where he was—his circumstances what they were. He knew his sister had been right that he needed some sleep. Haltingly, he climbed the stairs, turning left and opening the door into the small bedroom that was scarcely bigger than the single bed that was its most prominent feature. The small bedroom where he had spent most of his youth—or at least the nights of his youth as, even then, he found his house to be an unhappy place and tried as much as possible to be as far away as possible during the day.

Pushing these ghosts of times gone by into his minuscule closet, he put his suitcase at the foot of the bed, opened his holdall and took a healthy swallow of his favored cognac, took off his shoes, and literally fell on his bed, falling asleep almost before his head hit his pillow.

Brother Mike was bouncing along a potholed road winding through banana plantations, the worn springs of his pickup making him feel as though he were on a hobbyhorse. Up and down, up and down. Snap. He awoke. He realized it was not the suspension of his old Toyota, but the equally spent suspension of his old bed that was rocking his body, the power behind the movement coming from Femke who was trying to rouse him from his deep sleep.

"Mother is up and has had her breakfast. She'd like to see you in her room."

"OK," he grumbled as the sleep fell away like a scab off a skinned knee; the slight pain subdued the mild shock at finding himself in his old bedroom.

He rinsed his face, got a clean shirt out of his suitcase, put on his shoes, and crossed the hallway to his mother's room. He was pleased to see his mother had made the room bright and airy as opposed to the demeanor of the rest of the house. There were bright chintz curtains surrounding clean windows that let in a lot of light. The bedspread and carpets all matched the uplifting colors of the window dressings—the whole room seemed cheery, even if a bit overplayed for a woman of advanced years.

His mother was sitting in her wheelchair, her hair combed, wearing a clean pastel colored robe. Beside her was a small table upon which sat two mugs of coffee. Across from the table was a wing chair with patterned lilac upholstery and white doilies on the back and arms. She motioned for Brother Mike to take a seat in the chair, with the same expansive gesture, indicating the coffee was for him.

Brother Mike bent over and gave his mother a hug, then took his place facing her, "How are you doing Mom? It's been a long time. I've tried to write regularly, but know we've been out of touch."

She smiled and made a motion with her hands for him to continue.

"Femke said you can't talk after your last stroke, but that you hear just fine and can follow a conversation with ease?"

She again motioned for him to continue.

"Mom, you know I'm not much good at one-way conversations unless it's my prayers; and these I hope aren't all that one-way. Anyway, we'll try and move along. Femke had written to me that Dad is in the hospital and that I should come home. The politics have become kind of rough at the Abbey—not the internal politics, those are what they always are, but the external politics with lots of folks making a lot of fuss about changes in the name of democratization. Pretty sensitive times and things could go any which way. The Abbot felt it was a good time for me to be away for a while so I decided to follow Femke's advice and come back to check up on you all.

"Just to get it all out of the way, I am fine. I enjoy my work and still feel I have chosen the best course for me. There is a tremendous amount to do and lots of people who really need a helping hand and God's Love. I feel I am helping; I hope others find this so.

"But as you know, the Church is not a vocation that has a lot of extra benefits. We don't have regular home leaves or vacations. It is really just not possible for me to get all the way back to Belgium on any regular basis. However, I am happy I was able to work this out this time and be able to come to see you and Dad.

"I don't know how long I'll be here. The Abbot said to just play it by ear. So, to start with, what can I do for you?"

She smiled, pulling a tablet and pencil from a drawer in the table. She wrote just a few words: "go see your father."

"Alright Mom," Brother Mike quickly replied. "I'll ask Femke to arrange for us to go to the hospital, but can I do something for you?"

She shook her head and made a gesture indicating he should get a move on. He left, leaving an untouched coffee mug, and went down to the kitchen where he found Femke washing dishes.

"Mom says we should see Dad as soon as possible," he declared with just a little too much edge on his voice. He felt it was now he who was a spectator to his own life, having no real control over what was happening. This was not a sensation with which he was familiar and not a sensation he enjoyed—he was accustomed to charting his own course and following his own compass.

"I know," obviously all had been pre-arranged between Femke and their mother. "I've called the hospital and we can see Dad at two this afternoon. I'll drive us."

There seemed little else to discuss. All Brother Mike really wanted to do was to go to the nearest travel agency and book a flight back to the other side of the equator, but knew he had other tasks—tasks where he could only follow others' lead. Hence, awaiting the departure for the hospital, he decided to go to his room as he had done so often as a child when he knew not what else to do.

Once in his familiar surroundings, he took off his shoes, pulled out his bottle of cognac, and settled on his sagging bed to watch the dust motes float through the air, somehow in his mind unsuccessfully trying to merge their motion with the ballet of the banana fronds around the fishpond at the monastery.

ლ ლ ლ

Femke knocked at his door at half-past-one and Brother Mike was ready to go. When they reached the street, irrespective of his sister's declaration of driving, Brother Mike had assumed they would be taking a taxi. To his surprise, his sister led the way to a beat-up Renault R-4. Fixing him with a piercing gaze that she had so well mastered, she proudly professed was the first car owned by any member of their family.

With a low cry, the little car pulled away from the curb, and moved down the street in a rather hopping-rolling motion. Sitting in silence, Brother Mike realized Femke had been right. His old Toyota was the Abbey's, not his—he had never owned a car.

They continued in silence. To avoid thinking of his father, past and present, Brother Mike watched the city of his youth float by the dusty windows. It seemed to him this old jalopy, living, as it were, in a major European city, was dirtier and dustier than the vehicles that sat outside the Abbey throughout the tropical rainy and dry seasons. Strange, he mused. How many people here, he wondered, suffered from dysentery?

Then they were at the hospital.

As he knew she would, Femke had it timed down to the minute. They parked, took the elevator, and were standing at the door to their father's room at exactly 2:00 p.m. Before they entered, Femke squeezed his arm, saying softly in his ear: "get ready for the worst."

Their father's room reminded Brother Mike of an avocado split in half, the great seed protruding out, surrounded on all sides by the fruit's flesh. Their father, the seed, was surrounded by all manner of machines and devices, with blinking lights, buzzing and bleeping sounds, and an overarching hum that made it seem like the set of a science fiction movie.

His father had tubes coming out from everywhere, but his eyes were open and he held his children in a steely stare as they approached his bed.

There were two chrome and vinyl chairs to the left of the bed. Femke and Brother Mike took their seats as though coming to do homage to their lord. Perhaps the analogy was not too far off. They sat silently, listening to the machines that functioned in place of their father's organs, and hearing the hum as though they were in a hive of bees.

Their father shifted his gaze to Brother Mike. "So you've come," he said in a gurgly tone that seemed to echo off the roof of his mouth.

Brother Mike knew not what to say, so he simply nodded.

"Took me dying to bring you out of the heathen bush," his Father nearly spat out the words.

Again, Brother Mike knew not what to do, so he remained impassive.

"Someone with all the opportunities I never had, who threw them away to go and live with a bunch of wogs in the name of some loving God. My own son deserted this family, the family that gave him breath and clothes on his back. Left us for some mythical god. Left us for a village of wogs.

"You could have stayed in Belgium. You could have been somebody. You could have done something. But not you. Always going your own way no matter how hard your parents begged you to do the right thing. And now you come back to watch me die."

Brother Mike tried to think what he should say to someone on his deathbed when that person was his father. After all, in spite of the bitterness, he was more than his father, he was a dying man and he, Brother Mike, was a man of God, as his father had just so indelicately pointed out. The Church's role was to help ease the pain of death, to instill in the dying the hope of salvation. To bless the soul that would soon be leaving the temporal body. What should a servant of God do to help someone, anyone, meet their end. He knew he should know, but he could not think of anything to do, so he continued to sit in silence. The humming in the room consumed him, like a nest of wasps in his head.

"Worthless," their Father retorted with what looked like a sneer on his face as he shifted his focus to Femke, "You brought him here, you deal with him.

"Don't waste your time on me. These damned machines can only keep the piss pumping for so long and that ain't much longer. Go talk to your mother. She needs to look over our affairs with you. See what you need and if there's any extra. Before I leave here, I want to give something to the Flem-ish Brotherhood if I can. The hope for a free Flemish State has been a fire in my belly my whole life, the thing that got me through the worst times. We ain't seen it yet, but tomorrow is another day and I ain't giving up. Whatever we can spare must go to the cause. That's all I need to know. Now take this one away and let me rest."

Brother Mike followed Femke out of the room almost as though he were sleepwalking. He said nothing, not when he got into the car, not when he got home: he said nothing. When he got across the threshold, he nearly ran upstairs to the safety of his room. In some abstract way, his mind's eye was twitching at the irony. During his childhood when his father would rant and rail about whatever he was doing, sometimes taking off his belt to add physical to the mental anguish, he would run to hide in his room. Now, decades later, he was doing the same.

❧ ❧ ❧

Brother Mike took a long drag on his bottle of Courvoisier, stared at the four walls around him and wondered how he had come full circle. Unlike his feelings for the dilemma surrounding Angela, for the impasse regarding his father, he had no guilt or regrets. He had felt distain. He had felt hostility. He had felt frustration. Over the years he had felt many emotions. But, in recent years he had learned to simply accept his father in particular, and his family in general, for what they were: something very different from him. How they had spawned someone like him remained a mystery. Nonetheless, he now knew, or felt they were simply fundamentally different elements: oil and water. There was no way, there were no words, for him to explain or justify his life to his family. And, in his view, such a justification was unwarranted. He also knew there was no way he would be able to understand his family's inner workings—how they reasoned, what they valued, what they needed. They frankly were worlds apart. There may be no right and wrong, he did not know. Still, there were major differences, a chasm that separated Brother Mike from the rest of his family.

His deep thoughts were interrupted by a knock on the door. Getting up, he found Femke there saying their mother wished to see him. "Pshaw," he thought. "Here we go again."

When he was once again seated in the lilac chair across from his mother, this time she had her tablet out and was writing and writing and writing.

His sister had left a cup of coffee on the table. He sipped this while his mother continued to get her words down on paper. When she handed the pad to him, he saw big scrawled sentences angling across the page, reminiscent of the early grades when he was learning his ABCs.

The rough-hewn style aside, the words had been carefully chosen from the heart. Brother Mike read: "My son, do not hate your father. He is not a bad man and, through it all, he has been a good husband to me. Yet I know he has not been a good father to you. He is not an educated man. He knows nothing of the world. His world has been this little part of Flanders and the vision in his mind that his customs, his language, and his preferences could become the common currency. This is a mistaken dream, but he knows no better. He is unpolished, even boorish. He has a bad temper. He is impatient. He has many faults. But he is your father. I know you cannot understand him. I do not ask you to forgive him, for I know he has impacted your life with prejudice in many ways. But all this is past. Your sister does not think I know, but I do: he is dying. I rejoice that you have seen him before he goes. I ask you only to stay with us, by our side, while he meets His Maker. He needs so much to know his family, a family that in his own way he values so much, is with him at the end. Will you do this for him? Will you do this for me?"

"OK Mom, I'm here," Brother Mike said as he finished reading and handed back her sheaf of papers. "I'll try."

He finished his coffee and left, not noticing the glitter of tears in his mother's eyes.

He did not want to return to the mental and physical confines of his old room, nor did he want to face his sister. He decided the best thing was to go for a walk to clear his head. He grabbed his coat and hat and left unannounced.

In the gathering dusk, he wandered in a random way through his old neighborhood, memories flashing by as his own story had flashed though his brain on the flight here. The school, the playground, Herbert's house, the butcher's, the barber's—so much of his other life still seemed replete around him.

Perhaps not surprisingly, his ramblings took him to Saint Catherine's Church where he had been baptized, confirmed, and had his first communion. Where he had been introduced to God's Word. Where he had chosen God's Path. He had again gone full circle.

He entered through the great doors, passed through the narthex into the nave where he genuflected and sat in one of the back pews. He had not taken time to consciously pray since he had left the Abbey. That seemed like weeks ago when in fact it was only 24 hours ago.

He knelt on the *prie-dieu* and began an Our Father. His mind was just getting settled in that special place facilitated by prayer where he found truth and solace when he felt an intrusion into his spiritual space. He opened his eyes, looking up, to find a young bearded man in a black cassock smiling down on him.

"I am so sorry to disturb your prayers. As evening approaches, I was just checking to see if anyone had come for confession. I am Father Tuur.

"Well Father, I am a wayward son of the parish, Brother Mike of the Brothers of Piety. My life of religious devotion started right here, before this very chancel. From these doors, I have tried to carry the Word of God far and wide. And now I have come full circle and am back to pray at Saint Catherine's; pray for my sins and pray for the soul of my father who will soon be departing this world."

"Brother, welcome back to the source. I hope your learnings, your faith, and your humanity, all shaped by Saint Catherine's, have held you in good stead—our church having prepared you well for the path you have followed over the years."

"I dare not judge, Father, but I have tried and I take great solace in my efforts and hopefully the good seeds I have planted." The unintentional reference to seed brought a pang of remorse and an immediate image of Angela. But he pushed these into one of his mental closets, closing the door and refocusing on now.

"Well, I won't interrupt you any further. Welcome home. May God be with you." With these parting words, Father Tuur continued down the aisle, turning toward the confessional.

Brother Mike returned to his prayers. After some time, he stood up. He felt grounded. He felt better able to shoulder the challenges of being at home, being among family. He retraced his steps through the narthex, exiting through the great doors into a now dark and cool evening, as one would expect in February not far from the North Sea.

The cold darkness brought nostalgia for the Central African highlands, an area many referred to as the "Land of Eternal Spring." The soft perfumed night air of the tropics was a stark contrast to the biting drafts of these northern latitudes, dosed with the fumes of petrol and asphalt rather than frangipani and hibiscus. How strange things are, he thought. All those years ago when he was preparing to leave this church, this city, for the unknown, everyone told him how lucky he was, how he would have a truly unique experience, how he would make a difference. Now that he was back, even if for but a short stay, one might think the agents of the Church would be interested in hearing how he had done, how it had been carrying God's Word and doing God's Service in far-off places.

But no, for everyone, including Father Tuur and himself, there was the urgency of now. The needs and the demands of this minute that seemed to compete with the time and energy required to take a step back and look at the bigger picture. Today, life was complex. Few had the luxury of contemplating the whole, when struggling to manage just one small part. It was up to Brother Mike to care about what he himself did, what he himself accomplished—few others had the time or the inclination.

With those sobering thoughts, Brother Mike stopped at a small supermarket to get some bread, cheese, and wine. He had no idea if his family had planned on him partaking of the evening meal tonight. This way, if there was nothing, he had something. If there was a meal on the table, his additions would still be welcome.

When he got home, he found two places set at the table and his sister engrossed in an evening game show on TV. It had not occurred to him, but logically his mother would have a difficult time navigating the stairs. As he was to learn and see later, she could go up and down, very slowly, when partially carried by the formidable strength of her daughter. However, she tackled the stairs as infrequently as possible, taking her meals in her room.

Hearing the door open and close, Femke got up, almost robotically, going to the kitchen and serving two plates from simmering pots on the stove. Brother Mike hung his coat and hat in the cloak closet, following his sister into the kitchen. He put his provisions on the counter before taking his seat, assuming correctly that the chair at the head of the table was Femke's preferred place.

She put a steaming plate of boiled potatoes and vegetable stew in front of him, adding, "So you made it home." A statement, not a question.

"Uh-huh," he supplied to not ignore completely her comment, but to adopt a tactic of least said, fewest chances for an altercation. "There's some wine if you'd like a glass."

"Maybe tomorrow. It's too late now as I've been waiting for you, but I had to go ahead and feed mother and I'll have to go in a few minutes to collect her dishes. The normal routine is out of kilter for the moment."

He knowingly took the hint. "Look Femke, you asked me to come. As I am sure you know, mother has now asked me to stay. I have agreed, so we need to make the best of it. I will be out of your hair as soon as I can."

"You just need to know," she said uncharacteristically softly, but with great emotion, "you have left. You abandoned the family and followed your imagination. As always, you did what you wanted, leaving others to do what needed to be done. I have done, and will continue to do the heavy lifting for this family. When you are back to wherever you are going, doing whatever you do, I will be here feeding mother and helping her live out the rest of her days as happily as she can. You are here because she wants you here. When you have again left, things will be normal."

There didn't seem to be anything more to say. For the second time in the day, Brother Mike felt silence was the best, the only answer. They ate with the only noise the clicking their forks on the well-worn dinnerware Brother Mike had known his whole life.

Having cleared his plate, Brother Mike took his dishes to the sink, leaving them there, he took his leave of his sister and mounted the stairs to his room—a new sort of monk's cell to which he was relegated for the coming days or weeks, he did not know which.

ই ই ই

Once in his room, he took a big gulp of cognac before getting ready for bed. Waiting for sleep to come, marveling at life's ironies, he decided he needed to be proactive. If the *status quo* continued, as had happened in his childhood, he would be pushed and shaped by his family into someone very different from the person he knew he was. For better or worse, he was where he was and he needed to pick up the reins if he was to have any voice at all as to what transpired during this portion of his life. As a young man, he had been unable to take control of his own life without leaving his family. Now all these years later, he needed to be in control at the very least of his own actions.

The next morning, he rose early and prayed on his knees at his bedside. Once dressed for the day, he went downstairs to find Femke had made coffee and the baguette he had purchased the night before was on the counter.

He had no idea where his sister was, and no interest in finding out. He took a small plate from the cupboard, got some butter from the fridge, poured some coffee, and sat at the table for his solitary breakfast. After blessing the food—he thought it really needed a blessing as the coffee was weak with no heady aroma like the Arabica from the Central African Highlands. The bread was rubbery and the butter almost sour. Alas, he reminded himself, you do with what you have.

This time, when he had finished, he washed, dried, and put away his dishes. He then retrieved his coat and hat from the cloak closet and went out. Unlike yesterday's meandering, this time his walk took him directly to Saint Catherine's.

He took his same place in the back pew and prayed to the Lord to help him, to guide him, to give him the wisdom to know what to do, to give him the tolerance to accept his family, to give him the patience to put up with their nonsense.

Sometime later—he had honestly lost track of time, which had been so important when organizing all the logistics of the Abbey—Brother Mike left the church, walking a short distance to a small café where he had a really good coffee and a fresh croissant.

He had to confess he did not know his family's routine. He did not know when they ate, when they slept, or what they did during the day. Nonetheless, he returned home about 12:30 with two fresh loaves of bread for the household and a basket of welcome new ideas for himself.

As when he left, he could not find his sister. He stuck his head in his mother's room, but she was napping. He went to the kitchen, made a cup of tea, cut a piece of bread and sat at the table, organizing his thoughts—after all, he was the guy who was so good at organization.

He had been sitting there long enough for his left leg to have fallen asleep when he heard the door open and then saw Femke enter the kitchen with a small bag of groceries under her arm.

She looked at him as though he had been sitting in the kitchen await-ing her return for years. "I was at the hospital and stopped at the market on the way back since we've now more mouths to feed."

Brother Mike let the barb pass, got up and poured hot water into an-other mug for his sister. "Take a seat, Femke, let's talk a bit."

She deposited her grocery bag on the counter, put a teabag in the mug, and obligingly took her seat at the head of the table. "Go ahead," she pro-nounced with a bored look.

"As we talked last night, I am here at mother's request—or demand, I might say. I have devoted my life to Christ and it is my duty, both as a son of my father and a son of God, to help those in need. I will stay only as long as I can help my mother or my father—our mother and our father.

"Clearly our father is more comfortable with you, so I will not en-cumber his remaining days with my regular, obviously irritating, presence. I assume you will be seeing him on nearly a daily basis. As the end nears, he may wish to see his son, or he may wish for some prayers on his behalf. I will, therefore, ask you to keep me apprised of his condition and when it is appropriate, I will accompany you.

"In the meantime, I have my religious duties. I will go to Saint Cath-erine's at least once a day to pray and ask guidance of my Savior.

"To help offset the additional cost of my additional mouth, and to help our family home keep its value, I will begin painting some of the dreary rooms like the salon, trying to capture a gay and airy atmosphere as in Mother's room. I will do one room at a time so when I leave, at least some the rooms will have been fixed up.

"Not knowing your schedules, as today, I will have my *petit dejuner* when I come down, even if you have left for wherever you are going. I will handle my lunch myself, either outside or put something simple together here. I will assume you will be preparing the evening meal and that we will be dining here as we did last night.

"I hope that covers everything. To the extent I have any laundry, I will take this to the cleaners myself. If you need supplies, you need only to ask and I will stop at the store on my way back from Saint Catherine's."

He was an organizer. He hoped he had hit all the points. He sipped his tea, waiting for his sibling's reaction.

When it came it was unexpectedly muted. "OK," she said in a neutral tone, "we'll go ahead like that."

She picked up her mug, "I have to go and see mother."

15

THINGS UNFOLDED AS BROTHER Mike had described. After two weeks, he had painted the whole downstairs. When not focused on his labors, he visited a nearby café where he once and again he had several pints with Father Tuur. He also received regular updates on his father's condition from his sister. The old man was on the decline, but it was not precipitous. Furthermore, whenever Femke mentioned her brother, the old man immediately tensed and looked like he wanted to get out of bed to lock the door against an encroaching demon.

After a month, Brother Mike had painted all the rooms except his mother's. He had spent so much time with Tuur that the poor Father probably knew the Abbey as well as Brother Mike did; the more beer, the more numerous and elaborate the tales of the Brothers of Piety and their heroic duties in distant Central Africa. Whether he wanted to or not, Father Tuur was becoming an expert on international monastic services.

When month two started, Brother Mike started on the outside of the house. He was not comfortable working on a ladder and did not want to paint only the lower floor, so he put up his paint brush and brought out a box full of tools to smarten up the house and do needed maintenance where there were loose boards or bricks, rusty pipes, or broken fixtures. It was not difficult to find several hours of work a day on the multitude of small things that needed attention, but that had fallen to disrepair since his father had fallen ill.

Over these weeks, Brother Mike made a concerted effort to reconnect with his mother. Nearly every day he tried to drop by her room for afternoon tea—or, most often, coffee. He had provided his biographical sketch early on so there was really very little to say about his life at the Abbey if he did not want to bore her to death. His aim was just the opposite, to try and get her to be enthusiastic about her life in spite of all the difficulties. Slowly a rapport was established, along with a routine. She would typically have a subject picked out, described on her pad. When he came, she would show her notes to him and then he would outline his thoughts on this topic, be it of a political, religious, or personal nature.

At first, these exchanges targeted rather innocent topics: what he thought about the changes in the neighborhood, how about the much-enlarged port, did he think parochial or public schools were better, what about the price of petrol, what about all these immigrants? Slowly more sensitive subjects worked their way into the discussion: what did he think about Flemish nationalism, is there a God, should priests and monks marry, did the Church care about the common man, were people inherently good or evil? They delved into all variety of subjects and, through their discussions, became closer.

Brother Mike began to see his mother as a wise and caring person who did love her husband and who felt her role was to be subservient to this man she had married, even when she fundamentally disagreed with him. He began to understand his mother had so often played a part, donned a mask to avoid confrontation, but not to sacrifice her principles. Brother Mike began to realize, moreover, his mother had opted for the same sort of charade with Femke. She let her daughter dominate, rarely contradicting her. Nonetheless, in her own heart and mind she had very different priorities and approaches. She sadly found her daughter to be, in her own way, just as boorish as her husband. But she also felt great guilt. Guilt that, unlike her husband, her daughter's behavior reflected to a large degree how she had been raised. Guilt that her son's isolation, seen by his parents as a series of incongruous acts, also reflected how he had been raised. She knew that in the former case, the damage was wrought due to too close coverage—being overprotective and over controlling. She also knew that the latter case was due to neglect and a loss of connection—a young son with aging parents simply had been an addition to the family that the family was ill-equipped to accept and accommodate.

Brother Mike related far too well with his mother on the subject of guilt, albeit in a totally different context. In many ways, he had a great desire to unload, to share with her the whole story of Angela and her baby, soon to come into the world. However, he knew she would disagree and be disappointed in her son. He knew she expected self-discipline, all the more so for men of God. He knew it was a subject he could not broach.

This inability to confess his deepest sins to his mother was in no way to say that Brother Mike, now far from the terrace at the Crane and Philip's card table, had expunged his guilt over Angela and her condition, a condition that was very soon to give birth to a new soul on this planet. But his survival instincts had kicked in. It was not reasonable to expect any updates as to Angela's condition, only the Abbot knew how to contact him, and even then, this would only be by the Belgian *Régie des Postes*, a surface letter taking up to a month and an aerogramme taking almost ten days to reach him. He was out of sight and out of mind, a predicament to which he had grown accustomed in many ways. Hence, as was his coping strategy, he made a small room for Angela in his mind, closing the door until such a time that he would really be able to do something meaningful. In the here and now he had to try and re-energize his mother, bury his father, and tolerate his sister.

🍎 🍎 🍎

Brother Mike's mental whirlwinds had, when he arrived at his Belgian home, been whipped into a raging Sahelian sand storm. His thoughts were spinning uncontrollably. He was befuddled and off balance.

The tempest still blew. Calm winds were far off. But, some of the sand and dust was beginning to settle. The road ahead was slowly becoming discernible, if not self-evident.

Over and beyond his responsibilities to his family, Brother Mike acknowledged he had a responsibility to himself. He was truly, he knew, the author of his life's story. Here, in his birthplace, the back pew at Saint Catherine's had somehow nearly replaced the pond bank. Here he was, at times, able to pull away from himself and the daily trials to see what he imagined to be the clearer picture.

The Church was a refuge. It was not only a refuge to those threatened and abused by an angry world, it was a refuge to those plagued by inner threats and abuses. The Church offered what could be seen by some as a good career choice—an easy life with a chance for advancement. But, the Church also offered therapy and salvation to those otherwise handicapped by external or internal demons—hopefully allowing the afflicted to assume positive roles of faith where they could help their fellow man and strengthen the Holiness of God.

Brother Mike's pilgrimage to Belgium had provided a much-needed perspective. Each had his or her reasons to enter the Community of God, to dedicate his or her life to the Lord. He now realized his own motives, even if less than crystal clear, were his own, and as valued and justified as anyone else's goals and aspirations. He only hoped he lived up to the task. He hoped he made a difference.

Brother Mike recalled one of his brothers saying, "Home is where you have your bank account."

Well, just like with a car, Brother Mike did not have a bank account. Did this mean he did not have a home? He thought not. He believed not. In truth, having dug back into his past, Belgium was not his home. The Abbey was his home. He knew he would spend his remaining days in the service of "his" Abbey.

But, the worms of doubt that crawled between the chambers of his brain would not let him get off with such a simple declaration. His father would surely be forced to face difficult questions as he neared the end of his temporal life—the only life his father so far believed he would ever live. It was normal—no, it was a matter of fact—he too would have tough questions, questions whose answers so far eluded him or hid from the light of truth.

Was he running away from life when he enshrouded himself in "his" Abbey? Was he seeking salvation and being closer to God and His Holy Work? Or, was he seeking the ease of a bed and three meals a day with no family to feed and no debts to worry about? If he truly wanted to be closer to God, how could he have approached Angela? Were not his sins proof—actions and not words—that he was not at heart a religious man?

These and so many questions bounded around Brother Mike's head when he sought to have a moment of serenity. They whirled about like pieces of a jigsaw puzzle in a gale.

To these profound questions, he was, he hoped, looking for answers— looking for truth. Even so, regardless of the answers, he was certain of one thing: for whatever reason, the Abbey was his home.

🍎 🍎 🍎

Almost six weeks after his arrival, Femke announced one evening over a plate of boiled cabbage and ham hocks their father's health was declining more rapidly. She thought her brother might make an appearance at the hospital to see if the old man was in a more charitable mood as he too certainly saw the end looming.

Brother Mike organized his schedule to be at the hospital a half an hour after Femke got there, giving her time to prepare the terrain. However, when he poked his head in the door, before even crossing the threshold, the old man's keen eyes fell upon him and he screeched in a hoarse, guttural voice that made one feel the words were pealing the skin off the inside of his throat, "So you're still here living off others. Go back to your jungle bunnies."

He withdrew.

There was no mention with Femke of what had transpired. However, the next day, when paying his now habitual visit to his mother, she had a note ready for him when he had taken his place in the lilac chair. It was simple missive, "Come back tomorrow, I will have something important for you. For now, my son, have a peaceful night and do not worry."

The next day when he returned he found a neat pile of notepad pages stacked in front of his mother and another smaller stack in her hand. She handed the smaller of the two to him as he sat down. He read the hand-written pages: "Our son, and you are OUR son. Your father is afraid and ashamed. Like all of us, he is afraid of the unknown, afraid to die. He is ashamed that, as your father, he has not been able to bond with you and he knows now it was his fault. You have shown that what he considered a self-ish caprice was a worthy calling in the service of God—God he is only now recognizing as he sees his own mortality. He also now knows that his lack of education, lack of worldliness, lack of vision have handicapped his whole family, and he is humiliated. His unwillingness to be tolerant and open have led to his abuse of you and me, to his pushing your sister into some impos-sible role that has ruined her life, and to his absurd singing the praises of Flemish Nationalism, where he was able to surround himself with a lot of old white men just like himself. But we are never too old to learn, even on our deathbed. This pile of papers on the table is for him. Femke will take it to him today. Arrange your schedule to go back to the hospital next week to see your father. In the meantime, pray to your Holy Father for your paternal father's soul. And, never forget that in our own ways, even though we may not show it well, we do love you."

Brother Mike had wanted to talk with his mother. He had wanted to say he was beginning to understand. He knew he had made their lives difficult. He knew their lives were strenuous. They had raised a family in demanding times and at the end of the day they all had come out all right. He had wanted to say more. But his mother gently waved him away, signing that she would spend more quality time with him tomorrow.

As evening crept in, through the shadows of the street lights, Brother Mike walked briskly to Saint Catherine's, taking what he now thought of has his spot in the back, but staring long and hard at the altar, enveloping the cross that had been and continued to be his loadstone, his harbinger, his beacon. If the child Michel van Leuven, baptized within these very walls, had foreseen the path foreshadowed by this cross, would he have been sad or glad?

Brother Mike went to his knees. He thought of Jesus' request: "Father, forgive them, for they know not what they do." He too asked his spiritual Father to forgive his corporeal father, to bless him and to offer him eternal life as he reached the end of his mortal being. He asked God to give him, Mi-chel, the courage to forgive his earthly father and his entire family. He had many scars, some old, some new. He felt he had been misunderstood and maligned. His mother had now confirmed this. He had suffered through ignorance and dogmatism. He asked God to give him the strength to forgive and forget these adversities, this pain. He prayed and he wept.

The following week, Brother Mike felt he needed to give all fair warning of his plans, announcing to his mother and Femke that he would, as his mother had asked, go to the hospital on Wednesday to see his father.

On the appointed day, he did not ask Femke for a ride, assuming she would be at the hospital before he arrived. He told his mother goodbye and hailed a taxi. When he entered his father's room, he expected to see his sister, but knew not what to expect from his father. Curiously, Femke was nowhere to be seen and his father was sitting a bit upright in his bed, apparently expecting the visit.

There was no garrulous haranguing, no driving away the ill-favored son. In a gruff but modulated tone his father asked him to take a seat by the bed. He then pulled the sheaf of notepaper from under the covers, "I received this from your mother."

"Yes, I know," Brother Mike replied, taking his seat.

"It is impossible for a child to know how his parents were when they were young. We were very much in love. I think, I hope, we still are. Your mother deserved much better than me. When all is said and done, I am still at my roots an ignorant farmer. I saw things I could not have, I saw things I could not understand. I became angry. I wasn't always angry you know. When your mother and I were young we laughed a lot, we danced, we sang, we enjoyed life. But life is not easy. Little by little the songs ended. Life became drudgery. Life became worrisome. Life made me afraid as I saw we had a growing family and no going income. Fear grew—fear of poverty, fear of illness, fear of being left behind. I became angrier as the fear grew. I became unkind—unkind to your mother, unkind to your sister, unkind to you.

"But you were so different. You were so smart. You were so thoughtful. You were so caring. You were so different from us all. That made it so easy for me to target you more, making your life more difficult. Refusing to listen, refusing to try to understand.

"Michel, do not think what I am saying is coming chiefly from my ailing heart." He held up the note pages, "Your mother has, for the first time in our lives, taken me to task. She was always there for me, self-effacing, forgiving, supportive. She tried to temper my spirit, but she only received suffering for her efforts. She finally gave up, until now, trying to show by example when her kind words went unheeded.

"She has finally succeeded in opening my eyes, opening my heart. I have not much time left, but I do not want to leave you with words of hate or anger. I want you to know that I now know I have been so wrong. Forgive me. You are our beloved son. In spite of my harsh words, I have been proud of you—your dedication, your selflessness, your smarts. You are my legacy and I am so gratified.

"Your Mother invested a great deal of thought and soul-searching into this pile of papers. She has told me she knows and accepts that we may not meet again in this world, but that if I do the right thing, we will again be together in a better place. Showing her love for me, for us, she has tried to show me how to do the right thing. I am not a very quick learner, as you probably know all too well."

His Father's voice grew weak with all the effort and emotion—it was now barely a raspy whisper.

"I know she poured her heart and prayers into those pages," Brother Mike inserted encouragingly.

"I know not how to pray, but I would be most grateful if you would pray with me. Pray with me, pray for me, forgive me." His voice faded and he bowed his head, weighed-down by illness and regret, but not broken.

Brother Mike knelt beside his father's bed and prayed as he had never prayed before. Forgiveness. Redemption. Benediction. Consecration. He asked God to look after his father and thanked God for letting him know his father before he left. At the end of the prayers, his father was asleep. He left the room silently.

That night his father died peacefully in his sleep.

Brother Mike was working in the back of the house when Femke brought him the news. There were no tears—they had been shed long ago. Sister and brother went to their mother's room with three glasses of wine and drank a toast to the man each loved in his or her own way, but all wishing him Godspeed.

Brother Mike saw Father Tuur who agreed to officiate the funeral. Femke, in her role as general-in-chief, made all the arrangements save one. Following his wife's explicit instructions, there was to be no Flemish flag at the gravesite, nor was *De Vlaamse Leeuw* to be played during the services. The ceremony itself was Saturday. Brother Mike spent extra quality time with his mother over the following week, then took a Sabena flight back to Central Africa. He left with no regrets—he was glad to have come and glad to be leaving. It saddened him that he would likely not see his mother again. He was relieved that his father's death had not, and would not, precipitate a stroke or worse for his mother. But she was frail. His final trip to Saint Catherine's was to pray for her, asking God to keep her well, and give her more years to enjoy her home, her books, and, in some rather abstract way, her daughter.

16

THE ABBEY WAS PREPARING for Easter celebrations, falling in April this year, when Brother Mike's taxi dropped him off at the front gate, the trip having been much longer than expected due to the many police and military roadblocks. By his count, after he had cleared airport formalities and found a taxi south, he had had to show his papers at no less than six checkpoints where the authorities had barricaded the road, letting only one vehicle pass at a time.

He went straight to the Abbot's office, still carrying his small suitcase and holdall. No one knew he was coming, so he needed to promptly and formally announce his return.

He found the Abbot, as always, seated behind his desk, a dour but caring man of indeterminate years, a good manager—a good Abbot. "Ahh, the Prodigal Son has come back," the Abbot pronounced as his greeting. Brother Mike was unsure if it was a statement or a question.

The Abbot then came around from behind his desk, gave Brother Mike a strong embrace, and proceeded to fill him in on the goings-on during his absence. Fostan was back in his home area. Nothing major had happened at the Abbey, but they needed Brother Mike's skills when they ramped-up the Easter festivities. As Brother Mike had undoubtedly witnessed, however, the overall security situation had deteriorated. There was now a score of different political parties, each aggressively and often violently pushing their own self-centered agendas. The current government was under tremendous pressure. Their main response had been to make the police and military services more and more visible. Officers were stationed around all municipalities. In urban areas, there were dusk to dawn foot patrols. There were vastly more roadblocks. The police and soldiers were everywhere, yet this seemed to do little to quench the growing unrest. No one knew how long the *status quo* could be maintained and what would ultimately be its replacement, but many of the options were not good.

With this dire recounting, without asking about his father nor his stay in Belgium, almost certainly knowing intuitively most of the answers, the Abbot asked Brother Mike to drop his affairs off and get back to work as quickly as possible. Brother Mike was happy to be needed.

☙ ☙ ☙

At the first occasion, Brother Mike offered to drive some of his team into town to replenish supplies. It felt good to be reunited with his old Toyota, but his objective was not the monastery's kitchen but Angela's condition. Obviously, he could not go directly in search of her, so he sought out Philip after dropping the others off at the market.

He started at Philip's clinic, but found no one there. He then went by their house, only to be informed by Joseph that Monsieur was at the capital and Madame was visiting her family. This was all very strange. Upon Brother Mike's prompting, Joseph did add, without any other explanations, that Madame had had a healthy baby boy, and mother and baby were doing just fine.

Brother Mike asked Joseph to give the *Patron* and *Madame* his regards, informing them he had returned from Belgium and was once again at the Abbey. He then left, in many ways relieved that Angela was healthy and safe.

On the well-worn drive out of town, Brother Mike silently and fervidly thanked his Lord while the cab of the pickup was filled with the banter of the market crew, arguing loudly about who had got the best prices—prices for which they had had to argue loudly. The irony was not lost on Brother Mike as he swallowed hard, trying to shake the disquiet that was seeping into his pores.

Immediately when they returned to the monastery, Brother Mike was summoned to the Abbot's office. There he found his Leader had gathered together all the other supervisors who looked after other interlocking components of the Abbey's diverse operations. The Abbot informed all assembled that the Church's national leadership had decided to build on Easter's promise of new beginnings, expanding the celebrations to try and reach many of the rural youth—inviting them to festivities that would include sermons on peace and tolerance, as well as a feast that would fill all stomachs and hopefully instill in all participants the need to love thy brother.

Given the Brothers of Piety's rather central location in the inflammatory southern part of the country, they had been chosen as one of the sites for this special observance. Other religious communities from the southern region would join them, contributing both staff and funds to the event. This was all being organized hand-in-hand with the country's political leadership; the President's sister, as they all knew, was a member of one of their own congregations and a major liaison in the preparations. Through these arrangements, the military was giving large tents to accommodate the crowds. Their own chapel was far too small for the expected crowd, so the open-sided tents would be put up in the area between the clinic and the orphanage. The kitchens from all the different institutions would come together to prepare the meal. Brother Mike was responsible for ensuring the needed foodstuffs were ready when needed and that the tents were pitched as planned.

The Abbot concluded, asking all to pass the word that the whole community should pray hard for success, should work hard for victory—the victory of God's Word—helping their flock come together rather than tearing themselves apart. As he spoke, Brother Mike thought of his father. He hoped their final exchanges had succeeded, that his father had truly seen in his heart and his soul the need for change and that he was now more serene in a better place. If it could happen to his father, couldn't it happen to these young kids who, like his father, had too narrow a view of life, but who could, with God's help, see life as beautiful, diverse, and worth saving?

ಶ ಶ ಶ

The preparations for the Easter "spectacular", as some of the workers now called it, were considerable. The tents arrived in three 6x6 Mercedes transports, and the soldiers helped the monastery staff set up the big pavilions. Local parishes and nearby communities brought extra tables and chairs. As the celebration would take place on Easter Day, most of the celebrants were not assisting with Good Friday Mass. The Abbot decided to start off with Lenten decorations for the makeshift chancel under the main tent—a single wooden cross, covered with a violet veil and set out by bouquets of dried flowers. When the service began, clerics wearing bright white would replace the artisanal cross with the golden Crucifix that was generally placed on the Chapel's altar. The dried flowers would be replaced by bouquets of fresh frangipani. Monks in the processional would carry the statue of the Risen Christ, placing it in front of the altar.

The service itself would be held midmorning. After the devotional, there would be three speakers who would address the congregation—the local Burgomaster, a professor from the University, and Father Daniel. These orators would be tasked with describing in simple, easy to understand terms the political changes that were taking place, the risks of overreaction and zealousness, and the need for all to be peaceful and thoughtful as the country moved through this phase in its development.

Brother Mike wished them all luck. He was not a pessimist. He hoped he was a realist, and he hoped these efforts would be successful. Sadly, he had seen too much of extremism, intolerance, and bigotry to be convinced that people already indoctrinated in dangerous ways would be able to do an about-face. But he knew it was possible and prayed it would work.

His aspirations aside, Brother Mike had little free time to contemplate the results of the Abbey's efforts. The preparations were time consuming and challenging. On Easter Sunday they would be feeding five times more people than usual and, equally troubling, they were competing with limited food supplies in local markets as nearly all households in this predominately Christian country were hopeful of having some sort of Easter feast, even if modest.

He organized a trip to town to meet with all his major suppliers to try and reserve the needed provisions. Both going to and coming from the city center he passed by Philip's house. However, no one, not even Joseph, was present at either visit.

All his arrangements had to be made before Palm Sunday and the stores delivered between Holy Monday and Holy Wednesday, as much of the food was to be prepared in the kitchens over these three days. Maundy Thursday, the Mass of the Lord's Supper, and Good Friday were fully oc-cupied with religious obligations and there was only Holy Saturday to put everything in place before the invitees arrived the next day.

To the great satisfaction of everyone, and as a tribute to the efforts each had invested in the celebration, everything when off without a hitch. By sun-set on Easter Sunday the monastery had returned to its normal population, with those who left, leaving with full stomachs and hopefully full hearts.

Over the following two days the tents and extra furniture were picked up, the pots and dishes scrubbed, and the Abbey's chapel redecorated in its own subtle but glorious way. The old routine returned with a communal sigh. In many ways, the Easter tumult was the perfect way for Brother Mike to reintegrate into his community and his duties after his extended stay in Belgium.

The customary schedule of activities back in place, Brother Mike set about updating his tasks, making sure all the pantries were full, all the vehicles following their maintenance programs, the butchery, bakery, and general kitchen implements all working well—the orphans clothed and the students with notebooks.

This typically required periodic trips to town, and on each journey he would stop by Philip's, but for more than two days he found the residence void of anyone—apparently even Kasuku. He was unsure if this unknowing was good or bad. Maybe things just ending as though they fell off a cliff was the best solution?

Then, on one visit, the house was again a home and everyone was there. When Brother Mike crossed the threshold, all embraced him—hugs and kisses flowing. There was a sincere outpouring of friendship, or so it seemed to the trepidatious visitor.

After all the welcoming and polite complements, Philip disappeared for just a few minutes, returning with a tiny bundle in his arms, "So, Brother Mike, here he is, our newest arrival, who chose to enter this world during your absence—Michel. We hope you will be honored to be his namesake and his Godfather?"

Brother Mike looked at the baby's round, already smiling face that somehow looked familiar and was overtaken by mixed emotions. His eyes darted about the room, catching Angela's and seeing a hidden twinkle, or was it a smirk?

He took a deep breath, hopefully not too obvious, gathered his equanimity, calmed his voice, and thanked Philip, "This is truly an honor, an unexpected honor. I am so happy to be considered for this serious task of being young Michel's steward and perhaps spiritual guide in God's Holy Ways. I am equally honored and surprised that you have chosen to name him after me. This is undeserved, but cherished." He then gave Philip a great hug, nearly crushing the baby Michel between them.

"Please," Philip continued with a big smile that Brother Mike hoped was sincere, unsure of how much of the new Michel's story might have been told, "take a seat. Angela dear, can you get us some beer?

"Brother Mike, we did hear from Joseph that you passed by before Easter. We were sorry to have missed you. I have been called regularly to the capital to discuss the Belgium Cooperation's support to the University. With the current political precariousness, the Cooperation is reviewing all its assistance programs to the country and all its assignments of expatriate staff. I am part of a panel that is assisting in making the final decisions that will be implemented in the coming weeks. This brings me to the good-news–bad-news scenario. Certainly, our son's birth and his mother's health are good news. However, there is also, unfortunately, bad news.

"We are leaving. Most likely within a fortnight we will be transferred to Lubumbashi. I will be setting up an eye clinic in conjunction with the University of Lubumbashi. My work here will be taken up by a local NGO that is connected with the international Vision Society that will provide frequent backstopping and some operating capital. So, life goes on.

"While we are sad to leave a place we have for so long considered home, a place that was and is Angela's motherland and the birthplace of our two boys, this is in many ways a good opportunity professionally. The University of Lubumbashi, as you may know, was established in 1955 as the official university of Congo and Rwanda–Urundi in collaboration with the University of Liège. Today it is one of the largest universities in Congo."

This second shock to Brother Mike made him gasp audibly. There was a strange shadow in Philip's eyes. But, whether real or imagined, it was fleeting and he scarcely missed a beat as he tried to assuage his friend, "Sorry, no more poker games or afternoons on the terrace, but we are not far away. You will always be welcome at our new home.

"But let's not worry too much about tomorrow now, let's drink to my new son, to your return, and to our health."

Angela had put several glasses and bottles of beer on the table. Brother Mike drained his a bit too fast, but she quickly, in prescribed popular custom, refilled it and he took more time with his second pint.

They asked about his trip to Belgium and he filled them in with just the barest of details, mostly that his father had passed but that this mother, although not well, would likely have several more years ahead of her.

The discussion then turned to the local political situation. Philip and Angela had perhaps more information than the Abbot, but it was equally gloomy. The plague of *multipartism* had led to so many schisms—each rallying its affiliates with greater and greater promises of their ability to right all the wrongs, to remove all the malefactors, and to restore that specific groups' cultural and ethnic norms to the prowess they deserved, but had long been deprived of due to years of mismanagement and foreign domination.

Different combines, many seemingly crews of unemployed youth, would meet in what appeared to the outsider akin to throngs at a football match—each with their own flag, beret, or song. At times, groups would clash in the streets leaving many wounded, including innocent passersby. It was troubling and it was growing.

The disquiet and ethnic tension were becoming all-consuming, casting grave doubt on a peaceful future for the country. There seemed little at this point anyone could do to defuse the situation unless the politicians and the activists quickly had a change of heart. This seemed unlikely—very unlikely. Everyone appeared to already have a personal stake in the pandemonium; some would even reap greater benefits if the worst happened and civil war broke out. It was very sad.

They all sat in silence as if at a funeral—even the baby was voiceless. After a final pint for the road, Brother Mike bid farewell to his friends, agreeing with them to arrange a send-off dinner in the coming two weeks. Philip added it would have to be in a week's time as he had to go once more to the final meeting of the Cooperation's panel on reshaping their activities.

On the way back to the Abbey, Brother Mike forced all the news to the back of his mind, compelling his brain to concentrate on the falling dusk, the traffic on the road, and the need to order more potatoes from the North. In the chapel for Vespers, he kept the lid closed on his revelations; tomorrow would be soon enough to unpack all the disclosures and prepare a plan of action.

🍎 🍎 🍎

As luck would have it, he needed to make a morning trip to town, following another of the Abbey's vehicles that had to go to the garage. He asked the other driver to wait for him, taking a quick detour by Antonio's store for some sweets and then a stop at Philip's. He again found only Joseph at home, but told him he had a small gift for his godson, knowing the baby was too young to eat the offering, and slipped a piece of paper in with the delicacies, telling Joseph it was "for Madame." On the paper he had written, "Congratulations. I know with your love your son will grow into a strong tree on the morrow." He only hoped Angela would decode the crude cypher and meet him the next day in the arboretum.

The next day, Brother Mike left the Abbey after Lauds, telling the Abbot he had to be in the market early to make sure the potatoes coming in from the farmers in the North were not sold to anyone else. He did go straight to the part of the market where the trucks were unloaded; found the freighter used by his suppliers, and had the bags of potatoes moved straight into his pickup. He then parked the truck nearby, asking a vendor he knew to keep an eye on it. He took a taxi to a part of the University campus closest to the arboretum and walked the last few kilometers on foot.

He reached their previous rendezvous point, not knowing if his message had really been received. He sat down and leaned against the trunk of a custard apple tree, listening to the song of the forest. He must have dozed off because he was awakened by tap of small pebbles ricocheting off his shoulders. He looked up to see a laughing Angela, a handful of small smooth stones falling from her grip.

"I'm glad you understood my message," Brother Mike smiled as he got up and gave her a hug, a good solid hug, but with no kiss.

"I imagined you would find some way for us to chat," she replied, a smile adorning her face, but somehow sadness in her voice.

"I'm so glad everything went well."

"It did?"

"Well, you and Michel are both fine."

"Yes."

"But now you're leaving?"

"Yes."

Things did not seem to be going very well right now, Brother Mike thought. Angela seemed very guarded, as though she was fulfilling an obligation with no enthusiasm. He thought he would continue with the soft approach, "I'm sorry I wasn't here when you had the baby."

"You know he's yours, you can clearly see how much he resembles you!" she blurted out.

He could not tell if the catch in her voice was because she was close to tears or close to exploding. He tried to keep his own voice cool, "There is truly something familiar about his demeanor."

"Familiar! Damn it, he is your son!"

"Well, OK. Does Philip know?"

"I have said nothing. I have no reason to think he suspects anything. However, it was he who chose the name Michel. Was it a cruel joke?"

"Oh, I don't think so, we are friends after all."

"And?"

"Well, my father just died. Maybe he thinks it's a kindness to me at a time of difficulty?"

"Doubt it."

"You know, Philip is kind. This is probably a token of what we've shared—and I mean cards and beer, not you my dear."

"Don't try to be smug or clever. You've seen him. He's you!"

"It is perhaps only our gilt that paints that picture of the baby."

"Oh, that's enough. We've had this discussion."

"But what does your heart tell you. Surely you would sense something if Philip was making a statement about your indiscretions, our indiscretions, if he indeed suspected any?"

"I don't know. I just don't know. This is all too much. And now we are leaving. I just don't know."

He tried to give her a hug, but she backed away.

"As Philip told you, he is in meetings about the restructuring of the Belgian assistance program. When he comes back, he intends to ask you to have Michel baptized at the Abbey. This is the main reason I even came. I don't know if the others at the monastery will see how my baby resembles you. I don't know if this is the right thing to do. I don't know why Father Daniel cannot baptize Michel, but Philip wants it done at the Abbey, with you standing up as the godfather. I have not fought him on this as it might raise questions best unasked. I honestly do not know if he has other motives, or if this is just a way to cement the bonds between us all. Damn. I simply don't know. What should we do?"

Brother Mike thought for a minute then calmly stated, "We will just go ahead. I think this is very straight-forward. I will arrange it with the Abbot. Again, I am sure Philip is only doing this out of respect for my position as his friend—nothing more, nothing less."

"But there is so little time."

"It will be fine. I'll arrange with the monks, we will have the baptismal on Saturday next week. I will also arrange with the others and we will come back to town after the church ceremony and have the sendoff on the terrace of the Crane. This way we will not make a mess at your home as you are preparing to leave and we will be able to say all our goodbyes."

"I just don't know," she almost wailed, "there's so much, so many questions, so many things. It is too much!"

"You'll manage just fine. Please tell Philip you saw me in town and that I sent word that this Saturday I will go to the Crane as usual, for an afternoon beer. If he is back and would like a last pint on the terrace for old time's sake, I'll be there."

"Sure."

Brother Mike could see Angela was on the verge of collapsing. Even here in the forest she felt there was a good deal of risk of them being seen, of tongues wagging, of Philip connecting the dots, of everything being turned upside down. He did not attempt another hug, but just put his arm around her shoulder and said, "Now go home and give that boy a hug, have a nice glass of wine, and calm down. Everything will work out well. You'll have an exciting new life in Congo. The boys will have new friends and new schools. You will have a whole new life to establish and be far enough from your family to be much freer, but close enough to get home when you need to or want to. Believe me, it will all be fine."

She turned and silently was lost in the greenery. Brother Mike wished he felt as confident as he spoke. It was a difficult time and if Philip suspected, he could make a world of problems for Angela and baby Michel, as well as for he himself. But it was what it was. He could not change things, but only be happy that Angela and their baby were both fine. It needed to stay that way.

17

As promised, Brother Mike did go to the Crane Saturday afternoon. He was about to think Philip would be a no-show, this adding fuel to the possibility that he had some suspicions as to the paternity of the baby. However, just as he was finishing his second pint and thinking about leaving, Philip showed up, apologetic about his tardiness. He told Brother Mike he had only returned home last night after marathon meetings in the capital about the Belgian Cooperation's programmatic future. At long last, things were all sewn up, the various parties all having signed on to the new program that would result in a net reduction of 40% in the number of expatriates, but an overall budgetary increase of 15%—arrangements that sat well with those whose priority was the coins they could siphon off for their own use.

Philip himself was unhappy with the changes, but had no choice but to accept them as necessary steps given the deteriorating political situation coupled with the continuing need for improved services for the growing population across the country.

As Philip talked, Brother Mike ordered more beers and even took the liberty to get two plates of *frites*.

When the food and drink arrived, Philip took a break from his diatribe about foreign aid, cooling both his spirit and throat with the frothing beer. Brother Mike took advantage of the hiatus to prompt a subtle change in direction of the conversation, "So, are you still set to leave in about ten days?"

"Maybe. You know all too well from your own side the trials and tribulations of bureaucracies. The bean counters are moving slowly and it looks like there might be up to a week's delay. They have decided the best route for our personal effects is to go by the lake down to Zambia and then across by road to Lubumbashi. Nonetheless, for us they've decided we need to go to Brussels for a debriefing-briefing session. Fortunately, the baby is old enough to travel. They have devised an intricate itinerary that they think will work, but one that anyone else in their right mind would know was too complex to ever materialize. They want us to stay here in the hotel for some days after our effects are picked up and our house empty—it's cheaper to put us up here than in Belgium. Once they have word that the boat has sailed, they will have us fly to Brussels and then, after the formalities, take a direct flight straight to Lubumbashi where we will magically arrive at the same time as our freight."

"Indeed," commented Brother Mike, "that's complicated. All I can say is good luck."

"We're in the hands of the bean counters, with fingers crossed."

"That means you have about two and a half weeks here in the Land of Eternal Spring."

"True. Don't remind me. But that does remind me. Angela and I would like to have Michel baptized at your Abbey before we leave, you of course standing up with us. Do you think you can arrange it?"

"I don't think it will be any problem, but I will have to talk to the Abbot."

"Thanks. We really appreciate it. This is Angela's home and has been mine for a long time. We want Michel to have some roots here before he is transplanted next door to Congo."

"Well, I wish you were leaving under better circumstances. These are strenuous times."

"They are for sure. What of the Abbey? If things get worse, what will you do?"

"We are here for better or worse. We cannot leave. Our fraternity embraces many nationalities, but one faith. With this faith, we know that as things get bad, they will again get better. We will be here to help those who need it."

"I wish you luck. From all the briefings we had during those damn never-ending meetings last week, the one thing that was clear was that many well-informed people feel things will only get worse—and by some accounts, quickly."

"As God wills it."

"I guess."

There was a short silence as each man sipped some beer and munched some *frites*. Brother Mike then picked up the conversation with a bit of a twist, "Philip, I was just thinking. Why don't we try to schedule the baptismal for next Saturday morning and then we'll arrange a sendoff here at the Crane for the afternoon. If your family is already here as lodgers, all the better. If you're still packing up, we won't impede the process. Would this work?"

"Like a charm."

"OK, I'll see the Abbot for his part and then talk with Karl and Antonio and we'll organize the sendoff—all you and the family have to do is to show up."

"Impeccable."

"Indeed, impeccable."

They savored their tart, chilled brews as well as the breeze that picked up speed as it whisked down the street, creating small dust devils in its wake. Brother Mike knew this was likely the last time he would have a chance for quiet, even intimate conversation with Philip for some time to come. He had so much to say. He wanted to bare his soul to this friend he both liked and admired. But he had to think of Angela, of Michel. Some things are best left undone.

Their time was coming to a close and both sensed it like a change in season—those days before the rains come when you can feel their arrival, smell them coming.

"Well," Brother Mike said meekly, "you'll now have a chance to go to some good restaurants and maybe see a recent film when in Brussels."

"It has been a long time since we've been there," Philip concluded as if just realizing the fact himself.

"And what about the championship? Do you think Club Brugge will do it again like they did two years ago? K.A.A. can't ever seem to do better than third, even if they are over 125 years old. Ghent needs to do something about that team."

"I like the way Anderlecht plays, but feel Brussel's teams have all the advantages."

"They certainly have all the money."

"A great tradition we've transferred here, although they've still got to grow a bit."

"Hmm, if only all their aggressions and inhibitions could be taken care of on the pitch."

"Like you said, as God wills it. Say, before I forget, I've one more favor and don't know when I'll have another chance to ask."

"Sure."

"Can you take Kasuku? If we were going straight to Congo, it would not have been problem. In fact, that's where the bird originally came from. But it's really tough to get a parrot out of here, through Belgium and back to Congo via the airlines. We'd really appreciate it if you could take him, as we think you'd give him a good home."

Another unexpected turn of events and Brother Mike was not sure of all the implications or even if this would create problems at the Abbey. But this seemed a harmless enough favor and a way to have a living keepsake of important relationships.

"As long as you teach me all I need to know about parrot parenting, I am sure I can find a suitable place for him at the monastery."

"Wonderful! Many thanks."

"Well, maybe the next time you see him when you come back to visit he'll be able to recite the Rosary."

"That would be something to see."

They both laughed and drained their glasses.

Their last afternoon on the terrace was concluded. They seemed to jointly feel the need to make a clean cut, ending it with no pomp or regret. They simply paid their bill, stood up, hugged each other, and then separated, each heading in his own direction.

18

THE COMING DAYS AND weeks unfurled nearly exactly as planned. The Abbot had been unusually accommodating, both for agreeing to the christening and to Brother Mike's "parenting" of Kasuku. The whole community turned out for the baptismal, with Brother Mike standing elegantly at the font with Philip and Angela as well as, of course, the baby Michel.

Brother Mike found a sunny spot in his office for Kasuku. When he came in each morning, the parrot fixed him in his golden eyes and pronounced "asshole." Somehow, Brother Mike found this totally befitting.

Karl and Antonio had outdone themselves in the preparations for the sendoff at the Crane. It was a true bash to be forgotten by none and overtaken by few. By the time of the party, Philip and Angela had emptied their house and were staying at the hotel. When things began to wind down and a rather seriously inebriated Brother Mike had to get into his old Toyota pickup to drive back to the Abbey, he gave Philip and Angela great hugs, then slightly less enthusiastically embraced the two boys, and he was gone. It was over.

🐘 🐘 🐘

The next morning, Brother Mike left the Abbey before sunrise, having told the Abbot a tale of needing to be at the hospital the first thing in the morning. He expressed great contrition for foregoing his religious responsibilities that day and promised to double his efforts the next.

With a goulash of emotions swirling in his head, he drove through town, taking the route south, then turned east on a small side road that took him to a bridge on the Migina. The bridge was really nothing more than a few rough logs with some planks nailed across them to assist any of a variety of wheeled vehicles in crossing the river.

He parked on the shoulder in front of the bridge footing, the sun just peeking over the eastern hills, the water reflecting a black-blue light that seemed to come from the Earth's very core. As he stared down into the eddies of the swift-moving current, he withdrew from his pocket his emerald—what he now considered more "their" emerald, having hoped its crystalline energy could heal his spiritual wounds.

He walked slowly to the bridge's center, knelt, and prayed to his Savior for salvation and for safe keeping of all those he loved. He then dropped his emerald into the stream, seeing a small trail of bubbles as the water carried it downstream.

These were the waters carrying his tears onward, carrying them to the Kanyaru, on to the Nyabarongo, and then into the Nile. Finally, joining millions and millions of specks from humanity, his tears would flow to Alexandria where, two thousand years ago, he and Angela could have wed, she wearing a beautiful emerald around her neck.

Brother Mike's old routine continued. He avoided political discussions and meetings. He put all thoughts of Philip and his family into a small box in his brain. He set about making sure the Abbey was running smoothly.

Regrettably, outside the pastoral calm of the Abbey's domain, the political climate across the country worsened, changing from a regular flaring of tempers of opposing factions, devolving into a state of constant animus. Real hate now became more and more visible. In spite of the feeling of being on a sinking ship, as Brother Mike had told Philip, the brothers at the monastery asked God's help to remove the terror that was infecting the population. As circumstance deteriorated, increasingly greater numbers of people sought the aid of the Church—the religious community's role became truly a factor in life or death.

Some of Brother Mike's confrères found the stress too much, petitioning the Church for transfers outside the country. Brother Mike even received a query from a community in Burkina Faso enquiring if he were interested in relocating to West Africa. He found the promise of new lands, new people, and renewed security enticing, almost seductive. But, Brother Mike had decided he was here to stay. Going to his spot on the pond bank when the tension got too high, he knew with God's guidance he could persevere.

One day, nearly six months after the departure of Philip and his family, on a routine visit to the market's truck park to pick up his regular—and so far, uninterrupted by political turmoil—supply of potatoes shipped from the farmers in the North, he ran into one of the butchers he regularly used to supply meat to the Abbey. After exchanging pleasantries, this gentleman unexpectedly asked Brother Mike to wait in his truck for a few minutes.

The man ducked into a shed and then returned with a box that he put in the back of the pickup among the bags of potatoes. Brother Mike attempted to get out to inspect his new cargo, but the butcher asked him to only look at his gift once back at the Abbey, adding it was just a small token of his gratitude. When he got back to the monastery, he found, nestled among the gunnysacks of potatoes, a case of Courvoisier.

Brother Mike had helped the gentleman, as he would and did help any of his protégés, with some spare tires for his Isuzu trucks and some dry-cleaning supplies for the gentleman's cousin—these items surreptitiously added to the goods in a recent container arriving for the monastery. It was good to be appreciated.

That night in his bed, he mused over his friendships. He thought he might send Sister Alice a note. She too liked Courvoisier and it had been a long time since he had seen her.

The next morning after Lauds, Brother Mike decided to visit his favorite spot on the pond bank. He threw his baited line into the pond, leaning the pole against a banana tree stump, and leaned himself against the firm soil of the levee. He inhaled the deep aroma of the earth, heard the crackling of dried banana fronds in the wind, and fell soundly asleep, not seeing his line jiggle as a bream deftly removed the worm. His breath was deep and regular. He dreamed of fishing with his son.

19

SINCE THE SIMBA REBELLION of '64 and the Katanga Secession of '67 when Belgian mercenary Jean Schramme, his French compatriot Bob Denard, and about 125 other white mercenaries and 900 rebellious Katanganese, were surrounded in Bukavu, the political situation in Congo had been precarious. When Philip arrived in Brussels, he discovered the president of Congo had violently put down student protests at the University of Lubumbashi, resulting in the deaths of a number of people. The University was closed, at least for the moment. Philip and his family would need to find temporary lodging in Brussels until the situation stabilized.

Life next-door to Congo carried on in its tumultuous way. In Central Africa, experimentation in what was labeled "democratization" continued, but proved to be more polarization and fractionalization. The situation entered a downward spiral that culminated four years after the bloodshed in Lubumbashi in the twin assassinations of the presidents of the two countries that once comprised the German, then Belgian colony of Ruanda-Rundi. The violence that followed was about as bad as it can get. The area is still trying to make a full recovery. Some are prone to wondering if those seated on the hilltop are still closer to God.